STEALING HEAVEN

Previous novels by Heather Ingman, *Sara* and *Anna*, reached the bestseller lists in Ireland. *Stealing Heaven* is her second novel for Fourth Estate, following *Waiting at the Gate*, published in 1996. She has lived in Ireland, France and Ecuador. At present she lives in East Yorkshire with her two young sons and teaches at the University of Hull. Her book *Women's Fiction Between the Wars: Mothers, Daughters and Writing* is published this year by Edinburgh University Press.

STEALING HEAVEN

HEAVEN

HEATHER INGMAN

FOURTH ESTATE • *London*

First published in Great Britain in 1998 by
Fourth Estate Limited
6 Salem Road
London W2 4BU

A catalogue record for this book is available from the British Library.

ISBN 1-85702-657-8

The author would like to thank George Hepburn and Margaret Hepburn
for permission to reproduce 'Pilgrimage' by Anna Wickham.

'Try a Little Tenderness' by Harry Woods, Jimmy Campbell,
Reg Connelly. Copyright © 1932 Campbell Connelly & Co Ltd,
8/9 Frith Street, London W1V 5TZ. Reproduced by permission.
All Rights Reserved.

'Sitting on the Dock of the Bay' Words and music by Otis Redding and
Steve Cropper © 1968 Cotillion Music Inc, East Memphis Music &
Irving Music Inc, USA. Warner/Chappell Music Ltd, London and
Rondor Music (London) Ltd. Reproduced by permission of
International Music Publications Ltd.

Typeset by MATS, Southend-on-Sea, Essex
Printed in Great Britain by Clays Ltd, St Ives plc

For Ferdinand,
with love

Acknowledgements

For details about Laura's life in Paris, I am indebted to
G. Hanscombe and V. Smyers, *Writing for their Lives:
The Modernist Women 1910–1940*
(The Women's Press, 1987).

Pilgrimage

I think of the room at Bon Secours:
The clock on the shelf, and the bare-board floor,
The tallow smell from the out-blown light,
And the laughter and love of the prodigal night:
I wish I were young, dear,
As young and as poor
As when we stole Heaven
At Bon Secours.

Anna Wickham

PART ONE

Chapter One

Here it was. Streoneshalh, Hwitabi, Whitaby, Whitby, a town with many layers of history. Liz Miller walked out of the station and sniffed the sea air. She was conscious of English voices around her, higher and thinner than the American ones she had become used to. It was eighteen years since she had last been here. Whitby, town of her childhood, of her dreams, of her nightmares. Panic set in. She wouldn't, after all, go straight to Henrietta Street.

She lit a cigarette and set off round the harbour. She passed some fishermen painting their boat, then cut up by the National Westminster Bank to the narrow twisting alleyways, perfect for adolescent fumblings, that led to the West Cliff. Car fumes hung heavy in the air. What a difference unleaded petrol made. Boston, the city she had just left, smelled cleaner than this English seaside town. It was like stepping back in time.

Further up, the path widened. She passed the street where Roger's mother had kept her bed and breakfast. With its tall, narrow four-storey houses and the smoke-blackened church of St Hilda at one end, it reminded Liz now of north Dublin. Of those parties in crumbling Georgian townhouses with their peeling stucco and faded glamour. The gorgeous young men, some of them in dresses. Getting legless and throwing up in Stephen's Green. Smoking dope. Taking speed. Thinking you were making the most fantastic love in the world. The things she used to take. She wouldn't do it now. Or at most a bit of coke, after one of Louise's dinner parties.

Liz arrived at the top of the West Cliff, in front of a shabby crescent of Victorian hotels. A municipal noticeboard announced tea-dancing this coming Saturday in Whitby Pavilion. Amazing how that still went on. During the course of the summer various tired old 1960s stars were coming to entertain the town. She wondered how Kate stood it, but of course her sister lived in Hull; nowadays, she was as much a visitor here as Liz herself.

From the West Cliff, the town looked bigger than when she had lived here – there were new housing estates – yet also, in some undefinable way, shrunken as if, after the skyscrapers of Boston, she was seeing everything in miniature. Liz gazed across the harbour, the jetties and the sea walls to St Mary's church on the East Cliff, pressed between abbey and cliff edge, and reached from the harbour by one hundred and ninety-nine shallow steps. Red-roofed houses, piled on top of one another, climbed slowly up to the abbey of St Peter and St Hilda. Her glance swept along the harbour, inland to the narrow valley of the river Eske. Liz remembered how, growing up in this town, its houses clustered on either side of the valley had seemed to crowd in on her, making her feel claustrophobic, making her want to scream, so that she had known, from the age of fourteen, that the only solution would be to run away. Now what struck her, after the clapboards of America, was how solid the brick houses looked, how stubborn and immovable – like their Yorkshire inhabitants.

She sniffed the sea air again and smiled, remembering her father's words, repeated throughout childhood. 'Shoulders back. Head up. That's right! Breathe in that sea air. That'll put roses in tha' cheeks, my lass.' Nowadays it was said to have been proved scientifically that people who live by the sea live longer. Something to do with the ozone. It hadn't worked for her father. It had been the sea that killed him. Drowned, along with the rest of the trawler's crew one stormy winter's night in her sixteenth year. After that she'd gone a little wild . . .

It couldn't be put off any longer. Liz took a deep breath and plunged down the Khyber Pass to the harbour. She walked over the swing bridge into the cobbled streets of the old town. Her first impression was that the tourist industry had completely taken over; her second, seeing the headline WHITBY SEA TRAGEDY on a billboard, was that nothing had changed.

She walked up the cobbled street, past the cafés and the shops selling Victoriana and jet, past Nathaniel Cholmley's town hall and Hannah Cholmley's school. There was something fitting, she thought, about arriving on foot. The last image she wanted to present was of the emigrant returning home having made good in the New World. After paying for her B and B in London and the train fare up here, Liz had precisely eight hundred pounds to her name. Not much to show for so many years away. She had left, at the age of nineteen, to seek her fortune. And she had found fortune in many, many ways, only not in any way that translated into money.

She followed the curve of the street. On her right were the steps leading up to St Mary's church, on her left Henrietta Street and a view of the harbour. She gazed at the small terraced houses. The street looked almost exactly the same as when she had last seen it; some of the houses had changed colour, that was all. She felt her shoulders tense up, her palms begin to sweat, her heart beat a little faster.

She knocked on the door and stood back on the narrow pavement (there were no front gardens down this street). An iron object embedded in the wall by her foot caught her eye. It was in the shape of an inverted horseshoe with a bar running across it.

The door was opened by a tall, intelligent-looking woman in her mid-forties. She was wearing a white T-shirt, denim skirt and flat black sandals.

'Liz?' she said uncertainly.

Liz's eyes swept the pavement.

'I was looking at that old thing. Shoescraper, isn't it? Fancy it still being here after all these years.' She laughed, a shade nervously. 'Hello, Kate,' she added. She wondered what the etiquette was for meeting up with your elder sister after eighteen years. Did you hug or not? A handshake seemed a little formal after you'd shared a bedroom for God knows how many years.

Kate, too, seemed unsure what to do next. The sisters stood looking at each other for a moment in silence.

Liz took in the fact that in Kate the red hair which had run through the women in their family right back to their great-grandmother, so people said, was now faded to auburn. There were tiny criss-cross lines at the sides of her eyes and mouth. Don't grow old on me, Kate, she thought, in a kind of panic.

Kate took in Liz's grey-green eyes, her elfin face and elfin figure. She's not put on an ounce of weight in all these years, she thought, damn her. That boyish look wears well. Liz's thick red hair was cut short like a boy's, shorter in fact than most of the boys Kate knew. She'd picked up an American accent too. She was such a bloody chameleon, Liz. Lost her northern accent as soon as she had got down to London and, to judge by her random and unpredictable phone calls over the years, had become Irish in Dublin and French in Paris. Anything rather than be honest, thought Kate, who still spoke with a slight, soft, Yorkshire accent.

'You've not yet fallen down the cliff, I see.' Liz attempted a half joke. 'I thought you might have.'

'Not yet, though there's a chap at the university who thinks we should all sacrifice ourselves for the sake of Holland.' Kate gave a wry smile and let the door swing open. 'You'd better come in.' She stood back.

Heart in mouth, Liz stepped into the dark, narrow hallway. At a glance it seemed entirely unaltered since the day she had walked out. The same striped wallpaper on the walls, in two shades of brown, the same spotted old photograph of a sailing ship. She suddenly felt terribly claustrophobic. This wasn't helped by her consciousness of several battered-looking suitcases crowding round her legs, blocking her way.

'Some of Mother's things,' explained Kate. 'Odds and ends of china, old tablecloths, stuff I was sure you wouldn't want. I was going to take them down to the Oxfam shop.'

'Good idea,' agreed Liz, thinking, she might have waited until I came before she started packing Mother's things, burying our memories, bundling a life away. She looked at her sister. Or hadn't Kate expected her to turn up? No, probably she hadn't. After all, she had missed the funeral. She'd been out with Louise on Cape Cod, incommunicado for a fortnight, in a desperate attempt to save their relationship. By the time she had got Kate's message that their mother was dying, the burial had taken place. Now it looked rather, she supposed, as if she had come home for a share of the spoils.

'Kick them out of the way.' Kate thrust out a hand and pushed open a door to the left. 'Sit in the front room for a moment while I make us a cup of tea.' She hesitated. 'Or would you prefer something else?' Did her sister, living in America for the past eight years, drink tea any more?

'Tea's fine.' Thinking, Kate's obviously going to be touchy about my supposed cosmopolitanism. She was looking Liz up and down now, noting the designer-label jeans, the crisp white shirt, the silk waistcoat. All Louise's, thought Liz, if only you knew. Louise! The name stood quivering in her mind like a thrown knife. She bit her lip.

'How's Boston?'

'Boston's fine.' Despite Liz's best efforts, her voice trembled on the last word.

Kate hesitated, then said a little less guardedly, 'You must be tired? Jet-lagged.'

'Not too bad. I've had the night in London to recuperate.'

All the same she did feel a little light-headed. She was glad to sink into their father's old armchair. The springs had gone but it still had the white cotton antimacassars over the arms and back to hide the worn patches.

'Ages since I've been down to London,' responded Kate, a touch of asperity in her voice. 'The train fare's so expensive. Er,' she added, as Liz took a packet of cigarettes out of her pocket, 'must you smoke in here? It's a small house.'

Kate went away to make the tea, leaving Liz wondering precisely at which point in their conversation she had put a foot wrong. She shoved the cigarettes back into her jeans. What had upset her? It wasn't her fault she had travelled while Kate had stayed at home. Sometimes Liz thought that was all she had done in her years away Travelled from city to city, never quite finding what she was looking for, though almost, she'd thought, with Louise . . .

She gazed around the room. She took in the sagging sofa matching the armchair, the 1930s yellow tile fireplace, the leaved table pushed back against the wall out of the way, the carved walnut sideboard inherited from their grandmother who had died young. The furniture was all too large for such a tiny room. Liz imagined what Louise, used to designing exquisite interiors for the owners of mansions on Beacon Hill, would have made of it. Probably she would say this furniture ought to be preserved in a museum somewhere, a monument to English bad taste.

What did the rest of the house look like? Liz rose, taking two steps down the hall and into the kitchen where Kate stood by the kettle waiting for it to boil. Nothing had changed. The same electric cooker, bought in a sale two years before she'd left home. The same stone sink. No microwave, no toaster, no freezer. An American would have thrown up her hands in disbelief. There was, however, a washing machine. Liz could see it through the door that led into the scullery. That damp, stone-flagged scullery where their mother had stood on washdays squeezing clothes through a mangle.

Liz moved over to the sink and looked out of the window at the back yard, literally, a strip of paving stone – not at all what Americans meant when they described their beautifully manicured lawns as yards. In the old days, their mother's yard had been criss-crossed with clotheslines. Liz remembered the feel of damp sheets flapping against her face as she skipped in and out of the lines looking for a ball, until chased away by her mother and told to go and play somewhere else and not dirty the washing. In those days the children had played in the street: hopscotch, football, fives. From morning till night in the summer, the road had rung with their cries. Not any more, she supposed. Even in Whitby, mothers could no longer safely encourage their children to play out in the streets.

The trash cans were still there but the clotheslines had gone. In their place was a prim little umbrella contraption surrounded by flowers in tubs. The tubs were an innovation, a frivolity Liz was somehow surprised her mother had stooped to. In childhood, the back yard had been strictly functional. Now, there was even a wooden bench. Had her mother sat out, then? Liz found it hard to imagine their mother sitting about. She'd been a northern working-class housewife with red hands and arthritic joints from kneeling to wash her floors. Behind the yard, the grassy slope rose up steeply towards the cliff and Dracula's gravestones. As a child Liz had had nightmares about that cliff falling on top of them and crushing them all in their beds; its shadow hung over the rooms at the back of the house like a threat.

'The tubs are lovely. What have you got in them? Heathers, a miniature rose tree –'

'Lavender, thyme,' Kate went on. 'I did them myself. Latterly, when Mum couldn't get about much, she liked to sit in the yard.'

'I can't remember her ever just sitting.'

'She did latterly.'

'And you made her a garden to sit in.'

Kate the good daughter, the nurturing one, the one who had stayed behind. Liz gazed at the dark green cupboards, unchanged since her childhood. She saw her mother reaching up for a cup. She'd been a small woman, smaller than either of her daughters. In Liz's memories, her mother always had her back turned to her.

The kettle gave a shriek. Liz jumped. She was used to kettles that clicked discreetly.

'What's it like to be here?' asked Kate, pouring water into the pot.

'Strange. Weird. Like visiting a museum filled with childhood memories. Or reading a novel that you used to know very well. It's like reading Dickens. Yes, that's what it's like. Like reading *David Copperfield*. Same kind of feeling.'

Kate loaded a tray with the old blue and yellow cups.

'She kept them all these years,' said Liz, marvelling.

'She was careful.'

'Not like me. I smash things up. Louise says . . .' But she didn't want to talk about Louise. She let the sentence die away.

Yes, you smash things up, Kate thought. She carried the tray through into the front room. Liz sat down in the sagging armchair again. Kate perched on the sofa.

There was a silence. The sisters looked at one another.

'Well, here you are,' said Kate.

'Here I am,' Liz agreed.

Kate poured out the tea and handed Liz a cup. Liz began to feel she had made a mistake, coming back. Did she and Kate have anything at all in common? She started to feel suddenly unreal, her old familiar life in Boston retreating by the moment. To get rid of this slippery, quivery feeling she said quickly, 'Is there much sorting out to do?'

'A bit. I'm afraid there's not much left of yours though. Mum threw most things out years ago. Your school books, end of term reports and so on.'

'She liked to be tidy.' Or had it been a way of trying to forget her unsatisfactory younger daughter?

17

'There are some things up in the attic. I thought we could go through them together.'

'What sort of things?'

'Curtains, my old record player, your hockey stick –'

'You can give that away. God! How I loathed that game!'

'And a trunk. I haven't looked inside it, I can't find the key. I expect it's full of spare bedding or something.'

Liz smiled. 'Other families have secret wills hidden in their trunks, we have spare bedding.'

'There was nothing secret about Mum's will,' said Kate, a little sharply. 'As I told you on the phone, she left the house to us both, equally.'

Liz found it difficult to tell from Kate's tone whether her sister resented this or not. After all, Liz hadn't done anything to deserve being remembered. *She* hadn't made their mother a garden.

'We'll have to start organising the sale,' Kate went on. 'I've already had a word with the estate agent, Hamley's.'

Liz sat up with a jolt. 'Hamley? Roger Hamley?'

'Yes.'

There was a pause. Roger Hamley, bespectacled and stammering badly, had followed Liz around during their teenage years with doglike devotion.

'Good God! What's he doing these days?'

'Taken over the family business, as everyone expected. He's married now, with three daughters,' added Kate, in a warning tone that Liz rather resented. Why should her sister assume she made a habit of running after married men? It was the sort of thing you did only once in your life, if you were wise.

'Yes, I suppose the house must be sold,' she said slowly, setting down her cup. 'No thanks, no more tea. It seems a shame somehow, after all these years.'

Kate stared at her. 'You surely don't want to keep it on?'

What was Liz thinking of? Did she fancy having a base in England? A holiday cottage on the Yorkshire coast? That might be convenient for her but it isn't much use to me, thought Kate. Living in Hull, she could visit the Yorkshire coast any time she wanted. Besides, she needed the money. Perdita was starting university in the autumn, there were fees to be paid. And lately Duncan had grown rather extravagant.

'I don't know. I don't know what I want.' Liz sprang up suddenly and went over to the window to look out at the house opposite. 'Does Mrs Cuthbert still live there?'

Kate shook her head. 'She's in an old people's home across the other side of town. She has multiple sclerosis. None of her children wanted to cope with her. She's cheerful enough though. I pop in and see her from time to time.'

'Kate! You don't!'

'I promised Mum. She was good to us when we were children.'

'Yes, I remember. Always had a slice of bread and jam or a freshly baked scone for us. So who lives there now?'

'A young couple with a kid.'

'God! Fancy starting out married life here.'

'It's not so bad.'

Liz drummed her fingers on the sill.

'I've got to pick up my luggage. I wanted a bit of a stroll round after the journey so I left it down at the station. Why don't you come with me? I can't seem to stay still at the moment. I don't know whether it's excitement or jet lag or what.'

She turned and smiled ruefully at her sister who said, 'I'll get my bag.'

Kate noticed Liz didn't carry a handbag. She wondered what she did with her keys and her money. Carried them around in the pockets of her jeans, she supposed, like a man, like Duncan. They were so alike those two, in many, many ways . . . Kate's thoughts came to an abrupt halt. That was a road she didn't want to go down, not tonight at any rate. She would need all her strength and courage to get through this visit of Liz's, however long, or short, it turned out to be. She slung her leather bag over her shoulder.

'Have you a lot of luggage? Should we take the car?'

'I'd rather walk, if it's all the same to you. It's only a holdall.'

Really, thought Kate, imagine coming all the way from America with one holdall. You can carry the vagabond act too far. And how long a stay did one bag imply? You couldn't tell with Liz. She locked the door behind them.

'That never used to happen,' commented Liz, remembering the days when the children on the street had run freely in and out of each other's houses and no one would have dreamed of locking their front door.

'Tourists,' said Kate briefly.

Liz paused to light the cigarette she'd been made to forgo in the house. They turned the corner into the cobbled street Liz had walked along earlier. 'There're lots of new shops,' she remarked.

'Shops for tourists,' Kate replied. 'Now the fishing industry's decimated, they're selling Whitby as a tourist centre. Dracula, Captain Cook, even St Hilda has been roped in. And Victoriana.' She gestured towards a shop front hung with shawls and long white cotton nightdresses. 'Cashing in on people's yearning for an age that never was – a calm, stable time, presided over by a stout, motherly figure. They forget about the beggars on the streets and the hysterics locked up in asylums.'

Liz burst out laughing. 'Is that what you tell your students when they say they want to study the Victorian Greats?' Kate lectured in the English department at the University of East Riding, on the outskirts of Hull.

'Sometimes.'

'Incidentally, how have you managed to get time off? It's the middle of term, isn't it?'

'We don't have terms any more. We have semesters like the Americans – and I'm on sabbatical for this one.'

'Cushy!'

'I'm supposed to be writing a book,' Kate retorted.

'What on?'

'Inter-war women's fiction. It's the coming area. The Victorians have been done. Only I can't seem to get on with it.'

'So you don't have to rush back to Hull?'

'No, I thought I'd stay here a few days, carry on with sorting out Mum's things.' Kate swallowed and glanced sideways at the harbour. 'Duncan's away at present.'

'Mm.'

Liz hunched up her shoulders, dropped her cigarette butt on the ground and dug her hands more deeply into the pockets of her jeans. So that was that. The name had finally been mentioned between them, as simply as tossing a pebble into the sea. In the silence that followed, the two sisters heard the splash, watched the ripples subside, the water close over the pebble.

'How is he?' ventured Liz, at length.

'The same. At least he seems the same to me. Possibly you would find him aged.'

'Duncan? It doesn't seem likely.'

They crossed the swing bridge and paused for a moment beside the harbour rail where a solitary fisherman was tying up his boat. Unwillingly, almost, Liz conjured up an image of Duncan, unsummoned by her for years. Softly curling chestnut hair, brown face, white teeth, deep brown eyes, those long, sensuous, sensitive lips. Her perfect ideal of male beauty. In love with her sister. Lucky, lucky Kate. Married at twenty-two to Duncan Townsend, the colonel's son, brilliant local boy who, against all the odds, had won a place at Cambridge and then come home to teach art. Even their mother, who thought hardly anyone in Whitby fit to associate with her girls, was in awe of Duncan, proud that her elder daughter had done so well for herself, hopeful now for her difficult, discontented younger daughter just touching fourteen. And then, gradually, it had all gone wrong.

Liz banged the rail with her fist. 'Come on then,' she said impatiently, as if it were she who had been waiting for Kate and not the other way round.

They skirted the harbour, crossed the road to the station and collected Liz's bag from left luggage.

'Want a hand?' offered Kate.

'No thanks.' Liz slung the holdall over her shoulder. 'There's not much in it.'

They retraced their steps along by the harbour. The air smelled of fried fish, candy floss and toffee apples. Liz remembered coming down to the harbour on Saturday mornings with her father, buying winkles and whelks and cockles from one of the kiosks, walking home along the beach eating the shellfish out of cardboard cartons with wooden forks. The town was half Victorian fishing village, half day-trippers' delight. Prosperous in the nineteenth century when its fishing industry had connected it to the four corners of the world, the decline of that industry in the twentieth century, the drop in demand for jet, the shutting down of the alum works, had caused the town to close in on itself.

'How's Louise?'

'Fine.' Kate's question brought her out of the past with a jolt. 'Louise is fine.'

But I'm not, I'm not. Liz looked over her shoulder at the grey sea, thinking how often she had gazed out at the same scene during childhood, in hope, in boredom, in despair.

'And the writing?'

In her early twenties, Liz had had a book of poems published. Quite good poems, Kate believed. They had been favourably reviewed in all the right places. Kate herself had never read them. She had been afraid of what she would find. Since then, as far as she knew, Liz had had nothing more published.

'I haven't written much lately. What with one thing and another, there hasn't been time for it.'

'That's a pity.' Kate paused. 'So you've been busy working, have you?' What exactly *was* Liz's line of work these days?

'I've been living off my savings, such as they are, or were. Madness. I'll have to think about getting a proper job soon. I've been doing a bit of waitressing in a nightclub in Boston, but that's come to an end too.'

That's Liz all over, reflected Kate, living from day to day without a thought for the future. She *would* turn up here broke. I hope she doesn't expect me to keep her. I need every penny for Perdita.

Aloud, she said, 'We'd better sell Mum's house then. I'll try to get things set in motion before I go back to Hull.'

Liz hesitated, then said in a rush, 'What about Perdita? Doesn't she need you at home?'

Kate cast an ironical glance at her sister walking beside her. 'Perdita's eighteen. Girls grow up quickly nowadays. I don't do everything for her, like Mum did for us. Besides, at this moment, she's away, staying with her godmother in Pickering. She's been – er – given time off school.'

'What's she like?' asked Liz. 'I know so few people her age,' she added in a tone that was almost pleading.

'Ambitious, self-confident, like most young women these days.' Unconsciously Kate began walking faster, as if she wanted to get this conversation over with as quickly as possible. 'Knows what she wants out of life.'

'Which is?'

'A decent job, a decent income, a chance to travel and see something of the world. She's determined not to make a mess of her life, like her elders.' Kate gave a short laugh.

Liz halted on the pavement, drew in her breath and said, 'Does she . . .? She doesn't know anything? Or does she?'

Kate stopped too. 'Not yet. I thought that's one of the things we might discuss. if you're staying, that is.' She glanced doubtfully at the bag over Liz's shoulder.

'Of course I'm staying. I've got an open return. Thought I might travel around a bit, see a little of England again, now I'm back.' Though what on? Eight hundred pounds wouldn't get her far, even here.

'Perdita's got a place at Duncan's old college,' Kate went on, as they resumed their tramp up the hill.

Duncan's old college, which was to have been my old college, only . . . 'That seems fitting,' she said.

'I thought so.' Kate's tone softened. 'I thought you would like that.'

'I do.'

A sudden wave of irritation swept over Kate at her sister's casual assumption that she had any right at all to express an interest in Perdita's future.

'Yes, well,' she said sharply, getting out her front door key, 'it's what Perdita herself wanted. She's going to read languages. French and Spanish. That should provide her with a sound enough basis for the future.'

Liz glanced at her sister, then dropped her eyes and followed her meekly inside the house.

Chapter Two

....

Later that night, lying awake in her old room, in her old bed (surprisingly familiar even after all this time), Liz listened to Kate's light breathing coming from the other side of the wall, from what had been their parents' bedroom, and thought of Duncan as she'd seen him that last time, at the fag end of the summer of '78. He'd been grey, ashen, exhausted. The one time in his life he'd looked older than his years. The bright young man who had gone a step too far this time. Duncan Townsend who could never, Whitby folk used to say half-admiringly, see a top without going over it, reduced to this. His conversation flat and dull, so different from his usual playful self, lacing his words with quips, self-parody, double, triple meanings. He'd sat in the greasy café down by the harbour, hugging a mug of coffee, not looking at her, muttering over and over again, 'Will you be all right? You will be all right, won't you?'

'Yes,' she had said, wanting to put him out of his misery.

'You're sure?'

'Yes!' A trace of anger on her part, swiftly suppressed, for after all what was the use? 'Kate's arranged everything. It's what she wants.'

'It's what we all want. Don't we?' He sounded doubtful. 'Best for you.' He leaned across the table, his eyes on her mug. 'It is what you want, isn't it?'

Two women coming into the café at that moment glanced across at them, struck, perhaps, by the note of intensity in his voice. Glanced and then glanced again. Duncan always had that effect on people. Even now, even today, there was something charmed about him. That lithe, male, loose-limbed body, those boyish good looks in a town where good looks were conspicuously lacking.

'I don't think what I want comes into it, do you?' she had replied, gathering up the tatters of her eighteen-year-old's sophistication. Nor what you want, either, she felt inclined to add. Though what did Duncan want? Did he even know himself?

'Christ! What a mess!' He covered his face with his hands.

24

Liz sat opposite him in that filthy café feeling about twelve years old but with her woman's body, and wondered whether to take his hands in hers, whether to kiss them and hold them close to her, whether to comfort him. Her eyes dropped. No, she'd lost that right. To tell the truth, it had never been hers.

'It needn't be a mess,' she said softly. 'Kate's seeing to that.'

'Yes,' he mumbled and slowly took his hands from his face.

They looked at each other for the first time since coming into the café. Her grey-green eyes met his soft brown ones. What she saw in them prompted her to say urgently, 'Duncan, you know we're still free, both of us. We can still *choose*.'

There was a pause. His eyes slid sideways. She saw that he had already chosen. Kate would do everything for them.

How she'd left, how they'd parted, she couldn't clearly remember. Perhaps she had stood up then and stumbled blindly out of the café? Perhaps not. Her memory of that scene always ended there, at that point. Any other words that had been spoken between them had dropped out of her mind. For years afterwards, scrabbling to earn a living in London, Dublin and Paris, that last meeting with Duncan had remained burned into her memory. She had played it over and over again in her mind, a tape that always broke down at the same spot. Then she had met Caro, then Sarah, then Louise, and the memory had become dulled, robbed of most of its pain, an ancient war wound that was almost, not quite, healed. Now it was like running through an old movie scene from someone else's life. It hardly seemed real. She wondered whether she would see Duncan on this visit. On the whole, she hoped not. Kate hadn't mentioned him again that evening.

'There'll be a certain amount of family business to be got through while you're here, I'm afraid,' she had said, over their women's supper of scrambled eggs and yoghurt. 'Uncle John will probably pop in. He does most evenings when he knows I'm here. Can't quite get out of the habit even though Mum's gone.'

'I don't mind. I'd like to see him again.'

Shy Uncle John, their mother's younger brother, who had sat Liz on his knee as a child and taught her how to clean out his pipe and pack it with tobacco. Slow and inarticulate he'd been, like all the males up here. All except Duncan, that is.

So Uncle John had called in, a small, thin man wearing a pair of shabby trousers and a home-knitted jumper that looked like one of their mother's efforts. He'd sat in the front room and smoked his pipe (pipe smoking was apparently allowed under Kate's rules) and chatted with them a while. He'd been a painter down on the docks. Retired now. Or rather, laid off. He and some others had been fighting for compensation for years. Meanwhile he lived in a council flat in an area of town that had never featured on any tourist trail.

'Like Boston, do you?' he'd asked Liz shyly. He'd not known what to say to this niece of his who had travelled abroad for so many years, in far-off places he had no desire to see.

'Yes. It's a great place to be. Lots going on. The place where we – where I live, Beacon Hill, isn't so different from here, you know. It has terraced houses and narrow little streets and tourists.'

He shook his head. 'I never fancied living in a city.'

Their Uncle John had lived in Whitby all his life. Never married, for which Kate blamed their mother, saying that she'd taken care of him so well – doing his washing and ironing and baking him pies – that he'd never needed to look for a wife. Liz wondered how he was going to manage without her. Kate, living in Hull, would be too far away to help.

He'd turned to Kate. 'And how's my great-niece? How's Perdita?'

'In a state of constant rebellion.'

'Why didn't you bring her with you?'

'Whenever I bring her over here, she spends her time mooching around down by the harbour, complaining she's bored.' Kate laughed shortly.

'Does she? I was like that!' exclaimed Liz impulsively, then stopped under Kate's gaze.

Now, lying in bed, she remembered the hours she had spent drifting about the harbour, watching the boats going out, the words of that record they used to play down at the youth club echoing in her head. 'Sitting in the morning sun . . . Watching the ships roll in . . . I'm sitting on the dock of the Bay . . . Watching the tide roll away . . . Wasting time.' She'd been good at wasting time in those days. Still was, if it came to that: all those solitary afternoons on Cape Cod, walking up and down the half deserted beaches in Brewster, waiting for Louise to return from her mysterious trips over to Provincetown. Provincetown – one of the few places in the world where the alternative lifestyle was mainstream and two women could walk down the street holding hands without exciting any comment. Except that Louise hadn't felt like holding hands, hadn't really wanted Liz there at all. Now Liz knew why. Annie, her rival, lived in Provincetown. Annie who had finally, so it seemed, triumphed and taken Louise from her.

Forcing her thoughts away from Louise, Liz returned to the song. The words 'l left my home in Georgia' had never failed to send a shiver down her spine. Leaving home. Roaming the world. Liz wondered whether Perdita knew the song. Would she see the girl on this visit, or would Kate want to keep her all to herself? And what would she find to say to her if they did meet?

Chapter Three

In the morning, the sun shone so brightly it even managed to penetrate down the grassy slope and into Liz's bedroom at the back of the house. With a sense of excitement, she thrust back the sheets and pulled on her jeans and T-shirt. In the kitchen she found Kate bustling around, giving the impression she had been up for hours. The time signal sounded out softly from the radio. It was ten o'clock, early in the morning by Liz's standards. She yawned, stretched, gulped and said, 'What are you so busy at?'

'Yesterday's supper things,' muttered Kate, bending over the sink, scrubbing a pan. 'No matter what I do, when I scramble eggs they always seem to stick to the bottom. Mum kept these pans so nice.'

'Want a hand?'

'No thanks. The sink's too small for two. Help yourself to coffee,' she added. 'The kettle's boiled. I'm afraid it's instant. Mum never got round to owning a percolator.'

'Neither did I, till I met Louise,' replied Liz, pouring herself a cup and wandering out into the back yard with it.

She sat down on the wooden bench, lit her first cigarette of the day and lifted her face to the sun. On Cape Cod it had rained a lot of the time. She shut her eyes and conjured up the wild and lonely seashore, the white expanses of beach disappearing into the horizon mist, the feel of tough dune grass beneath her bare feet, the cry of gulls scavenging for clams and crabs. She saw the house among the pines, a nineteenth-century shipmaster's house that had been in Louise's family for years. She pictured it standing there with its white clapboards and dark green shutters and knew that was another place she would never see again.

To Kate, washing up at the sink, it seemed entirely unreal that her sister should be here under this roof, finally, after eighteen years away. If Liz had not reappeared this morning, Kate would have been perfectly prepared to accept that yesterday was a dream.

What had her sister's life been in the years since she'd left

England? Kate had no clear picture. Snatched phone calls, the odd postcard, hadn't told her much. Sometimes, especially in the early years, struggling with nappies and feeding and Perdita's tantrums, Kate had imagined her sister's life bathed in glamour. Living in cities among artists, writing poetry, working in nightclubs, being wined and dined by rich customers. But apparently, from something Liz had let drop last night, it hadn't been like that, or at least not all of the time. She heard her mother's voice comment drily, 'Not much of a life, is it? Living with a woman. Not what I'd call a proper life.' 'Isn't it?' Kate heard herself answer back. 'Liz can have holidays whenever she likes, live in a beautiful house filled with fragile lovely things, and never have to clean up after anyone but herself. A woman who lets herself in for a husband and a child ends up with a lot of drudgery. Liz's may not be the life the *Daily Mail* would like its women readers to live, but I bet it's the kind of life most women dream of. Yes, in lots of ways, Liz has been cleverer than me.' She pulled out the plug in her mother's sink and watched the water slowly drain away.

Liz came back into the kitchen. Bryan Ferry's song, 'Love is the Drug', was playing on the radio. 'I love this.' She set down her cup, turned up the radio and began stomping about the kitchen.

Watching her, Kate tut-tutted. 'Shouldn't you be past all that?' Memories of Liz at fifteen going off to a disco, a black felt hat pulled down low over her eyes, Bogart fashion.

'Music, like poetry, is one of the things in life that keeps me going. When I'm past dancing, I shall die,' replied Liz extravagantly.

Circling Kate, Liz grabbed her sister by the waist and waltzed her around the tiny room. Kate moved stiffly, as if she was unused to dancing, which indeed she was.

'Think what music can do.' Liz swept her around the kitchen. 'Think what the Beatles did for this country. They gave hope to a repressed little nation starved of joy. They told us it was all right to have fun. Look inside yourself, that's what Lennon was telling us. Don't waste your time. Life's richer than you think.'

'That's all very well,' retorted Kate, 'but we can't all earn vast amounts of money like the Beatles. Some of us have to go on working nine to five.'

The music stopped.

'You've grown old, Kate. What's made you old?'

Kate didn't reply but stood gazing at Liz. Slowly, Liz's arm dropped from her sister's waist. She flushed slightly, turned away and drummed her fingers on the windowsill.

'It's a beautiful day. Let's go up on the moors.'

'We ought to make a start on clearing out the attic,' Kate objected. 'And have a talk with Roger Hamley.'

'Later, later,' her sister said, rinsing her coffee cup. 'We can see Roger this afternoon, deal with the attic this evening, or tomorrow. Kate, come on. Before the day spoils itself.'

The moors had been Liz's saviour when she was younger. Tramping through heather and bracken with her father at weekends, she had shaken off the worries of the week. That bleak, purple-clad landscape expressed something important about the soul, she'd always thought. Living in tree-covered Massachusetts, the moors were the one thing she had missed about England. Besides she felt restless, found it difficult to stay still today. Was it the effect of jet-lag? Was it that, having come back to this house after all these years, she couldn't wait to leave it again? Or was it because, ever since she had read Louise's note, the words of that song, 'Try a little tenderness', had kept echoing in her mind, lying in wait for her no matter what she was doing?

Louise. She'd been running, running ever since Boston to get away from her. 'Soft words, they are spoken so gentle, It makes it easier to bear.' There had been no soft words spoken. She was left with only the memory of the two lines at the side of Louise's mouth, like two small commas, of her long dark hair swinging over her shoulders, her crooked dark eyebrows, one slightly higher than the other. Thinking, oh well, she had died so many times in her life, what did one more death matter? It did matter though; it mattered more than all the rest, except one, *the* one which had started everything off and which came back to haunt her at the end of every relationship. Was it Louise she was afraid of, or Duncan? This house was full of memories of him. The clever Cambridge graduate, standing on the hearthrug in the living room, asking their parents' permission to marry Kate. Later, the son-in-law, allowed to help their mother in the kitchen; still later, the brother-in-law who had held her in his arms when her father died, the only one who had been able to calm her during that first, wild, terrible stage of grief. Coming back here, the lid had begun to be lifted on things suppressed for years. Keep away from me, Duncan, she thought, keep away, else I shall crack. She set her cup down on the draining board with a clatter, causing Kate to glance anxiously in her direction.

They fetched their jackets and walked up the street to collect Kate's Fiat, parked on a piece of wasteland overlooking the harbour. Cars, apart from those belonging to residents, weren't allowed up this street.

'He's still curing his kippers then?' remarked Liz, as smoke from a tiny building on their right blew across their faces.

'Yes.' Then, a little defensively, 'Don't they do that in Boston?'

'Not in a back yard. They have factories.'

'Curing kippers has been going on in that yard since 1872,' stated Kate, as if that clinched the argument.

Or had it been an argument? Liz stared across the harbour to the Victorian hotels and the whale's arched jawbones on the West Cliff. I must be more careful, she thought. All the same, she couldn't help noticing yesterday, as she'd walked through the town, how very poor the people looked, how cheap their clothes, how unhealthy their complexions, compared with the inhabitants of Boston. And the litter was shocking. On the Cape, where there was a two hundred dollar fine for littering, you wouldn't find a scrap of paper or a broken bottle anywhere. She wondered what it felt like, never to have got away (for you couldn't call Hull getting away).

'How do you like living in Hull?' she asked, seating herself in the car.

'It's all right.' Kate shrugged and started the engine. They drove slowly through the town. 'Hull's a bombed-out city trying to rebuild itself after the war.'

'The war? That was a long time ago.'

'I know. Meanwhile the Germans have rebuilt the whole of Germany. However, we're doing our best. We've been rather forgotten about up here. The poetry's good,' she added, changing gear as they started to climb up on to the moors in the direction of Goathland. 'And we have a marina, an art gallery, two theatres and concerts in the City Hall.'

'Sounds great,' said Liz, thinking, *Boston has more theatres than I can count.* She wondered what it must be like to live in a place where so many names were a subject of mirth in other parts of the country – Cleethorpes, Scunthorpe, Grimsby, Goole. She looked out of the window. Green fields and rape gave way to an explosion of colours. Browns shaded off into fawns, purples into dusty pinks with, here and there, patches of dark shadow.

'It's like being on top of the world,' she said.

Kate pulled into a lay-by. 'This all right for you?'

Liz stepped out of the car. There was a smell of peaty water and sweet scented ferns.

'It reminds me of Dad.'

'Yes.'

They began to walk in single file along a narrow sheep trail, pushing their way through the heather and bracken and fern.

'Do you have countryside like this around Hull?' called Liz, over her shoulder.

'No. We have the Wolds. Gentle little grassy hills. Actually I prefer them to this barrenness.'

I wouldn't, thought Liz, gazing across the expanse of purple moorland. *This is reality. This measures up to the best moments in life. When I'm dying, it's these moors I'll see, not the town or the coast. These moors and Louise's face, or . . .*

The path widened. Kate came up beside her.

'You are lucky to be near all this.'

'To tell you the truth, it's years since I've been up here. In the past few months I've been dashing back and forth between classes to see Mum. Once in Whitby I hardly stepped out of the house, or hospital, as it was latterly. Before she got ill, Perdita and I used to visit her three, perhaps four, times a year.'

'Oh.'

Over the years, lying in strange beds in foreign cities, Liz had envisaged cosy mother-daughter meetings on a monthly or even a weekly basis. Kate and their mother shopping or having afternoon tea together in some country hotel. Evidently it hadn't been like that.

'You know Mum,' Kate went on, trudging through the heather, 'she was always self-sufficient. Or pretended to be. She never wanted to be a burden on us.'

Liz stopped for a moment. She broke off a piece of fern and held it to her nose. 'Kate, did she ever . . .? I mean, do you think she . . .?'

'Guessed? I don't know. I was never sure. She certainly distanced herself from us all over the years and she went off Duncan pretty shortly after you left.'

'Did she?' said Liz, surprised. 'I thought he was the apple of her eye? The son she'd never had.'

'She didn't think painting pictures a respectable way for a man to earn his living. Or not earn his living, in Duncan's case. She preferred him as a schoolteacher.'

'He hated it.'

'Yes.'

They walked on. In some part of her mind, Liz was convinced her sister was lying, or if not lying, then hiding something. She decided to change the subject. A curlew cried. Sheep nibbled at ferns, making a steady champing noise that accompanied them as they walked.

'Kate, what's it like living in England? I feel so out of touch with things here.'

'England?' Kate thrust her hands into the pockets of her denim skirt. 'England's still England. Women get thrown into prison for fiddling benefits or not paying their gas bill because they've got to feed their kids. There was a period when women prisoners about to give birth were chained to their hospital beds in case they ran away. They may have stopped that now. But prisoners are still kept in remand cells the size of a double bed for twenty-three hours out of twenty-four. The poor are punished for being poor, women for being women. Nothing changes. Everything's much like it was in Dickens's time, in fact.'

This was a new Kate, a Kate that hadn't been there before. Politicised, angry about impersonal things in a way Liz could never bring herself to be. But then living in England *was* depressing, she remembered, people complained about things so much. Just the other week, after a recent hurricane had razed their shops to the ground and lifted the roofs off their houses, the inhabitants of Florida had gone on television talking about community spirit and working together to get the show on the road again as quickly as possible. Faced with a similar situation, the English were apt to stand around looking helpless, saying somebody ought to be blamed and when were they going to get compensation? All the same, Liz wondered how this new Kate had come into being.

'Do you campaign?'

'I'm a member of the Labour Party. Not that I expect much from them – they've become rather more right-wing than when you were last in the country. I'm a founder member of a women's group in Hull.'

'I bet your students love you.'

Kate shrugged. 'It's difficult to know what they're thinking, half the time. The age gap between myself and them gets wider every year.'

'But you like working at the university?' persisted Liz, wanting, suddenly, Kate to sound happy about something.

'I don't know. The job's changing, like all jobs nowadays. We assess students, they assess us, we assess our colleagues and then all of us are assessed by someone from outside. It's not enough to be a teacher any more, to love books. You have to be an accountant, an administrator, a social worker and, above all, published.' She sighed, plucked off a piece of bracken and began rubbing it through her fingers. 'The whole process is making me feel old and jaded. Year after year the students look at me with their fresh enthusiasms – there's something sacred about that – and I find it harder and harder to respond, overwhelmed as I am by the examining, the marking, the classifying that's always slightly corrupt. I sometimes think we take their enthusiasms and turn them to dust.' She let the bracken stalk drop from her fingers and gazed across the moor. 'I want out, Liz, but I can't afford it and I'm too young for these early retirement packages they keep foisting on my colleagues.'

'What about your book? How's that going?'

Kate sighed. 'It's been dragging on for years and somehow I can't seem to get it finished. The thought that I must have it completed and out before the next research assessment exercise is creating a kind of block in my mind.'

'Sounds deathly,' agreed Liz. 'You can't be expected to be inspired when you've a deadline to meet.'

'I don't think inspiration comes into much of what's published in the academic world these days. Sweat and lit. crit. jargon are what most of the books reek of. Churn out the volumes, that's the name of the game. I even know people who have published the same book over and over again – well, almost, they simply change the title.'

Liz laughed. 'I wish I could work out a way of earning money.'

Kate glanced at her sharply. 'I thought that flat in Boston was quite ritzy?'

'It is.' A beautiful, beautiful apartment built in 1836 and overlooking a quiet leafy square where Louisa May Alcott once lived. But it belongs to Louise. 'Oh yes, I'm not starving. I just wish I could earn enough money to give me time off to get some poems together for another collection. When I had that first volume published I thought, this is it, I'm made. This is going to be my life from now on, writing, giving readings, doing a bit of reviewing on the side, to earn money. I felt so lucky, so privileged. When I wrote I felt, this is what I was born to do. Then somehow, I don't know, the inspiration went. I had to go back to waitressing. I've never felt settled enough since to do more than the odd scribble.' All these years, she thought, I've been waiting for that feeling to come again, waiting to start over. My life's been twisted away from its roots.

Kate shaded her eyes against the sun. 'I wonder if we've done as well as we might?' she murmured. Then she looked about her. 'We ought to have brought a picnic.'

'I know!' exclaimed Liz. 'Let's go to Egton Bridge.'

'Bit extravagant.'

'Just this once? The check's on me. After all, I've been eating your food.'

So Kate drove skilfully down narrow twisting lanes to the village of Egton Bridge, nestling by a river, in between two folds in the hills. They parked the car beside the Catholic church and walked down through the village, passing large stone houses, their gardens filled with daffodils and tulips and the sounds of children at play.

'Why on earth,' said Liz, pausing and looking around, 'would one want to live anywhere else?'

Kate smiled. 'Roger Hamley lives somewhere around here. I'm not sure exactly where. He did up the old schoolhouse. Oh yes,' she added as Liz turned and made a face of astonishment, 'nowadays, he's quite the lord of the manor.'

'Turn up for the books,' commented Liz. 'A change, I should think, from his mother's B and B.'

They arrived at the stepping stones that led over to the old inn. Looking down at the brown water swirling around them, Kate had a qualm.

'Did we really leap over these as children?'

'We had courage!' said Liz, springing lightly from stone to stone. 'Besides,' she stopped on a large flat stone in the middle, 'Mother was watching us. We had to impress.'

Kate, following her sister gingerly over the stones, let this remark pass. She had long ago come to the conclusion that Liz's view of their mother was quite different from her own. Kate had never felt the need to impress that short, sturdy woman who had stood like a rock between the world and herself for twenty-two years, then had suddenly and apparently so light-heartedly relinquished her to Duncan and had from then on kept out of her elder daughter's life – out of tact, self-effacement, or indifference? No, surely not indifference, it wasn't possible.

They safely negotiated the stepping stones and made their way up the path smelling of wild garlic to the inn.

'I mustn't go on like this.' Kate studied the menu. 'Moaning about everything. Perdita said to me the other day, "Mum, why are you always so miserable?" Now I try to lift my voice a notch or two when I talk to her. It's becoming a bit of a strain. I think I'll have pasta.'

'What I want,' said Liz, from behind her menu, 'is roast beef, Yorkshire pudding, onion gravy, horseradish sauce, the works.'

'You can't be serious!'

'I am. You don't know what it's like to live in a country where everyone eats with a calorie counter propped up in front of them.'

Putting down the menu, Liz wondered what it felt like to be called Mum.

They gave their orders to a blowsy middle-aged woman with dyed blonde hair that showed dark at the roots.

'And a bottle of mineral water, please,' added Liz.

'Right you are, love.' She went away.

'Nice to be called love again,' Liz murmured. 'It hasn't changed much, this place.' She looked about her. There were only two other lunchers beside themselves, men in business suits with mobile phones and calculators by their plates. 'Is it still owned by Miss Thingie?'

'Bennett. No, she died. It was taken over by a chain last year. But you're right. They don't seem to have made any changes.'

The two sisters looked around, remembering the special occasions when they had dined here. Not so very many of them. Mum's fortieth birthday, Kate's twenty-first, Kate's engagement to Duncan. The inn had been in the Bennett family for years. Smells of roasts and thick gravy and Yorkshire puddings had seeped their way into the walls hung with hunting scenes and painted dull yellow with, here and there, dark brown stains. Smoke, damp, or had someone been flinging gravy around, wondered Kate.

The blowsy waitress brought their food.

'Mm!' Liz leaned over her plate and sniffed. 'This is what I call food!'

'I don't suppose you'll put on an ounce even if you eat all of that.' Kate plunged her fork dismally into her pasta swathed in low-calorie sauce.

'Want a piece?' Liz held up her knife, on the end of which dangled a slice of Yorkshire pudding.

'Go on then.' Kate pushed her plate across the table.

'Wise decision. It's heavenly. Melt in the mouth stuff. If I lived here, I'd eat nothing but Yorkshire pudding.'

'No you wouldn't, not if you still wanted to get into your jeans,' retorted Kate, swallowing the pudding and instantly regretting it. 'Do you remember Miss Bennett?'

'I do.' Liz pictured a tall, fair-haired woman, rumoured to be in her seventies but with the brisk walk of someone twenty years younger. 'She was terribly upright in the way she held herself, wasn't she?'

'Forthright in the way she spoke.'

'In fact, just right.'

They laughed. Things are getting better, Liz reflected. Together, we're beginning to cut through the vanished years. She leaned across the table.

'Do you remember the time she offered us raspberries fresh from the garden for our dessert? I shall always remember that − her coming straight into the restaurant from the lawn, a basket over one arm, her gardening gloves on and showing us the raspberries she'd just picked.'

'It was like a scene from some 1930s film,' agreed Kate.

'She made you feel you were guests in her private house rather than in a hotel.'

'That was the time when . . .' Kate stopped and looked down at her plate.

The time when you'd had that first miscarriage and been told you might not be able to have any children and we were all desperate to find ways of cheering you up, Liz finished the sentence in her mind. Mother, Duncan and me (Dad was already dead by then); we invited you out and you sat for the entire meal toying miserably with your food. Was that when everything started to go wrong? Duncan and I laughing and making bad jokes together, the first time he'd really taken any notice of me. You, sitting silent and wretched. Mother . . . but what her mother had thought remained a mystery to Liz . . . No, it wasn't going to be easy after all. The dead weight of the past hung over them still. For the rest of lunch the sisters conversed in monosyllables.

Chapter Four

Roger Hamley was taller than Liz had remembered. He had got rid of the glasses and the stammer. His greying hair made him look vaguely distinguished. He spoke without hesitation. Someone must have been kind to him, Liz thought guiltily.

He rose from behind his desk as they came in.

'Hello, Kate.'

'Hello, Roger. You remember Liz?'

'I do. How are you?'

He shook hands. His manner was urbane, without a trace of embarrassment. Had he forgotten, then, how he used to follow her around, begging her to go out with him? And that one time she'd finished with him, more for his sake than hers, because she'd thought he ought to have more of a life than this, and he'd cried noisily all the way down the street. Had he forgotten this, or had Kate mentioned she might turn up and so given him time to prepare himself?

'We've come about Mum's house,' said Kate.

He gestured to a couple of chairs and perched on the edge of his desk, swinging his legs.

'We've decided to sell,' she added.

Liz glanced at her sister. Had they indeed?

Roger pursed his lips. 'Well, you can try. As I explained before, the market's fairly stagnant at the moment. People round here are worried about hanging on to their jobs, they're not thinking of moving. We could advertise in one or two of the national news-papers in the hope that someone down south might want a holiday cottage on the Yorkshire coast. But it can get expensive if you run the ads for more than a couple of weeks.'

'Besides, I would rather have somebody local,' said Kate. 'I mean someone who was going to live in the house all year round.'

Roger let this piece of sentimentality slide past him in silence. Yes, he had definitely changed.

'Why don't you rent it out?' he suggested.

'Yes, why not?' Liz turned to Kate. 'That way it would bring us in a steady income and mean we could put off the decision to sell until we're absolutely sure.'

I am absolutely sure, thought Kate, irritated. Aloud, she said, 'I don't know. There's the problem of the upkeep of the house. It would need repairing and painting from time to time. There'd be tenants' complaints to deal with.' And I'd be the one lumbered with seeing to it all. For Liz in Boston there'd be nothing to do but pay in the monthly cheque.

'We could arrange all that for you,' said Roger. 'It's one of our services, finding suitable tenants, drawing up contracts, making sure the property is kept in good order. We've had to diversify,' he added, with a nod to Liz. 'It's the only way we've been able to weather the recession.'

'Oh,' said Liz.

It was never any use talking money with Liz, reflected Kate. She hadn't the slightest grasp of economics.

'Mr Hamley.' Roger's secretary, a smartly dressed middle-aged woman with penetrating eyes, interrupted them. 'Lady Wheeler's on the phone about letting the lodge.'

'Tell her I'll call back in a couple of minutes, Joan.' He slid off the desk. 'Well, think about it. There's no hurry.' He glanced at Liz. 'How long are you staying?'

'I'm not sure.'

'Still scribbling?'

'Not as much as I'd like. The inspiration doesn't seem to come these days.'

'How's Boston?'

'Great,' she replied, wondering whether there'd been an edge to his question. 'A bit like here – sea, seagulls, crabs – only bigger.' And with less litter and less pollution, but this she kept to herself.

'Wow!' she exclaimed as they left Roger's office and walked back down through the town towards the swing bridge. 'He's changed.'

'Yes, I believe he's doing very well. Expanded the business in all sorts of new directions. Why?' Kate glanced mischievously at her sister. 'Feel you made a mistake?'

'No, but I suppose I never thought he'd turn out so well.'

His name had been against him from the start. At fourteen, it had been hard to get romantic about someone called Roger when there were people around with names like Jason and Wayne – and Duncan. He'd not been stupid, one of the brighter boys in the class in fact. But he'd been so clearly heading for the family business and Liz had already made plans for moving away from Whitby.

'Roger's one of the most eligible men in town,' remarked Kate airily.

'I thought you said he was married?' Had Whitby's mores changed so much then? Liz kicked bad-temperedly at a fish and chip paper that had got itself entangled around her ankles.

'Widowed.' Kate relented. 'His wife died four years ago.'

'What was she like?'

'I only met her a couple of times. Petite would be the word, I think. Petite and dark, with a pretty oval face.' Kate glanced at her sister. 'Oh, all right, she was a crashing bore. Only ever talked about her house and her children. It was rumoured even Roger got bored with her.'

Liz couldn't avoid a smirk. 'What did she die of?'

'Car crash. It was tough on the children. They've been looked after by their grandmother.'

'Oh God, his mother!'

'Precisely.'

In Liz's opinion Charlotte Hamley, widowed early, had been responsible for most of what had been wrong with Roger – the thick vests, the awful glasses, the appalling crew cut, his general fussiness and prissiness.

'She must be getting on a bit.'

'She is.'

'Does she still do B and B?'

'No, she stopped that years ago, when Roger started bringing in the money.'

'Someone ought to rescue those children.'

Kate turned. 'Were you thinking of taking them on? They hardly need it. The two eldest must be into their teens by now.'

She wondered what was running through her sister's mind. Had

41

something gone wrong in Boston? Liz seemed in no hurry to return, didn't even seem to have a job to go back to. This talk of keeping on the house in Whitby simply wasn't practical. I hope she hasn't come back here to dump a load of problems on my doorstep, thought Kate.

Chapter Five

That evening they went up to the attic. It was surprisingly large for a fisherman's cottage, big enough to stand up in and with a window at one end; spacious and airy, not like those cluttered attics full of romantic family secrets you read about in Victorian children's novels. Liz looked around. Their mother must have got rid of a lot of stuff over the years. Apart from the shabby brown trunk, there were a couple of broken lamps, an old-fashioned wireless set that had belonged to their father, Kate's gramophone, some records and a pile of children's board games in a corner.

'I remember this!' Liz exclaimed, pulling out a battered snakes and ladders. 'God! The hours we spent playing with it.' She opened the box and ran her fingers over the board. 'How familiar it seems,' she murmured. She remembered every dent in that board and the scuffed patch where the dice wouldn't roll straight. It's been waiting here all these years, she thought, with a lump in her throat.

She put the board down and pulled out a record. 'Gerry and the Pacemakers. Good God!' She picked out some more. 'The Animals. The Shadows. The Monkees. Dear me, I wonder if these are collectors' items?'

Kate, fumbling at the lock of the trunk, glanced over briefly. 'I shouldn't be surprised.'

'It's like a museum of ancient music up here.'

'Do you mind? I'm not that much older than you.' She sat back on her heels. 'Damn it! None of these keys seem to fit.'

'We could break it open.'

'I'd rather not. It might come in useful.' For Perdita going off to university, she was thinking. 'Wait a moment. Yes, I've got it.' The lock sprang open. Kate undid the clasps, pushed up the lid and looked inside. 'Oh!' She took a step back. 'It's not bedding.'

'What is it then?' Liz came and peered over her sister's shoulder.

'A lot of old papers, it looks like.' Kate leaned in and brought out exercise book after exercise book. Then a couple of hardback books that looked like diaries. Then a blue folder.

'What is all this?' Liz picked up the folder, untied the ribbon around it and opened it up. A heap of yellowing newspaper cuttings fell out. She glanced at the date on one of them: 1925. 'What on earth . . .?' She picked up a cutting and began to read. It concerned the death, in mysterious circumstances, of Arthur Chapman, shipbuilder and property owner, late of St Anne's House, Whitby.

'Arthur Chapman. Wasn't Arthur the name of our grandfather?' muttered Liz.

'Yes.' Kate crouched on the floor, poring over the exercise books. 'Arthur and Laura Chapman, Mother's father and mother, the grandparents we never knew. Laura's name is inside these books, they must have belonged to her.' She looked up. 'Our grandparents died in the same year. Yes, it was 1925, come to think of it, I remember Mum telling me. But there was nothing mysterious about his death. Mum told me grandfather had a stroke and that Laura died a few months later, of a broken heart. It was after that that Mum and Uncle John went to live with the Braithwaites, if you remember.'

Liz frowned. 'Then I don't understand. It says here that Arthur Chapman was found murdered. Cyanide poisoning, apparently. Oh my God!' She read from another cutting. '"MRS ARTHUR CHAPMAN TO STAND TRIAL FOR THE MURDER OF HER HUSBAND."'

'Let's see.' Kate dropped the exercise books and came to kneel beside her sister. 'Goodness. What a horrid photo of her!' They stared at the grainy, blurred picture in the newspaper. A tall woman, looking ill and bedraggled and with her hair coming down, stood handcuffed to a policeman. 'It's nothing like the photographs Mum has – had – of her.'

'I don't think I've ever seen a photograph of our grandmother,' said Liz, brought back to her childhood when her mother and her elder sister had seemed to share confidences from which she was excluded.

'Mum had several. She showed them to me once. I can hardly remember them now but I do remember thinking Laura looked beautiful and that I wished I'd known her. Did she stand trial then?'

'I don't know. Hang on.' Liz scrabbled through the cuttings, reading out bits of them as she went. '"Arthur Chapman, shipbuilder and popular man about town" – man about town! Where do they think they are?'

'Get on with it,' urged her sister.

'"– was found dead in suspicious circumstances shortly after nine o'clock on Tuesday morning. Foul play suspected." Then another: "Autopsy confirms cyanide poisoning. The police are questioning a number of suspects." Then it comes. "Laura Chapman arrested on suspicion of murdering her husband. To stand trial." Kate, why did we never know about any of this?' Liz closed the lid of the trunk and sat down on it with the folder in her lap. 'Why did Mother tell us our grandmother died of a broken heart?' She glanced suspiciously at her sister. 'Or did you know about it?'

Kate shook her head. She sat down beside Liz on the trunk. 'Perhaps Laura did die shortly after her husband? Perhaps she was hanged for murdering him?'

Liz flicked through the rest of the cuttings. 'These are the reports of the trial. March 22, 1925. Statements read out in court by the cook, the housemaid, the gardener, the gardener's boy. Neighbours say blah, blah, blah. Arthur Chapman's mistress. Mistress! Good Lord! Ah, here it is. "TRIAL HALTED FOR LACK OF EVIDENCE. The judge in the Chapman case has ruled that the prosecution has provided insufficient evidence for the trial to continue. He has directed the jury to find Mrs Arthur Chapman not guilty." Well, thank God for that!'

'Is that it?' Kate sounded disappointed. 'Was the murder never solved?'

'There are no more cuttings. No, wait, here's one more. Not from *The Times* but from the *Daily Mail*. July 1925. "Housemaid discovers empty bottle in the cupboard under the stairs in the house of Arthur Chapman Esquire, the Whitby gentleman who was so brutally murdered earlier this year. The bottle is thought to have contained cyanide. The *Mail* calls upon its loyal readers to support its campaign for a change in the law to allow suspects to be charged twice for the same crime if fresh evidence comes to light. It is cases like this and the recent one in Shropshire which highlight the importance of restricting women's influence in public life. Even in private, the fair sex, it seems, cannot be relied upon to behave rationally and responsibly. The *Mail* urges those in power to resist calls to extend women's suffrage to women under thirty. THE FLAPPER MUST NOT BE GRANTED THE VOTE!" Well, it's clear whom the *Mail* suspected of murdering Arthur Chapman. I wonder if Laura really did do it?'

'It looks like they never found out,' replied Kate. 'As the *Mail* points out, you can't be tried twice for the same offence. It's like them to bring the flappers into it, I must say.'

'Yes, of course, it's slap bang in the middle of your period . . . So Laura got away with it.'

'If she did it.' Kate paused for a moment. 'I wonder what happened to her afterwards? I wonder whether she did die of a broken heart or whether –'

'Kate, do you realise?' Liz interrupted excitedly. 'Our grandmother may still be alive!'

'She'd be a very old lady by now,' objected her sister. 'And wouldn't we somehow have got wind of her over the years if she had still been alive? Besides, if she was, why did she let her children be brought up by the Braithwaites?'

'Perhaps she had to leave Whitby? It must have been pretty awkward for her living here in this small town with everyone suspecting her of having murdered her husband.'

'But in that case why didn't she take her children with her, or at least try to get in touch with them later?'

'Perhaps she did. Perhaps Mum didn't let on. She seems to have been pretty keen on keeping quiet about our grandmother, doesn't she? Kate, what else do we know about Laura?'

'Not much. Mum always said she was odd.'

Odd. Their mother's word for anything that didn't fit in with her, quite narrow, view of life. Pragmatic, their mother had been, reflected Liz, down to earth. Not an ounce of creativity in her veins. Good old Yorkshire stock through and through. While other women in the town might think up fancy dishes to please their families or spend hours planting things in their gardens, their mother had been content to be a good plain cook and there had been no flowers in the yard till Kate took over.

'I can count on the fingers of one hand the number of times Mum mentioned her mother,' continued Kate. 'Mum never spoke about her childhood much, did she? She never talked about the Braithwaites either, though she must have lived with them a good many years.'

'Braithwaite. Braithwaite. Hang on.' Liz flicked back through the cuttings. 'Wasn't that the name of Laura's cook? Yes, here it is. "Mrs Braithwaite, who has worked for Mrs Chapman since her marriage to Mr Arthur Chapman, swore in court that the sugar bowl had been put out as usual on the sideboard at eight o'clock, in time for Mr Chapman's breakfast at half past." The cyanide was mixed into the sugar. apparently. "In response to a question put by Mr Allsop, the prosecuting lawyer, Mrs Braithwaite replied that Mrs Chapman always breakfasted half an hour earlier than Mr Chapman, on a tray brought up to her room. She never took sugar."' Liz put down the paper. 'I wonder if it's the same Braithwaite?'

'Must be. Mum would have been about five at the time. She *was* quite small when she went to live with the Braithwaites. You know, Liz, we should ask Uncle John about this.'

'He'd have been even younger when all this was going on.'

'He must have been told at some point what happened to his own mother!' Kate gestured at the newspaper cuttings. 'He must *know* about this, mustn't he?'

'Presumably. Or he'd have heard rumours, growing up. Whitby's a small town, this must have created quite a scandal at the time, especially if Arthur was as popular "about town" as the newspapers claimed. Kate, are we descended from a murderess, do you think?'

'I don't know. Creepy thought, isn't it?'

'Not the kind of behaviour one normally expects from grandmothers,' agreed Liz. 'What's in Laura's exercise books?'

'They seem to be full of stories.'

'What! Another writer in the family? Let's see!' Liz picked up one of the exercise books. They were children's books, soft-backed, filled with spidery black handwriting.

'And these are a diary of some sort.' Kate turned over the two hardback notebooks. 'With the initial L on the inside. Laura's then, presumably.'

Liz's head jerked up. 'Perhaps they'll provide the solution to our mystery. What year do they begin?'

'Nineteen twenty-four. And,' Kate looked inside the other one, 'this is for 1925. Only a few entries. It tails off in early March.'

'When the trial began.'

Kate held the books open in her lap. 'I wonder if Mum knew what was in these?'

'Perhaps she didn't dare look.'

Kate got up and studied the lid of the trunk where she had been sitting. 'The initials on here are LRC. Laura. R something – Ruth, I think. Chapman. All this must have come from St Anne's, like the sideboard downstairs.'

'I wonder if it's the same sideboard mentioned in the trial?' said Liz, excitedly. 'On which the sugar bowl was kept.'

'Bound to be, I should think. Would one possess two of the things?' Kate stretched and groaned. 'My back's killing me. Let's take this stuff downstairs and read it in comfort.'

'Over a glass of wine,' added her sister.

'You'll have to fetch a bottle from the off-licence then,' said Kate sharply. 'There's nothing here. You know Mum would never have alcohol in the house.'

'I know. It was hard on Dad, I always thought.'

'He didn't mind. It gave him an excuse to go down to the pub.'

Reflecting that it was almost impossible to get Kate to agree on anything to do with the past, Liz went out to hunt for an off-licence. She returned ten minutes later a bottle of Chablis under her arm.

She simply doesn't know how to economise, thought Kate. Aloud, she said, 'Is that the kind of thing your customers buy you?'

Liz stared at her.

'I'm a waitress, Kate, not a whore. When I've finished my work all I want to do is go home to bed. On my own.'

She stalked off down the hall to the kitchen and began rooting through drawers for a corkscrew.

'Here.' Kate came up behind her. 'Use this.' She held out a Swiss army knife and flicked open the corkscrew part of it. 'Mum didn't possess a corkscrew. I'm sorry,' she added.

'My life isn't quite as sleazy as you seem to imagine.' Liz smiled wryly and took the knife. 'Natty gadget.'

'Perdita gave it to me last birthday. She always gives me practical presents for some reason. I think she must think they suit my personality. One year it was a tool box. Occasionally I feel I wouldn't mind something from the Body Shop.'

Presents, thought Liz, yes, I suppose daughters do buy their mothers presents. I used to buy Mum talcum powder. The same brand every birthday I don't know whether she really liked it, or was only pretending. She thrust the corkscrew into the cork, twisted it, pulled out the cork and poured the wine.

'Cheers.'

'Cheers,' said Kate. 'Mm. Quite a while since I've drunk good wine.'

It was true, but it was also an attempt, as Liz knew, to make up for the remark about customers. How well we know each other still, she thought. Perhaps you never get off the wavelength of someone you've grown up with. Kate's remark had been closer to home than Liz was prepared to admit, out loud at any rate. Those two years in London employed by the Stars in Your Eyes escort agency. It was a period she tried not to think about now, but it had been part of her life, there was no denying it. Between the ages of nineteen and twenty-one, when most of her contemporaries were pursuing some form of higher education, broke, unable to earn money by her writing, unwilling to earn money by waitressing, that's what she had done – gone with men for money. Creeps and sadists, perverts and bullies, she'd had them all. Now she only felt romantic about women.

'Which do you want? Stories or diary?' asked Kate, when they had seated themselves in the front room.

'Stories.'

'Here you are.'

Secretly pleased, Kate handed her sister the exercise books. Fiction was distancing. What she wanted to find out were mundane details about Laura's life and the diary would be better for that. There was a long silence as the sisters read, broken only by the turning of a page or the clink of a wine glass being set down on the hearth.

Kate read:

February 23rd. 1924. I, Laura Chapman – but who is this 'I'? This Laura? I have so many selves: I am Arthur's wife, the mother of Jessica and John, Mama's daughter, the respectable middle-class lady who visits old Mrs Thornton. And beneath all these surface lives beats a steady pulse – Laura the writer. Yes, I am Laura the writer. That is who I am, if only in this diary.

Well then, I, Laura Chapman, the writer, am starting this diary in the hope that it will help ease me back into writing short stories, for which inspiration seems sadly lacking these days. I am twenty-six years old. My father is dead. My mother still lives in the farmhouse where we grew up, with my youngest sister, Bessie, and my brothers, George and Percy, who run the farm. This is to set the scene and to remind an older Laura of things she may have forgotten. If she cares to read this diary, that is.

I wonder if the sixty-year-old Laura will have got any further with her dreams of becoming a writer? I wonder if by then she will have had anything published? I mean in places that count, not the women's magazines I have been published in so far.

This diary is not to be a dull, tedious document of daily events. I want it to be a writer's diary. I want it to contain my stray observations, random thoughts and reflections on life. All the things I cannot talk about to anyone here.

February 25th. Goodness knows how I ever came to wish to be a writer. It was an unlikely enough dream for someone from my background – and a female at that. Everyone knows that literature is men's business. Never mind, the desire is there. I am stuck with it. I run after words as we used to run after butterflies up on the moor near our farm and just as vainly, I sometimes think. Oh dear, Carr is calling. I hear one of the children crying. I must go. Motherhood and writing definitely do not mix.

February 26th. I have just had a story sent back. 'Beautifully written but not enough plot to interest our readers,' says the magazine editor (who shall be nameless in these pages). Everything smells of failure today.

March 2nd. Who am I? Why do I feel that being a writer is the only thing I am fit for? And what does it amount to, this phrasemaking, this trying to pin things down in words? Why do it? Why impose a pattern on life where there is none?

March 6th. I am determined not to be despondent but to go on writing, calmly and patiently, whenever I have the time. What is one rejection? I write to please myself. Nothing else pleases me so much, not even my children. Is that a terrible thing to say? I expect it is. Oh these words, these words, why do I go on with them? Are they simply a protection against living?

March 10th. I have finished reading Jacob's Room *by Virginia Woolf. It is remarkably good. A work of genius, in fact. It makes me proud of my sex for a moment – the thought that somewhere out there is a woman writing as well as this. Beside her, Rose Macaulay, who is far better known, reads as thin and merely fashionable. Fashionable – that is something I am in no danger of becoming, living up here. I wonder how much it matters? A different place, a different time, different people to talk to – would these things have made me a better writer? I wonder.*

March 17th. Another windy day. That is what you get for living on the north-east coast of England. Wind and rain and mist. I have just come in from a 'blow' along the pier. I was wondering, as I walked, whether men and women have anything in common. It is a year since I have seen Mama. I miss her. Yet in another part of my mind I am relieved. If she came here she would see at once that there is something wrong. The wind has given me a headache. I shall go and lie down.

March 23rd. Jessie is not at all like me. She reminds me of Mama. She is practical and already, at four years old, she watches and judges me. I wonder if Carr is having too much influence over her? Little John – but it is too early to tell how he will turn out. I love the way, when I pick him up, he curls his soft body into mine. What a pity that he will have to grow up to be a man and – oh, the front door bell has rung. I can hear Gladys at the door saying, as I have trained her to say, that she will see if Mrs Chapman is in. It is only a matter of seconds before I shall be interrupted. So life goes on.

Kate continued reading. Presently she laughed. Liz looked up queryingly.

'Listen to this.

'April 5th. I can't help feeling that my management of household affairs is rapidly descending into farce. Arthur makes it plain he thinks so too. Cook has quarrelled with Gladys over the mysterious disappearance of some cold mutton left in the larder overnight. Gladys has "followers" and Mrs Braithwaite thinks that one of them is hard up and Gladys feeds him on the sly. I think myself that the culprit was Arthur on one of his midnight prowls around the kitchen after coming back from his card game. But I could hardly say so to Mrs Braithwaite.

'Carr has quarrelled with Baines over which part of the garden the children should be allowed to play in. Baines is worried about his begonias. I feel he should stop worrying. I've never liked begonias. A wretched little plant for people who have no imagination. All this has created "an atmosphere" in the house, for which Arthur blames me. Though, since he is out most of the time, I can't see what he has to complain about.

'To cap it all, today I've gone and engaged the sulkiest-looking gardener's boy. Joe Perkins is his name. Baines vouches for him so I suppose he's all right. "A good lad," he said. I wonder if Baines knows what he is doing? Master Perkins scarcely opened his mouth during the whole of the interview. Simply stood there and glowered at me. Sometimes I wish we didn't have a garden.'

Kate paused. 'Great, isn't it?'

'Marvellous,' agreed Liz. 'Read some more.'

'Let me see, the next entry is April 16th. She doesn't have entries for every day, too busy, I suppose. "*April 16th. I am writing this sitting at the walnut escritoire*" –' Involuntarily Kate glanced over at the sideboard. 'It must have matched that.

'– at the walnut escritoire which was my mother's and, before that, her mother's and thinking, as I look at Mama's portrait hanging on the wall opposite, that things were definitely better managed in her day. There were nine of us – and not one of us ever dared answer Mama back. Children should be seen and not heard was the prevailing rule. Mama kept a big stick on the highest shelf in the kitchen and if we were unruly she would start to reach up for it. One of my brothers would shout "Watch out! Battle's on the warpath!" and we would scatter and creep back later, very quiet and subdued.

'She ruled the servants with a rod of iron too. Mama always entered rooms with a pounce, I remember, as though hoping to catch someone unawares. That sort of firm management was possible in the pre-war days, before our servants tasted the freedom of factory work and got to know their rights. Good servants are scarce nowadays. Indeed I don't know why anyone would choose to go back into domestic service after the freedom of working outside the home. Gladys was laid off when the munitions factory closed down, so that's why she has come back. But she hates it, I can tell, though she has every Sunday evening off and alternate Wednesday afternoons, which is more than most housemaids get. Well, I would hate it too, always living in other people's houses.'

Kate paused. 'Gladys – isn't that the name of the maid who found the empty bottle of cyanide under the stairs?'

'Hang on.' Liz picked up the blue folder and flicked through some cuttings. 'Yes, here it is – Gladys Simpson. Must be the same person. Laura would hardly have had two maids called Gladys.'

'I wonder why she went to the newspapers? Revenge, do you think? Getting back at her mistress because she hated her work?'

'Or perhaps Gladys murdered Arthur herself and planted the evidence? After all, as housemaid, she'd have had plenty of access to the sugar bowl.'

'What would have been her motive though?'

'Maybe Arthur had seduced her? He seems to have been a bit of an old scoundrel, having a mistress and all that. Poor Laura.'

'Perhaps Gladys simply wanted money?' suggested Kate. 'She went to the papers rather than to the police because she knew they would pay her for information. Perhaps she found herself pregnant and needed money for an abortion?'

'Did women have abortions in those days?'

'They did, but it was a risky business. And illegal. Women's novels of the period are full of deaths or near deaths by abortion. Also it was expensive.' Kate fell silent. 'I wonder what happened to Gladys afterwards? I suppose she couldn't go on living under the same roof as Laura after betraying her to the papers like that.'

'Read a bit more of the diary. We might find out.'

Kate flicked through the pages until she came to a long entry in the middle of the diary. 'This might tell us something.

'*August 2nd. The days go on and my life is endlessly the same. Wake to the sound of Gladys rattling irons in the hearth downstairs and Arthur snoring in his dressing room. Gladys brings me my tray. I eat toast and drink coffee and glance at my letters. Get up and go into the nursery to see if the children have had a good night. Plan their day with Carr. After that, downstairs to see Mrs Braithwaite and order the meals for the day. Do the flowers. Discreetly supervise Gladys. Phone the meat order to Mr Bridges. Write letters. Pop in to see the children. If it's Monday, visit sick old Nancy Thornton. Lunch at one with Arthur. Then a lie-down with the papers. Then out to pay a few calls. Or a walk along the seafront to take the air. Nursery tea with the children and play with them before their bath. After that, an hour's writing (in secret, of course, because Arthur disapproves). Change for dinner at eight. That lasts until nine. Then another hour for writing, if Arthur's going out. Or a game of bridge with Arthur's friends if I am unlucky. Then bed. Alone, thank heavens, since John's birth. Arthur has what he wanted. He has his heir . . . Not much of a life, is it? Even writing it down makes me feel dreary. Goodness knows what it's doing to my unconscious – we know about that now, even in Whitby, thank you, Dr Freud, we know all about repressions and sublimations and the Oedipus complex.*

'*I feel so hemmed in by things. All this heavy furniture we've inherited from Arthur's mother and mine. These dark green and dark red walls. The clutter of ornaments. The Wedgwood, Sèvres and Crown Derby to be dusted every day by Gladys, then inspected by me*' on the sly for breakages. How I long to sweep it away. To live somewhere light and bright and bare, to get rid of this red plush and wash the walls in plain distemper.

'August 4th. I have made a small start. The potted palms about the place were starting to irritate me so yesterday I asked Baines to dispose of them. Naturally Arthur, who normally never notices anything, noticed at once that they were gone. On the spur of the moment I invented a Paraguayan palm disease which came in on one of the ships. I don't think he believed me. Later in the evening he found an excuse to pick a quarrel with me, did his usual thing, then took up The Times and flounced off with it to his dressing room. But it was worth it, to be rid of those palms. Or almost worth it. I must be careful though. Philippa is coming for tea today. A bright spot. I must wear my highest collar. She notices everything.'

'Who is Philippa?' Kate flipped back a few pages.

'July 20th. Miss Philippa Hamley is coming this morning. She is looking for work as a governess. I met her at one of Lady Cholmley's 'at homes'. She had got the ages of my children wrong, Jessie and John are a little young yet to need a governess. But I said I would help her find work.'

'Hamley. I wonder if she was a relative of Roger?' said Liz. Goodness, my head's beginning to spin.'
'Yes,' Kate glanced at her watch, 'it is late. I think I'll turn in. What are the stories like?'
'I've only managed bits of them so far. Light, glancing stories about modern life.'
'Like Elizabeth Bowen, perhaps?'
'I've never read Elizabeth Bowen.'
'Can I take them with me to bed? In case I can't sleep?'
'Of course.' Liz collected up the exercise books and handed them over. 'I'll take the diaries. Don't you sleep? You always used to.'
Whereas I was the one who woke up at three and tossed and turned and eventually crept into my elder sister's bed for comfort.

'It varies,' replied Kate vaguely, disinclined to go into the things that were keeping her awake – Duncan being away and Perdita, always Perdita to worry about.

'You go on, Kate. I'll lock up.'

They both knew what Liz meant was she was going outside for one last smoke.

She leaned against the railing, looking down over the twinkling harbour lights to the boarding houses on the West Cliff where Roger and his mother had lived. Six hours west of here by plane, was Louise looking out at the sunset over Boston harbour? Was she sitting on the deck of the house on Cape Cod, drinking wine and listening to the cicadas? Was Annie with her?

Liz inhaled deeply, blew smoke out through her nostrils and switched her thoughts to her grandmother. What lives those middle-class women must have led. Not tragic, particularly, just slow grinding misery and boredom. No colleagues, no proper work to do, shut up in their large houses, surrounded by sullen and often hostile servants. What a life, she thought. If Laura was anything like me, she must have hated it.

She lit another cigarette and gazed down at the beach. As a girl, she had spent hours exploring these beaches, looking for ammonites, amber and stray fragments of jet. She used to take them along to the jet works and the old man would give her a few coppers and let her browse round his workshop. In the olden days it had been a proper factory, with a team of men working there. Their coats and aprons still hung on the pegs, as if the factory had been vacated just the day before. Now there was only the old man and his assistant, working away at the jet to make necklaces and earrings for tourists. He used to show her his treasures – his fossils, the piece of amber with the insect trapped inside, the mother of pearl, the fragment of bright green copper from the Congo – and she would dream of the far-off places she was going to visit when she grew up. Well, she had visited some of them, though not nearly as many as she had expected. That dream had died, along with all the others. Smoking her cigarette, Liz gazed out to sea.

Meanwhile in bed Kate was reading one of Laura's stories. It was set in the ancient Yorkshire fishing town of Monkshaven. The heroine, Delia, was married to a prosperous businessman, Alfred Rodway. Alfred was a drunkard. Delia's life was centred around her two children, a girl of six and a boy of three. One day a sick captain was brought to the house off one of the boats. Captain James Lockhart was a Creole, from the island of Dominica. Delia, who had worked as a VAD nurse during the Great War, nursed him back to health and found herself falling in love with him. Witnessing the brutal behaviour of her husband, Captain James begged Delia to come back with him to the West Indies. His family owned an estate in the wilds of Dominica where they grew coffee; they could live there.

As he lay convalescing in her sunny breakfast room, Captain James described his island to Delia for hours at a time. He spoke of its beauty, its mystery, its three hundred and sixty-five rivers, its dense, unexplored rainforest. He described to her the flowers that grew rampant there – the hibiscus, the orchids, the stephanotis and jasmine. The lilies that blossomed overnight and decayed in a day, leaving behind a sweet sickly smell, like death. 'Come with me,' he would say, taking her hand. 'Come away from this grey, cold country.' It was the height of summer, but he was never warm in England.

Delia was tempted to go with him. She even began making plans. But in the end she resisted him. She would stay with Alfred for the sake of her children. At least it seemed she would stay. The ending of Laura's story, in good modernist fashion, was ambivalent.

Kate put aside the exercise book and lay back in bed, going over the story in her mind. It was a wonderfully crafted narrative, centring on feelings and states of mind. The developing relationship between Delia and Captain James was presented with great delicacy. Sentences from the story ran through her mind.

They brought him to me, a stranger from a foreign country I had not even heard of. He was ill with fever. They carried him into the house on a stretcher. For several nights I never left his bedside. Then gradually the fever receded. 'Why have they brought me here?' he muttered.

'You have been very ill. I am a nurse. Hush now.'

He lay on the sofa in our breakfast room and told me about his island, about the tall green mountains and the volcanic springs that lie underground. 'You have only to prod the surface and boiling water gushes out.' He told me about the Valley of Desolation where sulphur fumes have made a black hole in the forest and about the Abomination of Desolation, a semi-active volcano where, twice a day, fountains of scalding water explode upwards. I was reminded of Alfred when he described this, I don't know why.

Today he suddenly seized my arm and pushed back my sleeve to reveal the ugly red weal where Alfred grabbed me last night and dragged me around the room. He said nothing, but lay gazing at me with his soft blue eyes. 'Where I come from, we have a way to deal with a man like your husband. It is called obeah.' He refused to say more, or explain what he meant. Later I looked up the word in our dictionary. It means black magic.

He has asked me to come away with him. How can I wrench the children from all that is familiar to them in order to follow this man, whom I hardly know, halfway around the world? It would need more courage than I possess.

He is going away now and my whole life will be changed because they brought him to me, a stranger from a foreign country I had not even heard of.

The more she thought about it, the more Kate found herself becoming excited by Laura's story. It was a find. A definite find. Good women writers in the inter-war period were not so numerous that one could afford to ignore the discovery of a new one. Laura might be a minor writer, but she was a skilful one; Kate recognised echoes in her story of other writers of the time. The fashion had almost died for publishing unknown women writers from the past; the brutal economics of the marketplace had slowly extinguished the 1970s dream. Still, if she presented them attractively enough, perhaps some publisher might be interested? She lay awake for a long time, trying to think of a way to get her grandmother published.

Chapter Six

....

'I've discovered something,' Liz announced, at breakfast the next morning. 'Listen to this – it's from 1924.

> *May 16th. John fell and cut his head today. Doctor Walker came and put in stitches and gave him something to calm him down. We all fussed over him no end, for which Arthur punished me afterwards in the usual way.*

'Punished her?' said Kate. 'What does she mean?'
'Wait. Listen.

> *May 17th. This business with John has left me feeling shaky and upset. If only I had someone to talk to. I have to be on my guard the whole time with Arthur. Weeks can go by without it happening, then he gets drunk and the horror breaks. Yesterday he tied me to a chair. I have learned to scream with my mouth shut, for the children's sake. I wonder if any of the servants guess? Do they know why I wear high collars and long sleeves, even in hot weather? Oh, why am I writing all this down? Whom do I hope will read it? And who would believe it if they did? Arthur is so popular in the town. A generous man, entertaining in his conversation, always ready for a card game or a day at the races. No one would believe that my body is covered in bruises.*

'Oh my God!' murmured Kate. 'He beat her. Like the story,' she added, remembering Laura's tale about Delia and Alfred Rodway and Captain James. 'How foul!'
'Yes. I almost hope she did poison him.'
'I wonder why she married Arthur? He sounds such a brute and Laura was sensitive and cultured.'
'She's a good writer,' agreed Liz.
'I know,' said Kate defensively. She didn't see why Liz should assume that, because she wasn't creative in any way, because she was

only an academic and a teacher, not a poet, certain things lay outside her angle of vision. Kate had enough of that from Duncan. Then she observed that Liz was looking a little startled. Perhaps she hadn't meant anything after all. 'I wonder why Laura never tried to get her stories published?' she went on, in a more conciliatory tone. 'They're not even typed up.'

'Perhaps after the trial no publisher would touch them? Or maybe she couldn't bear any more publicity.'

'She could have published them under a pseudonym, like the Brontës.'

'Do you think she felt guilty about them? Didn't women in those days often feel guilty about giving time to writing instead of looking after their children or their husband or the house?'

'Women still do,' muttered Kate. She buttered a slice of toast. 'Liz, I want to go and see Uncle John this morning. I want to find out what happened to Laura.'

'I thought we were going to sort through Mum's things?'

'That can wait.'

'You might be opening a can of worms here, Kate. What if Uncle John knows nothing about the murder and the trial?'

'He must know something about it. Anyway I've got to find out whether Laura is still alive.'

Liz raised an eyebrow but said no more. When Kate became interested in something, she tugged away at it obsessively. It was her talent. Whereas I waste mine, reflected Liz sadly, thinking of her poetry and the many opportunities lost to make it her life's work. She sipped her coffee and presently went outside to smoke the first cigarette of the day.

She leaned against the railing, looking at the whale's jawbones on the cliff opposite. Looking, but not seeing. In her mind, she was going over the poems in that first volume, poems of love, of forbidden love in shabby, borrowed rooms. The candlelight, the rumpled sheets, the bottle of wine on the table, a man torn between two women. From time to time over the last eight years, she had sought to recapture the intensity that was necessary for her to write, then, always, something would interrupt her. Louise would come in. 'You're not still scribbling, are you? Come on, honey, put those old

60

notebooks away, we're going off for the weekend.' They'd fling a few clothes into a bag and head out of the city in Louise's open-topped Mercedes to spend the weekend on the Cape or in Vermont, skiing. Life with Louise had contained so many different possibilities; too many, perhaps, a poet needs peace and quiet and undisturbed routine . . . Abruptly Liz turned from the harbour and, to distract her thoughts, went down to the end of the street and began climbing the one hundred and ninety-nine steps that led to St Mary's church.

The church hadn't altered since those Sundays when she and Kate and their mother had attended. Not every Sunday but once a month or so, until Kate turned fifteen and put her foot down and the whole thing petered out. Liz wandered up and down the boxed pews left over from the days when the grander Whitby families each had their own pew reserved for them. She supposed Arthur Chapman must once have had his name on one of them.

Over her head were the wooden balconies built by sailors using wood from ships that were no longer seaworthy. The extraordinary three-decker pulpit was still there and the stove to warm the congregation when the wind blew in bitterly from the sea. There was the Cholmley pew erected by a vandalising lord of the manor who had, in the process of elevating his family, ruined one of the finest Norman chancel arches in the country.

All was pretty much as it must have been in Laura's time. Looking round now with eyes that were so much more travelled than when they had last been here, Liz thought the church reminded her of nothing so much as one of those Cape Cod whaling churches she used to wander in with Louise. She smiled wryly to herself. No matter what she did, her treacherous thoughts circled round Louise, trying desperately to find a way back to her. But she feared there was no way back. She sighed and left the church.

Uncle John lived in a council flat overlooking the river Eske. At least, he didn't overlook the river since his flat was at the back and faced on to more shabby council flats climbing up the hill. Washing hung on lines in the tiny back yards. Kate and Liz walked up the steep stone outside staircase to his flat. There was a sewer smell that reminded Liz of Paris.

Uncle John, forewarned by Kate, was looking out for them. He had his front door open before they reached the top of the stairs.

'Fair old climb, isn't it?'

He smiled at them, and his tanned face showed its lines. He was wearing a pair of shabby trousers, a shirt that looked none too clean around the neck and worn old slippers. Looking at him, Kate felt a pang. How was he managing without their mother? Perhaps she should offer to do his washing? But that would be no use to him. It couldn't be a regular thing. A couple of days and she would be gone from Whitby. She bit her lip and began to feel quite worried about her uncle.

'Come in,' he said. 'I was lighting the fire.'

The front door led directly into his sitting room. As the sisters walked in, the heavy walnut table almost filling the small room caught their eye. They glanced at one another.

'That's a nice table,' began Kate cautiously. 'I'd never realised – it must match Mum's sideboard.'

'Aye. It does.' With a grunt, their uncle bent down to see about his fire.

'Did this table, like the sideboard, belong to our grandmother?' Liz rushed in.

'Aye. They both came from St Anne's.' He crouched in front of the hearth and applied a match to the pile of newspaper and coal in the grate.

'Where exactly was St Anne's?' Liz persevered, ignoring a nudge from Kate.

'Over yon side of town, up St Hilda's Terrace, overlooking the park. It's still there.' From his crouching position in front of the hearth where thin bluish wisps of smoke were beginning to rise, he shot Liz a glance. 'Why do you want to know?'

'I'll tell you.' Kate, resigned to bringing everything out into the open, sat down on one of the hard dining chairs that went with the table while Liz sat on the sofa. 'We knew nothing about our grandmother, your mother. Last night, sorting through Mum's things, we found some newspaper cuttings, about a trial, and –'

'That old story!' He turned back to his fire and fanned the flames vigorously with an old pair of bellows. 'It drove my mother away, folks said. I was too young to remember. Two at the time. The only mother I ever knew was Nellie Braithwaite. A good mother she was.' He laid down the bellows and stood up, brushing his trousers. 'Sixteen stone of solid Yorkshire flesh. And a saint.' He sighed. 'She died when I was twenty. They don't make 'em like that any more. She raised us two, you know. I called her Mam, but she was always Mrs Braithwaite to Jessie – your mother. Jessie never forgot that she'd started out life as a shipbuilder's daughter, with a nursemaid and piano lessons.'

Liz nodded, remembering the times her mother had corrected her accent. 'Don't say that, dear, it's common. Do you want to be like everyone else?' Like their father, a common trawlerman, she had meant. Kate and Liz had learned to speak with different vowels at home from the ones they'd used with their friends at school.

'Jessie married your father to have a future,' Uncle John went on. 'And to get out of that haberdashery where she worked –'

'Oh yes, I remember her telling me about that once,' murmured Kate.

'– but she always felt she'd married beneath her. That was why she was so keen on you two having the best of everything, as far as she could manage it. She was so pleased, Kate, when you married Colonel Townsend's son.'

'I know.' Kate looked down at her lap. 'I was pretty pleased too.' Duncan was the kind of man – intelligent, respectable, a middle-class professional – they had been brought up to want. 'The thing is, Uncle John,' she went on carefully, 'Mum told us our grandmother died young. That she died, in fact, in 1925 from a broken heart. We know now from the diaries that may not be true.'

'Aye, well.' He glanced at them a little sheepishly then looked at the fire. 'I went along with your mother's story. Jessie were ashamed of our mother, you see. She didn't want you children to know about the trial.'

Kate hesitated. 'What happened to Laura afterwards? We were wondering if she's still alive?'

He shook his head. 'She's not alive.'

'How do you know?' put in Liz, disappointed.

'I know.' There was a silence. 'If we're going to go over the past,' he said eventually, 'I'll need a cuppa. Want one?'

'No, th—' began Liz, remembering the thick Yorkshire brew of her childhood.

'Yes please,' Kate cut across her. 'Never get anywhere without tea,' she whispered to her sister, as their uncle went through into the kitchen. 'You've been out of this country too long. And make sure you drink it up or else he'll be insulted.'

'What happened to St Anne's, Uncle John?' she asked, when he returned carrying a tray with three large mugs of tea. Just looking at the colour in hers set Liz's teeth on edge. She'd got used to Louise's herbal brews.

'It was sold after the trial.' Their uncle sat down in the armchair. 'Nellie Braithwaite put some of the furniture in store for Jessie and me. The rest was auctioned off with the house. The money hardly covered the debts.'

'Debts?'

'Yes. Oh, my father lived in great style but it were all show. He had been in hock to the bookies for years, Mam, that is Nellie Braithwaite, told me later. He'd sold his shipbuilding business back in 1910 and after that by all accounts he lived the life of Riley. By the time he died, Arthur owed money all over town. But he was still popular. Would always stand his round. No one wanted to be the first to pull the plug on 'im. Mind you, they were said to be closing in on him around the time of his death. He had a fortunate escape, in many ways. From what Mam told me about him, he couldn't have stood being poor. The mistress could, she said, but not him.' He took a mouthful of tea.

'Uncle John, do you know what happened to Laura – your mother?'

'Mam kind of pitied my mother. Wouldn't hear a word said against her. Not that many people dared, in Nellie's presence. And I must say, whatever she did or had done, the cheques kept arriving regular from Paris.'

'Paris!' exclaimed Liz.

'That's where my mother went.'

'And did she never come back?'

'Never. Never came back.' He looked into his mug. They

wondered what distant hurts lay behind that 'never'.

'Didn't you ever want to go and see her?' asked Kate gently.

'In Paris? Nay, lass.'

Kate perceived she might as well have suggested a trip to the moon. The furthest her uncle had been in his life, to her knowledge, was Scarborough.

'But didn't you miss your mother?' persisted Liz, with less than perfect tact, Kate thought. She hadn't touched her tea, either.

'Nay, I war nowt but a bairn when she left. I didn't know her. Nellie was my mam. She brought me up as one of her own. It was hardest on your mother. Jessie never really accepted Nellie. A girl needs her mother. Jessie learned to do things for herself from an early age. She would never let Nellie.'

'What happened to Laura when she got to Paris?' asked Liz, ignoring Kate's frowns. 'How did she live?'

'I know nowt about that.' He rubbed one bony hand over his face. 'All I know is that, when I was twelve or thereabouts, the cheques stopped coming. That's how I know she's dead. If she'd have been alive, she'd have kept on sending the money, I know she would. She would have known how much we needed it. Nellie had four bairns of her own to rear besides us two. I had to leave school and find work down at the docks. It war no great hardship. I warn't great shakes at schooling. But Jessie, now – she war real bright. The teachers said she should have been sent to college. Instead she had to leave and take that job in Simpson's the haberdasher's, in Baxtergate. Long gone.'

His nieces fell silent. The one question they longed to ask – did Uncle John think his mother had poisoned their grandfather? – was clearly an impossible one. They sat drinking tea and chatting about the weather and the shocking price of beer, and left with their question unasked.

Outside their uncle's block of flats, Liz looked across at the harbour where the sun was sending silver rays over the water.

'Poor Mother,' she murmured.

'Yes.'

'Knowing about her past sort of puts a lot of things into perspective, doesn't it?' Liz glanced at her sister but if Kate was surprised at this sudden sympathy from Liz the rebel, she didn't show it. 'You know, Kate, Laura could still be alive. Uncle John doesn't have definite proof she died.'

'He seemed fairly sure.'

'I know, but . . .' Liz looked at the sea again. 'I feel like a walk. Coming?'

'No, you go on. I have to get back and make a start on the sorting out,' replied Kate, anxious to return to the house on the off-chance that Duncan might phone.

'Leave some for me to do,' said Liz, who knew that Louise wouldn't be calling.

She turned and walked along by the harbour, past Captain Cook's cherry-coloured house. She went over the swing bridge and cut up through Baxtergate where their mother had worked in that haberdasher's Uncle John had spoken of. Liz dimly remembered her mother having mentioned it once. It had been a period of her life she'd seemed anxious to forget. She hadn't got on with the owner and it had been a humbling experience for the daughter of Arthur Chapman to serve behind a counter. Yes, it must have been hard on their mother, having to grow up in the town where her parents had left behind an enormous scandal. Marriage – their mother had married at nineteen – must have been a welcome escape from all that; a chance to assume a new identity, to be Mrs Miller instead of Jessie Chapman and to obliterate all traces of the past by making up a new version to tell to her daughters.

Liz cut through to Flowergate and followed the street up to St Hilda's Terrace. Here the road widened. On the right was a terrace of prosperous-looking four-storey houses with iron gates and long front gardens. Homes for the gentry, away from the dark polluted alleys down by the harbour that had been a breeding ground in the eighteenth and nineteenth centuries for cholera, typhus and other diseases. These houses had been built high up on the hill where the air was fresher and from where they could look over the heads of the slum dwellers to the moors and the church of St Mary on the opposite cliff.

But which number had their grandmother lived at? She'd forgotten to ask her uncle. She walked along the terrace. Then she saw, written into the ironwork of a gate, the name St Anne's. It was larger and more imposing than its neighbours, with bow windows on the ground floor and a balcony running the length of the house on the first. She counted the windows across. Six on each floor. It was a massive house. No wonder their mother couldn't bear to talk about it. What a come-down it must have been, after this, to live the rest of her life in that tiny fisherman's cottage. Liz took a step back and gazed at the house. This is where it all happened, she thought, the boredom, the misery, the beatings. And Miss Philippa Hamley, the one bright spot.

She retraced her steps and turned left along Skinner Street. She walked past street after street of Victorian boarding houses until she came to Abbey Terrace where Roger's mother had kept her B and B. It was still there. It was still a B and B. A three-storey house with basement. Less imposing than her grandmother's, but still impressive by modern standards. Liz remembered how Roger used to smuggle her down to his room in the basement, after the rest of the household was asleep. Lying on his bed, both of them still partly clothed, they'd never actually gone the whole way, although she'd wanted to, to see what it would be like. But Roger was the cautious type. Besides, he'd explained, it would be an abuse of his mother's trust and hospitality. Liz had never understood the line Roger seemed to draw in his mind between heavy petting and intercourse. But it had definitely been there. Perhaps he had been saving himself for marriage?

He'd always insisted on walking her home afterwards, though she would have much preferred to go home alone. Her mother never worried when she was out with Roger. She approved of him. He might not be handsome, like Duncan, but he was reliable, safe and above all, middle class, with a job ready and waiting for him when he left school. For the first time in her life, Liz felt a flash of sympathy with her mother's ambitions. It hadn't all been social climbing; more an understandable wish to get back to her childhood.

The general thinking, among friends and neighbours of her mother, had been that Roger hadn't Duncan's dash, but that he would do for Liz who, small and skinny, lacked her sister's mature beauty. They didn't know that Liz had made other plans for her future. They didn't know about her midnight prowls around the town on the nights she wasn't seeing Roger. They didn't know about the people she met, the sailors she talked to. Then, unexpectedly one night she had bumped into Duncan, coming out of a bar arm in arm with a foreign looking young man. He'd been startled to see her.

'Lizzie! What on earth are you doing here?'

She'd thought he was about to scold her, tell her she'd better go home at once, perhaps threaten to shop her to her mother. He did none of these things. Instead he stood on the pavement for a moment, looking at her with the sort of expression in his eyes that said, Kate's kid sister has finally grown up. The world can turn on such a moment.

He slapped his companion on the back. 'Catch you up later, André.' And added drily, as André gave him a knowing wink, 'Lizzie is my sister-in-law.' So he established the point. Safe relationship, safely out of bounds to one another. He put a hand under her elbow. 'Come for a drink.'

They went back inside the bar. He pulled up a stool. 'What are you having?'

Liz, coming from a dry house, was momentarily confused by the array of bottles behind the counter and asked for a double whisky.

Duncan burst out laughing and ordered her a single, with plenty of water. He had a beer. She felt proud to be sitting up beside him at the bar, proud that he looked so handsome, in his jeans and white shirt, a denim jacket thrown over his shoulders, and proud that, for once, his attention was entirely focused on herself. She was borrowing some of Kate's happiness for an hour.

'Well, little Lizzie, what are you doing out so late?'

'Wandering around. I like the town at night. The people are more interesting.'

'You've found that too?' He was treating her as an equal, then he spoilt it all by asking, 'Does your mother know about these nocturnal ramblings?'

She shook her head, took a sip of whisky and choked on it.

'You can tell you come from a teetotal household.' He thumped her on the back.

'Thanks. I'm all right now.' She shook the tears from her eyes. 'Mother doesn't know. She goes to bed early. I have my key. It's easy enough to slip out of the house. Promise you won't tell?'

He looked at her doubtfully. 'I suppose you won't come to any harm. Whitby's a safe enough town. But why do you do it?'

'I told you. I like watching people. I like night life. All the middle classes tucked up in bed.'

She didn't tell him she had once seen a man in a dress being kissed by a sailor on the pier. She thought he'd be shocked.

'Lizzie. Lizzie.' He shook his head. He'd always called her Lizzie. She rather liked that, that he had a different name for her. 'What is to become of you, eh? What does the future hold for you?'

His brown eyes stared at her with amusement from beneath that boyish lock of hair. Duncan had always managed to seem both sophisticated and at the same time youthful enough to talk to Liz on her own level (very different from the big sister approach Kate was adopting more and more these days). Liz struggled to match his sophistication.

'I want to get away from Whitby. That first. Once I've done that, I don't really care. I want to travel, see the world. I might become a singer in a nightclub,' she added defiantly.

He smiled. 'Or a poet? Kate says you're a good writer.'

'No one earns a living by writing poetry these days.'

'I thought you were trying for Cambridge?'

'I am, but it seems pointless.' She looked down at her feet perched on the rung of the bar stool. 'How many people from our town get into Cambridge? Only you.'

'I could coach you.'

'Would you? Would you really? Why?'

'It would please your mother,' he said simply. 'I like to please your mother.'

'Oh.' Her tone was sullen. The idea of pleasing her mother had never once entered into Liz's plans for the future. In fact, so far, the whole of her adolescence had been directed towards very much not pleasing her mother. 'I don't know why Mother's so keen on me trying for Cambridge. Didn't Kate go to Sheffield University – isn't that good enough for her? One clever daughter in the family's enough, I should have thought.' She kicked morosely at the leg of the bar stool.

'You'd have more fun at Cambridge. There the night life *is* interesting. Besides, it would avoid having to make those contingency plans for singing in nightclubs.'

'I'm a good singer. I sing with some of the girls from school.'

'What? Not nightclub songs, I hope?'

She tilted her chin. 'All sorts.'

He laughed, leaned forward and tickled her under the chin. 'I love it when you do that.'

He went off to make a phone call. As he went something dropped out of his jacket pocket and rolled along the carpet. Liz bent down to see what it was. Duncan's lucky charm, a silver florin, always carried with him. On impulse, she picked it up and thrust it into the pocket of her jeans.

'Got to go, I'm afraid,' he said, coming back a few moments later.

'Sure,' she replied immediately, disappointed but trying not to show it. Leaving the rest of her whisky undrunk, she slid off her stool.

They went out of the bar arm in arm. She hoped he might insist on walking her home, like Roger. But he didn't. Instead he released her outside the bar and said, pulling his jacket more tightly across his shoulders, 'Well, cheerio then.'

'Goodbye. Thanks for the drink.' She turned. 'Er, Duncan?'

'Yes?'

'Don't tell Kate.' She saw him hesitate. 'Please!'

'All right.' He smiled slightly.

This was their first secret from Kate. Only many months later did it occur to Liz that Duncan might have had his own reasons for wanting to keep this meeting secret. What on earth had he been doing wandering around Whitby late at night without Kate? Yes, in many ways, when she'd bumped into Duncan that night she'd still been incredibly naive. She had had no idea what was in store for her.

Liz turned back in the direction of the town and found herself by chance walking past Roger Hamley's estate agency. She glanced at her watch. Twelve thirty. On impulse she pushed open the door. The agency was on the ground floor of an imposing Georgian townhouse, very different from the shabby backstreet premises the firm had occupied when she was a child. As Kate had said, Roger was doing well.

'Just a minute,' said his secretary, Joan. 'I'll see if Mr Hamley is available.'

She went through into the back room. Almost immediately Roger came out.

'Liz! This is a nice surprise!'

He seemed genuinely pleased to see her. Liz was aware of Joan's sharp eyes appraising her. Perhaps she sized up all the women who called on Roger. What had Kate said? The most eligible bachelor in town? But even in the past, Liz's feelings for Roger had not been romantic, more of the brother–sister variety. She felt sisterly now, as she gazed at him. It was nice to see a familiar face. She had spent so much of her life among strangers.

'I was wandering around, mulling things over, when I saw your name on the door and realised this is where I came with Kate yesterday. When did you move office?'

'Six or seven years ago. The ground floor was going cheap and this is the kind of building that impresses clients.'

Against the odds, he'd acquired a bit of style, a touch of worldly cynicism that hadn't been there before.

She smiled. 'Have you time for lunch?'

'Have I, Joan?' He turned to his secretary.

'There's Mrs Cadwallander coming at two and –'

'I'll make time.' He grinned. 'Let me fetch my jacket.'

They wandered down the street, avoiding the tourist fish and chip shops, to a wine bar tucked away in a back alley. It was already filling up but Roger was obviously a regular here. They secured a table for two without any problem. He ordered crab salad, the most expensive dish on the menu, and a glass of Sauternes. Liz ordered prawns.

'Are you sure? Have crab if you like. This is on me.'

'No, let's go Dutch, I'd prefer it,' she replied, echoing an argument they'd had dozens of times in the past.

They smiled at each other.

'Have you decided what to do about your mother's house?'

She shook her head. 'Kate's keen on selling, but I don't know. After all, small and humble as it is, it is our family home. I'd like to keep my options open.'

Roger threw up his hands in mock horror. 'Liz, you're surely not intending to come back here to live, are you? You, of all people, who couldn't wait to get away from – what was it? – this narrow little town with its narrow little minds?'

She smiled ruefully. 'Perhaps I've changed as I've got older, started to appreciate things I never used to.'

A trace of smugness flitted over his face. He took a sip of wine. 'Yes. I've heard America is terribly violent. They have to frisk children going into their schools on a morning, don't they, and post armed guards to patrol the corridors?'

'Not in –' Boston, she had been going to say. She stopped herself. She hadn't come back to play a game of oneupmanship. 'Yes, it is quite violent,' she agreed. 'But tell me about yourself. Kate said you have three children.'

'Hardly children any longer. Two of them are teenagers.' He began picking his way through the crab, deftly prising the meat from the claws with a special two-pronged fork. 'Samantha, the eldest, is fifteen. Charlotte is fourteen. The little one, Elizabeth, is twelve.'

'Elizabeth?'

'My wife liked the name,' he said shortly.

His wife. She ought to say something about that. 'I was sorry to hear about the accident. Kate told me. It – it must have been dreadful,' she added lamely.

'It was terribly hard on the kids. To lose their mother at such a young age,' he returned conventionally. He didn't mention his own feelings on the matter. Liz supposed that, living in such a small town, he must have grown tired of being an object of commiseration. There was a moment's silence, then he said, 'I was sorry to hear about your mother, Liz. We ran into one another in the town from time to time over the years. I always liked her.'

'She liked you.' Liz sighed. 'I don't know what I feel about her death. Sort of numb at present, as though it hasn't yet sunk in. I've spoken to her only on the phone for so many years that somehow it doesn't feel real that she's gone.' And when I learned she had died,

I was still reeling from Louise's cruelty. Perhaps the human brain can only take in one piece of bad news at a time.

Roger nodded. 'The loss of a parent takes a while to sink in.'

His father had died when he was twelve. Four years later, her own father had died. As a teenager, Liz had felt that their both being fatherless had given them something in common and had been grateful that her mother didn't cling to her daughters, as Charlotte Hamley clung to Roger.

'Charlotte is well, is she?'

'Oh yes. Still going strong. She lives with us now, you know, since my wife died.'

'She'll like that.' Try as she might Liz couldn't keep the irony out of her voice. He looked up. 'Give her my regards,' she added hastily. And a good kick up the backside when you next see her.

'I will.' Roger studied his crab, hunting out the white meat. Presently he said casually, 'You never married?'

'No, I never did. Several long-term relationships, but in the end none of them worked out.'

This gave him a certain satisfaction, she could see. It wasn't because of any flaw in himself that their relationship had foundered, he was thinking. After all, two years after Liz had left Whitby, he had embarked on a marriage which, despite its faults, lasted twelve years, which was longer than most marriages lasted these days. No, the fault had lain, as he'd suspected at the time, with Liz herself. She was simply too flighty, too fickle for a permanent relationship. All the time she'd been going out with him, he'd had a feeling there'd been someone else lurking in the background.

Liz could see this running through his mind. Roger had never known exactly why she had left. Kate had said the fewer people who knew, the better. At the time it had seemed to make sense. Whitby was such a small, gossipy town. Now Liz wondered whether it would have been kinder to have told him the truth. The truth might have left less of a scar or a chip on the shoulder or whatever it was that seemed to be bugging Roger, just below the surface of their conversation. She left it unstated, but implicit, that these long-term relationships had been with men. No point complicating things further.

'Roger, one of the reasons I wanted to see you was to ask if a Miss Philippa Hamley is any relation of yours? Kate and I have been sorting through Mother's things and we found an old diary of my grandmother's in which she mentions this Philippa Hamley coming for tea and '

He gave a short laugh and threw down his fork. 'Here I was, thinking you wanted to meet me again for old times' sake. I should have known better.' He smiled ironically at her.

She smiled nervously back at him. 'It is important to me, Roger. There's just a chance my grandmother may still be alive. She may be living abroad somewhere.'

'What date is the diary?'

'Nineteen twenty-four.'

He shrugged. 'There was an aunt of my father's called Philippa. A maiden aunt. I never met her. She went off to live in Paris when she was quite young. Got a job as governess with some wealthy Jews, I believe. She wasn't much spoken of in the family. I grew up thinking she must have done something terrible.'

Liz's eyes widened. Perhaps Philippa Hamley *had* done something terrible? Perhaps she had murdered Arthur Chapman? What would have been her motive though? '*I must put on my highest collar. Philippa notices everything.*' Had Philippa wanted to rescue Laura from Arthur, never dreaming that Laura would be put on trial for his murder? And had Laura stood trial to protect her friend? There was a long history in Whitby of defying authority, stemming from the days when sailors hid from press gangs and smugglers outwitted excisemen.

'Do you know what happened to Philippa? Is she still alive?'

'Haven't a clue. Shouldn't think so. She'd be awfully old by now, wouldn't she?'

'Old, but not necessarily dead.' Liz paused as the waiter came to clear away their plates.

'Coffee? Pudding?'

'Just coffee, please.'

'Two coffees,' he ordered.

As the waiter went away again, she leaned across the table and said, 'Roger, you don't have an address for your great-aunt, do you? Even an old one would do.'

He shook his head. 'I doubt it. It was the other side of the family and Mother cleared out everything when my father died. I can ask her, if you like.'

'Thanks.'

'I still don't see the connection with your grandmother.'

'I think your great-aunt might be able to tell us what happened to our grandmother. You see, like Philippa, Laura left Whitby in the 1920s to live in Paris. We don't know what happened to her after that. It is just possible she's still alive.'

Liz looked at him closely but Roger's face remained a blank. Clearly the scandal over Laura's trial was unknown to him. He glanced at his watch and yawned surreptitiously, finding this talk of maiden aunts less than enthralling. She made an effort.

'So what do you do when you're not at work?'

'I play golf.' He brightened up and gave his coffee a stir. 'I was president of the club last year. And I'm involved in Rotary. I'm likely to be put forward as chairman next year.'

He went on in this vein for some time. It was Liz's turn to grow restless.

'I suppose I should be getting back,' she said at last. 'Kate's sorting out things in the house. I can't leave it all to her.'

Roger paid for their meal. He insisted. With a gold card, she noticed. Business must be good.

'We must do this again sometime,' he said casually, at the door of the wine bar. 'Or perhaps one evening . . . if you wouldn't find it too much of a bore.' Again the prickly tone.

'I'd love to,' she said quickly. 'Can I bring Kate?'

'Sure. If that's what you want.'

Roger turned on his heel. Liz was left on the pavement feeling that she had offended him in some way. Perhaps it had been the mention of Kate. But when they had so few days together and so much to catch up on, she didn't want to go out and leave Kate on her own. And she hadn't been thinking of it as a proper date. Had Roger?

Chapter Seven

Meanwhile, in the little terraced house Kate, far from getting on with sorting her mother's things, was staring at old family photographs she had rooted out from her mother's bedside table. Among them were several of Laura. Black and white studio portraits mainly. Head and shoulders. There was one full-length one. Laura was standing on the pier at Scarborough dressed in a long skirt and jacket and a plain hat. She looked tall, gaunt and graceful, with high cheekbones and thoughtful, searching eyes. Kate wondered what colour Laura's eyes had been. The red hair which she had handed on to her daughter, granddaughters and great-granddaughter, was of course black in the photograph and tucked up under her hat. Even so, she looked striking. The date on the back of the photograph was 1923, the year before the diaries began, two years before the murder.

There was a pre-war photograph of Arthur Chapman, too, looking round-faced and florid, with a nasty little moustache above his fleshy lips. There was a studio portrait of Kate's mother as a young child, sitting on a chair, dressed in a white frock with buckled shoes, her long hair tied back in an enormous bow. She was holding baby John in her arms. Then a gap of many years before the next photograph. Presumably Nellie Braithwaite hadn't had the money to spare for such frivolities. Her mother, aged sixteen or thereabouts, looked neat and respectable in a striped shirt and a calf-length skirt. Perhaps she had paid for the portrait herself out of her wages from the haberdashery.

Kate ran a finger over her mother's face. She missed her. There were a lot of things that had never been discussed between them, but she missed that down-to-earth approach to life which no one else in the family seemed to possess – not Duncan, not Perdita, certainly not Liz. She would have liked to have been able to talk over with her mother this latest escapade of Perdita, excluded from school for a month for smoking cannabis in the school grounds. The school would have preferred to exclude her for longer, but they hadn't dared. Perdita was one of their brightest pupils and this was her A-level year. They needed her results.

On being told about this Duncan, of course, had simply shrugged his shoulders and said, 'Cannabis is less harmful than tobacco or alcohol. It's only a matter of time before they legalise it,' a remark which Kate hadn't found helpful. All Duncan's friends seemed to smoke, drink or snort some substance or other. He hadn't been a good example to Perdita growing up. After giving her a stern lecture, Kate had packed Perdita off to stay with her godmother in Pickering. This much she had told Liz. She hadn't elaborated on the reason. Liz's response was likely to be something like Duncan's and anyway, Kate felt obscurely defensive about Perdita as far as Liz was concerned. As if any flaw in Perdita indicated some fault in herself and her mothering abilities. She didn't want Liz to know anything about this episode.

Oh, I suppose I wouldn't have told Mum either. Kate gazed at the photograph. For that generation, drugs were frightening, horrific things, whereas Kate knew perfectly well that just because Perdita smoked a joint from time to time ('It's my way of relaxing, Mum'), it didn't mean she was about to start sticking needles in her arm.

The front door banged. Liz strode into the sitting room.

'How's it going?'

'I got sidetracked.' Kate scrambled guiltily to her feet, clutching the photographs. 'I was looking at these.'

'Let's see.' Liz took the photos from her. 'So that's Laura. Beautiful, wasn't she? Fancy allowing herself to be pushed around by that old brute. He *does* look a bit of a brute, doesn't he?'

'Mm, but that's because we know what he got up to. If we didn't know, wouldn't we think it simply a portrait of an Edwardian gentleman?'

'He's much older than Laura.' Liz pored over the photographs. 'He gives me the shivers. Why on earth did she marry him?'

'For his money and the status marriage would bring her, I suppose.'

'Surely not. Surely she wouldn't have stooped so low?'

'Perhaps she didn't have a choice. Women often didn't in those days.'

Liz took the photographs over to the window to get a better look at them. 'I had lunch with Roger,' she threw out casually.

'Roger!' Kate looked at her wonderingly. 'How did that happen?'

'I was walking along the street and suddenly noticed it was the street his office is in. I called in on the off-chance,' replied Liz, still studying the photos. 'I wanted to find out about Philippa Hamley.'

'And?'

'She was, or is, his father's maiden aunt. Disappeared off to Paris to work as a governess. Hasn't been heard of, or spoken of, since apparently.'

'Paris? Like Laura.'

'Exactly.'

'Do you think they went together?'

'I . . .' Liz was interrupted by the phone.

Kate picked up the receiver. 'Oh, hello, Duncan. Yes. Yes. She arrived two days ago.'

Abruptly Liz dropped the photographs and fled the room, alarm in her eyes.

Kate bent over the receiver. 'How are things?'

'All right.' Duncan cleared his throat. 'I may have to stay here a bit longer. Chris's case comes up on Tuesday. I said I'd . . . I want to be here to give him support.'

'Yes.'

'You don't mind too much, darling? I mean, I thought you'd be busy clearing out things.'

'Oh yes, there's lots to do.'

'And with Liz there.'

'Yes.' Uncertain. How did Duncan feel about this? Was he going to want to see Liz, or would he avoid her?

'How is she?'

'The same. You know Liz,' Kate replied, then could have bitten off her tongue.

There was silence on the other end.

'How long's she staying?' he asked eventually.

'No idea. She's talking of touring the country.'

'Good. Right. Well, I'd better stay here.'

So it was going to be avoidance. What would Liz feel about that? Kate remembered what Duncan had said when she'd told him Liz was coming home and wondered aloud whether she would have changed, like everyone else they knew. 'Oh but Lizzie was never like anyone else,' he'd answered. 'I can't imagine her growing old like us.' Then, looking horrified at what he'd said, he'd shuffled off out of the room. No, it was better they didn't meet.

'Any word from Perdita?'

'She rang a couple of days ago. Didn't say much but she sounded all right. Jenny's keeping her busy around the farm. Hopefully cannabis hasn't reached Pickering in large quantities yet!'

'Don't worry about her, Kate. She'll be all right. She's a bright kid. She has a great future ahead of her.'

'That's what I'm worried about. I don't want it ruined.'

Again there was silence on the other end. Kate thought about what she'd just said. In the past someone else's future had been ruined. Duncan blamed himself. That was why he was so keen on picking up these hopeless young men and trying to set them on their feet. An endless replaying of old guilt.

'I meant –' she began.

'I know what you meant.' There was a sound of voices. He must be standing in some hallway. 'Kate, I've got to go.'

'OK. Give me a ring when you can,' she said, well practised in giving Duncan his freedom.

'I will. Take care of yourself old thing. See you soon.' He put down the phone.

Kate dropped the receiver and stood in the middle of the sitting room, pressing her hands to her temples, going over the conversation in her mind. There was nothing, simply no clue, as to whether this time this particular young man would emerge triumphant and carry Duncan off with him.

'What on earth are you doing?' Hearing silence next door, Liz came back into the sitting room.

Kate's hands dropped to her sides. She picked up the receiver dangling on its cord and replaced it. Then she sat down on the arm of a chair. 'I was thinking. That was Duncan on the phone.'

'Yes.'

'He . . . he's got to stay up in Teesside a few days longer. So you may miss seeing him.' Out of the corner of her eye, Kate watched for Liz's reaction.

'Will I? It's probably for the best,' Liz responded, as lightly as she could. She shut off her feelings (she would examine those later) and sank on to the sofa. 'What's he doing up there anyway?'

'This friend of his, Chris, he's in trouble with the police. His case comes up shortly. Duncan wants to be with him.'

'Is it serious?'

Yes, it's serious, thought Kate. But she knew that wasn't what her sister meant. 'Not very. Chris stole some bread. He's unemployed. He was starving on the streets when Duncan found him. He'd been kicked out of his home by a violent stepfather. He's sixteen so he can't claim benefit. He drifts around. He's been in and out of our lives for over a year now . . .'

'You're a hero, Kate,' Liz said softly.

'By the skin of my teeth.'

Kate grimaced and turned her head away. She hadn't always been heroic – those times after Perdita was born, when she'd come into Duncan's bed in the middle of the night and practically forced him to make love to her. She didn't do that any longer. And sometimes she was lucky. Sometimes he came to her of his own accord. Not in the last year though.

Observing the expression on Kate's face and hearing the wobble in her voice, Liz thought that, on the whole, she was relieved rather than disappointed that she wouldn't be meeting Duncan. He still seemed to possess the art of making his life, and everyone else's, as complicated as possible. She'd had enough of that with Louise. What she wanted now was to get some simplicity into her life, simplicity and peace, for out of those two things poetry might come.

Kate stood up. 'Well, we'd better go on with the clearing out.'

They spent the rest of the afternoon sorting through their mother's scanty wardrobe. A few Marks & Spencer dresses, a couple of skirts, five blouses, three cardigans, all terribly shabby. Louise, who went shopping twice a week in Newbury Street, Boston's most fashionable area, would never have believed a woman could possess so few clothes. There were no trousers. Their mother had never worn trousers as far as Liz could recall. In some ways she had been a generation behind her own generation.

'I'm going to give these to Oxfam,' said Kate, bundling clothes into a black plastic bag. 'There's nothing you want, is there?'

'No,' Liz replied. She was busy wrapping ornaments in tissue paper and packing them into a cardboard box.

'No, I don't suppose you would want any of this stuff.' Kate cast an envious glance at Liz's jeans. 'You can't be used to wearing second-hand clothes.'

Liz looked up. 'As a matter of fact I am. These belong to Louise. They're her cast-offs. I'm shorter than she is. I had to take the legs up.'

Kate hesitated. 'Liz, I was going to say, phone Louise if you like. We could afford one transatlantic call. So long as you're not on too long.'

'It's all right, thanks.' Liz's head bent lower over the box. 'She's not expecting me to phone. We've agreed we'll write to each other.'

'What's she like?' asked Kate curiously. This relationship with Louise had lasted a long time, longer than any of the others.

'Louise? She's rich, spoiled, promiscuous.' Liz gave a short laugh. 'Only kidding.'

'Rich?' That explained the designer labels then.

'Yep, that part's true. Her family's rolling in it. Plastics. They own a factory. Or several. Louise doesn't need to earn her own living. In fact she doesn't. She dabbles in interior decorating but it's really only furnishing homes for friends.'

Kate blinked, this kind of lifestyle being outside her range of experience. If Louise is so rich, why isn't she phoning every night, she wondered. 'What does she look like?'

'Tall, with long thick black hair, dark brows and black eyes. There's Spanish blood in the family from way back. It's come out in Louise.'

Liz bent lower over her box, remembering. Drowning her face in Louise's velvet hair that smelled of all the spices and scents of the

Orient, being carried away by it to strange, exotic places. Racing along the beach at Provincetown, in the days when they'd gone there as lovers, making love among the sand dunes, Louise's hair spread out around them.

'Sounds a beauty,' commented Kate.

'She is. She thinks I'm an elf.' Liz got up from her knees and ruefully surveyed herself in her mother's dressing-table mirror.

Kate sat back on her heels. 'Where did you meet her?'

'In a bar in Paris. I was waitressing. Louise picked me up.' It's a thing Louise often does, she added, though not aloud. She returned to her ornaments.

'But you do love her, I suppose?'

'Oh yes, I love her.'

Something in Liz's voice made Kate glance sharply at her, but her sister's face was hidden as she bent to wrap an ornament. She doesn't have things all her way either, thought Kate, with a flash of intuition. The thought didn't please her or give her a cheap feeling of triumph, as it might once have done. The thought of both of them being in the same situation made Kate feel rather bleak. Packing these clothes didn't help; she felt as if she was packing away part of herself. With Mum dead, there was no one to stand between herself and death. She and Liz were now the older generation. The future belonged to Perdita and to Duncan's young men. Wearily, she wiped a grubby hand over her forehead.

'Shall we take a break? This is a grim business, isn't it?'

'Yes.' With a sense of relief, Liz abandoned the tiny, cheap china ornaments and stood up, brushing her hands on her jeans.

'We should be able to finish this room tomorrow. Are you sure there isn't anything you want?'

'I might take some of the bedding.' Making contingency plans, supposing Louise had gone for good this time.

'Fine. I'll look out some of the better stuff for you. It's only sheets and blankets, I'm afraid. Mum never had duvets.'

They went downstairs and poured themselves a glass of wine.

'Let's go on with Laura's diary,' suggested Liz. 'Read it to me. If you're not too tired.'

'I'm not too tired.'

Welcoming a distraction from her gloomy thoughts, Kate went to fetch the blue hardback books.

She joined her sister in the front room.

'Let's see what she says about Philippa Hamley,' Liz suggested. 'Their friendship intrigues me. I can't help thinking it might hold a clue to the murder.'

'Where was she mentioned?' Kate flicked over a few pages. 'Yes, here it is – this is still 1924.'

July 21st. Miss Philippa Hamley called yesterday. She came, looking most unlike a governess, in a pale green knee-length linen frock, with a velvet cape and a little velvet cap. The height of fashion. I am sure nothing like it has been seen in Whitby before. I expect it will get round to us in about five years' time. Her fair hair is bobbed, a thick, straight bob with a short fringe. I have to say she looked rather racy for a governess. Whereas I was wearing my biscuit-coloured frock and brown low-heel shoes and my hair was coming down from playing with the children. To anyone watching, it would have been I who looked like the governess.

'"I speak French fluently," Philippa said, dropping on to the sofa and casually tossing off her cape and hat, with none of the fussy accompanying gestures ladies usually make, ladies in Whitby at any rate. "I have spent a year in Paris," she added, in a matter of fact tone, as if this is an entirely normal occurrence in the lives of the inhabitants of Whitby. As a matter of fact, I don't know anyone, any lady that is, who has lived abroad. As long as I live I shall remember those two sentences spoken in my drawing room. "I speak French fluently" and "I have spent a year in Paris." They brought fresh air from the outside world into our stuffy little room (I'm speaking metaphorically here, it's not actually little).

'I sat on a chair opposite, wishing I could be more like her – cosmopolitan and sophisticated and sure of myself. Then perhaps Gladys and Carr and Baines and all the rest of them wouldn't bully me so much. There would still be Arthur, however. There is nothing I can do about him. Only this being in constant terror is affecting my writing. It's getting harder and harder to make up stories. Perhaps that is why I am writing so much in this diary. I never used to keep a diary;

this is quite a new thing. I don't know whether it is good or bad for my writing. I only know it consoles me, makes up for Mama being far away and anyway I couldn't tell her the things I tell my diary; it would break her heart.'

Kate paused.

'Sad, isn't it?' said Liz.

'Yes,' said Kate quietly. Perhaps I should start a diary, she thought. It might be one way of getting over Mum's death. She swallowed, glanced at her watch and said, 'Strange that Uncle John hasn't looked in. He's usually here at this hour. I hope he's all right, I'd better give him a ring tomorrow.' She went back to the diary.

'To return to Philippa. "I had a good job in Paris," she told me, "but I had to give it up and come back to Whitby because of Mother. She's ill with her nerves," she explained, and I saw then that she was as trapped as I am. We are all trapped, we females. I wonder if any of us ever succeed in getting away?

'"I will ask around," I said. "I know Mrs Conyers was looking for a governess for her two girls. Call again next Tuesday and I will see if I have any news for you, Miss Hamley." I had been about to say I would send her a note but something made me change my mind and think, I want to see this woman again. Though Arthur dislikes me having callers, I will risk it this once.

July 22nd. I have been inspired by Philippa's visit to get down to work again. I am trying to write a story based on C's experiences in Dominica. It is coming on so slowly. I cannot get it right. I have the atmosphere, pages of description based on C's accounts of the island, but where is the story to hang it on? Where is the plot, as that magazine editor would say.

'I wonder who C is?' Kate turned the page.

July 27th. I have tried out the Dominican material, but at a slant. That doesn't satisfy me. I want to get at it in a more direct way. Perhaps actually set a story there. Dare I? Never having been there myself. Ah, but there's always imagination. How I prefer it to reality!'

'Then the entries for August we read yesterday, then:

'August 16th. Arthur returned from York in a foul mood yesterday evening, having lost heavily on the horses again. There was no hot water for his bath. Gladys had let the fire go out. Added to this, the rice pudding was burnt (I shall have to speak to Mrs Braithwaite, she will keep letting her mind wander at the vital moment). Arthur threw the dish on the floor. "Never mind," I said quickly. "I'll ring for Gladys." "No, you do it." "What?" "You heard, you bitch. Get down on your hands and knees and clean it up." So I did. It could have been worse. He could have thrown the pudding at me.'

'Christ!' muttered Liz.

'Arthur spent a good hour after dinner enumerating my many deficiencies as housekeeper, wife and mother. He ran out of faults after a while and had to keep repeating himself. He drank a good deal of brandy, then he slammed me up against the wall and hit me in the face. My cheek is all colours of the rainbow this morning.'

'Loathsome brute!' exclaimed Kate.
'Shitbag!' agreed Liz, more pithily.

'I will not be able to see Philippa looking like this. I had to tell Nellie Braithwaite that I ran into a door. I don't think she believed me. What a failure I am! I cannot help thinking it must be my fault that Arthur gets so angry. Something about me must irritate him. After all, he does not behave like this with anyone else. He is as nice as pie with Jessie. Sits her on his knee and lets her play for hours with his watch. John he is not so fond of. I have to be careful not to show him too much affection in Arthur's presence. I think he is jealous . . . No one in the town would believe what Arthur does to me. He is so popular with everyone. Perhaps it is my fault he drinks and gambles. Perhaps he does it to get away from me.'

'I can't believe this!' exclaimed Liz. 'She's blaming herself for Arthur's lousy behaviour. God!' She stood up. 'I'm going to have to go outside for a cigarette, Kate. I can't take much more of this.'

'Oh, smoke it in here.'

'Are you sure?'

'There's no one here but us two. I don't have to worry about Perdita's lungs.'

'Is that why you gave it up?' Liz fumbled in her jacket pocket for cigarettes.

'I was never very keen on it, if you remember. Besides, there's the little matter of cancer.'

'Mm. I'd love to cut down but I reckon I inhale so much of other people's smoke, working in bars and clubs, that I may as well smoke my own and get a little pleasure out of it before I die.'

'Oh well, it's your life, or rather death. Just don't smoke in front of Perdita, that's the last thing she needs.'

Liz's head swivelled round. 'Am I going to see Perdita?'

'I'm not sure.' Kate glanced down at her hands. 'That depends how long you stay. Do want to?'

'I don't know,' admitted her sister. 'Who does she look like?'

'Mum.'

'My God, does she? That's one possibility I never thought of.' She gave a few drags on her cigarette. 'Go on with the diary.'

'Jotting, jottings, jottings.' Kate skimmed the pages. 'They look like ideas for short stories. Perhaps she was getting going again.

'August 24th. I am writing away at my desk, pretending of course to be busy with my correspondence, in case Arthur should come in. The sky outside is blue, for a wonder – this has been a very grey August so far. Joe is weeding the rose beds. He has just given me a shy little wave. Now he is disappearing off to the greenhouses. That boy is a mystery to me. There are hidden depths to him that I have yet to plumb. Goodness, what a cliché! I had better stop at once if this is how my writing is going to be this morning.'

'No mention of Philippa in that one. Ah, here we are.

86

'September 3rd. Philippa stopped and looked at me today as we were walking arm in arm in the orchard, looked at me with those searching blue eyes of hers. "You don't seem at all well, Laura," she said. "It's nothing," I replied. "A slight migraine. I banged the back of my head last night." Or rather, it was banged for me. Philippa took her arm from mine and scrutinised me for a long time in silence. I wondered what she was thinking. Finally she said very softly, "What on?" I trotted out the usual story about slipping on the hearthrug and hitting my head against the fender. I do not think she believed me. I must be more careful. I cannot let anyone find out. At least I will not. It would ruin Arthur's reputation and I do not want people in the town pitying me. It is not as though I can leave. Where would I go? I have no money of my own. Not a penny. And it would break poor Mama's heart. In her eyes I have made a brilliant match, marrying into the Chapman family. And Arthur is not so bad really. I expect a lot of gentlemen hit their wives, it just does not get talked about. He was all contrition this morning, I must say. Brought me a huge bunch of flowers and said he hadn't meant to hurt me. He pushed me, he said, and I fell backwards.

'September 4th. I have no right to complain. I went to visit Mrs Potts again this afternoon. I took her some of the children's old clothes. She is in a very bad way. She has found out that she is expecting again, in spite of the advice I gave her. Her fourteenth. She and her husband and their eight living children (she had two stillbirths and three died in infancy) inhabit two rooms down by the harbour. I don't know how she manages. She is on her feet from six in the morning when Mr Potts goes out to work (he is a dustman) until ten o'clock at night. She has half an hour 'off' in the evening to do the mending and darning. The family eat their meals in three sittings. She eats hers standing up while she serves them or rather, she eats the scraps that are left over. I believe she exists on bread and dripping and tea. There is no bathroom. Every time she needs water, she has to go three floors down into the yard for a bucket of cold water which she then heats over the fire in the living room. She has backache, indigestion and rotten teeth. Every time I go to visit her, I come away thinking what on earth am I complaining about? If I had her life I would curl up and die.'

87

Kate turned over a page. 'That's the end of that entry.'

They sat for a moment in silence, mulling over what Kate had read.

'Isn't it quiet in this street when the tourists and the schoolchildren have gone home?' remarked Liz, then nearly jumped out of her skin as a thundering din filled the room. 'What the bloody hell is that?'

Kate smiled across at her. 'Have you forgotten the church bells?'

'They haven't toned them down, have they? How long is this racket going to last?' her sister shouted, above the pealing bells.

'Only a short while. It's their weekly practice. I'll make us a coffee and by the time we've drunk it, they'll be finished,' Kate shouted back. 'Be patient.' She went through into the kitchen.

That was Kate all over, thought Liz. Be patient. Think before you act. Don't do anything rash. Her elder sister had always pulled her back from the unsafe bridge, the crumbling cliff edge. She hadn't saved her from Duncan though, Kate hadn't foreseen the danger there. Kate came back into the room with two mugs and they sat drinking their coffee in silence, both going over Laura's diary in their minds. As the last peal died away, Liz asked, 'Do we know where Laura was brought up?'

'The family farm was somewhere up on the North Yorkshire moors, near Goathland, I believe. I remember Mum saying a few years ago that she had been back to see it and it was derelict.'

'Nine children on a moorland farm! No wonder Laura's mother was pleased to have married one daughter off well,' commented Liz.

'Shall I go on reading?'

Liz nodded.

'September 5th. Arthur is a puzzle to me. At times he can be so charming and attentive, almost as he was before we got engaged. Last night, for instance, he pleaded with me to forgive him, said he loved only me. And of course I forgave him on the spot.'

Kate stopped. She thought of Duncan, then thought, that's absurd, there's no comparison between Arthur Chapman and Duncan. Duncan, the gentlest of men, has never laid a finger on me.

'This is harrowing stuff,' she said aloud. 'I don't know if I can bear much more of it.'

'We know she escaped in the end.'

'Only just, it appears.'

'Read something from the next year, 1925, the year of the murder.'

'OK.' Kate picked up the other hardback book. 'There aren't many entries in this one. The first is January 9th.

'I am so tired of Whitby's endless social round. The jumble sales, the bazaar teas, the amateur theatricals. Everything we do is amateur. I long to meet some professionals. I live too narrow a life here. I need to get away, to see new things, gather material for my stories.

'The worst of it is, I fear this amateurishness is creeping into my writing and I do so wish to earn money from it. It is humiliating to have to depend on Arthur for everything. Though, heaven knows, it's unlikely that anyone will want to pay me for my writing. The scraps of education I've had! Poor Miss Roberts, it wasn't her fault, I suppose. There were six of us girls to be taught and she didn't know much herself. She could just about keep up with my sisters, but she found me a trial. Mr Samuel, the boys' tutor, said I was bright enough to go away to college but of course such a thing was not to be thought of; even if he could have afforded it, Papa would not have deemed it proper for a girl to have a college education. Our purpose in life was to marry and thus relieve Papa of the problem of financing us. It was what we girls had been brought up to expect. We were to marry and we all have except Bessie, my youngest sister, who keeps Mama company at home. The boys were to farm. Two of them did. Charles ran away to join the Navy. That was the extent of our rebellion.

'Well, I have to make do with what I have got. But my writing does not come out of thin air. No one's writing does. It is affected by the houses we live in, the people we marry, the food we eat, whether we have a headache. My writing is growing gloomier and gloomier. At this rate, I cannot hope for readers and as for thinking that anyone will read me after I have gone . . . If only I had a clean, bright, silent room where I could work absolutely undisturbed for at least a couple of hours a day. But of course that is impossible. I have to do my writing in secret

and hide it under my blotter if anyone comes into the room. *Arthur doesn't like me writing. It gets on his nerves. I suppose I can understand that. You cannot expect a man like Arthur to put up with having a clever wife. He hates these modern "flappers". Thinks they should be locked up or married off. He does not think women have the right to use their vote, those of us who have it, that is.*

'*How I long to be professional and sharp. My time is frittered away on trivialities; I feel dowdy and futile and my back aches. Whitby makes me feel like this. The pettiness of it all. I never felt like this at home on the moors. Here, people are constantly judged on what they have, or pretend to have, rather than on what they are. Of course we do very well out of this. Our status in the town is still high, but we are living off the past, I am afraid. The house is crumbling around us. It needs repapering and repainting and the roof needs seeing to. When it rains, Gladys, Mrs Braithwaite and I have to run round with buckets.*

'*Ten bedrooms, two bathrooms, three sitting rooms, two kitchens, a pantry and lots of passageways – houses like these are doomed. We need at least three more servants to do the work. No wonder Gladys is constantly short-tempered. I caught Lady Cholmley scrutinising the patch of damp on our drawing-room ceiling the other day. She probably noticed the mantelpiece hadn't been dusted either. Not that I care about this, not really. The maddening thing is, living here, one is almost forced to care. How Philippa would despise me for that! She says I should be above that kind of thing, social respectability and all the rest of it. I suppose I should, but it is hard. Some days I think I am drowning in domesticity. I must go. Gladys is banging the gong for dinner. She always makes it sound as though she is summoning us all to the Last Judgement. Come to think of it, that will probably be her job in the afterlife. Gong-banger to the Almighty. She would like that. The trouble is, I don't think I believe in Him any more, the Almighty, I mean.*'

'That's the end of the entry.'

'Do you think she did murder Arthur?'

'It's sounding increasingly likely, isn't it? Or perhaps they plotted it together? That Philippa seems as if she had courage enough for anything.'

'Yes, I think I rather like her.'

'Laura was awfully fed up of Whitby, wasn't she?'

'I thought it was only I who felt like that,' commented Liz, remembering that frustration, that terrible feeling of being trapped, and her mother's admonitions, understandable now because of what they were learning about the past, 'Whitby is a small town, we have a position to keep up, Elizabeth. Don't let the family down.'

'She sounds like Perdita in one of her moods. Perdita goes on and on about the Range Rovers of Swanland – that's Hull's stockbroker belt – and the women who drive them. The way they dress in gold shoes and gold jewellery and look as though they've spent the day in a beauty parlour.'

'Is Perdita a bit of a rebel then?'

'Not really.' Kate's tone was sharp, as though she regretted having said so much. 'Even I steer clear of the Swanland set. The Avenues, where we live, is quite different. Sort of shabby and bohemian and filled with students and academics and artists.'

'Sounds nice.'

'It is. At least it suits us.' Kate flicked through the pages of Laura's diary. 'Nothing, nothing, nothing. Ah.

January 28th. "Come with me to Paris," Philippa said today. "Paris!" I sat on the sofa, stunned. "Why Paris?" "It's a wonderful city. Women can live in freedom there, and cheaply. I have many friends in Paris, wonderful friends who would help us. Writers and artists. Natalie, Gertrude, Djuna, Mina . . ."

'What? My God!' Kate glanced up. 'If these names are who I think they are, Philippa Hamley must have been right in the thick of the modernist circles in Paris. Natalie Barney ran a lesbian salon. Gertrude – can that be Gertrude Stein? Djuna – that must be Djuna Barnes, the painter and novelist, and Mina, I wonder if that's Mina Loy? Yes,' she said excitedly. 'It must be them. God, what a find!'

'I'll take your word for it,' replied Liz. 'Apart from Gertrude Stein, I've never heard of any of them.'

'I know, that's the trouble. They've got lost,' Kate said tartly.

It had always been secretly galling to Kate that her younger sister, who never read anything, should be the poet, while she, who had been a voracious reader from childhood, had never managed to produce more than commentaries on other people's work: Christina Rossetti, Elizabeth Barrett Browning and her as yet unfinished book on inter war women's fiction. Kate sighed and turned back to the diary.

'"What would we live on?" I asked her. "My friends would help me find work giving English lessons. I have done it before," Philippa replied. "I would earn the money and you could go on with your writing. It would be so much easier for you to get published out there. There are several women editors living in Paris, and small magazines always eager to take on good new authors. Oh Laura, it would be the making of you as a writer!"

'Something leapt in my stomach at her words. I had to sit very still and dig my nails into the palms of my hands to keep myself from crying out "Yes! Yes, I will come with you! With all my heart!" What I said eventually was, "It is impossible. I cannot leave the children." "Bring them with us," Philippa answered. "We will find them a French bonne." "I couldn't uproot them like that, with the future so uncertain. Besides, they are fond of their father. At least Jessie is. Anyway," I added, "what about your mother? You said she needs you." "Mother doesn't need me as much as she thinks she does," said Philippa drily. "Her nerves have settled down. She has her bridge circle and the Women's Institute to keep her occupied. And she has my brother Hubert – he is always going to be here, running the business. Besides," she added, "Whitby doesn't seem to be exactly crying out for French-speaking governesses." It is true that I have failed to find her a post. I did arrange a couple of interviews for her, but she was never offered a job. Lady Cholmley told me privately that mothers were afraid of entrusting their daughters to her. "She seems a little too spirited for a governess, my dear," she added.

'"My resources are dwindling," Philippa went on. "I shall have to go back to Paris soon. There I know I will be able to find a post."

'Listening to her, I felt here is the woman of the future. Without ties, unmarried, free to go wherever she pleases and earn money whatever way she can.

'January 29th. I am not a woman of the future. My life is beginning to repeat that of my mother. The ceaseless drudgery is wearing me down. Added to which, I don't sleep well at night. Arthur has taken a dislike to Philippa and forbidden me to see her, the usual thing when I start to make friends with anyone. He has frightened off my other friends but, amazingly, Philippa is not afraid of him. I feel safe with her. From now on, we will meet in secret, away from this house. I suspect that someone, Gladys probably, has been telling Arthur about Philippa's visits. She is not to be trusted. She takes Arthur's part in everything. He can be charming when he wants to be and I expect he finds Gladys useful. As for myself, I am beginning to see through his charm at last. He accuses me of deliberately setting out to annoy him. I am sure I try my best not to – I am on my guard the whole time. He says I don't love him enough. I think that that is beginning to be true.'

Kate paused. 'Shall I go on? The next entry is February 3rd.'
'When was the murder?'
'February 24th.'
'Yes, go on, we're getting closer.'
'I'm frightened of what we might find.

'February 3rd. We have quarrelled. "You want to get away but you keep looking back all the time," Philippa said. "You keep accepting other people's false standards." And, grabbing me by the shoulders, "You are giving in, Laura! Don't give in. Don't do what they expect. You will be dead, dead inside. Do you want to be dead?" Then she went away and I was left all alone. I wonder if I shall ever see her again? In my heart of hearts I know that she is right. She is like a mirror. When I look into her eyes, I see myself reflected back. She is me, she is more myself than I am.

'February 6th. Everything is dry as dust without Philippa. I love her, I think – though what does it mean, love between women? Is it – can it be – the same as the love between a man and a woman?

'February 10th. Saw Philippa today. We met in the park. No, loving a woman is not the same as loving a man. There is a tenderness between Philippa and myself such as I cannot imagine finding with any

man. She knows me through and through in the way a man never could. False ideas about women prevent honest relationships between men and women. Philippa is no longer angry with me. I want to sing for joy! I must not fail her again.

'February 20th. I am afraid that if I go away my heart will break to leave my children behind; if I stay, I am afraid I will be suffocated. I feel so helpless. I must pull myself out of this morass in which I am slowly foundering. "You are living in a dream, Laura," Philippa said. "Wake up before it is too late." I have to save myself. Even mothers have that right.'

'So they do,' commented Liz.

Kate turned the pages. 'That's the last entry before the murder on the 24th.'

'Do you think she did do it?'

'I don't know. She desperately wanted to get away and yet she lacked courage. Poisoning has always seemed to me a cowardly method of killing someone. Perhaps Laura, hemmed in as she was by all the social pressures on her, could see no other way out.'

'Are there no more entries?'

Kate flicked through the pages. 'None until June, after the trial was over. Then there are a couple.

'June 27th. Gladys has gone to the newspapers. I suppose I should have expected something like this. I wonder how she came across the bottle? "Now will you come with me?" Philippa said. "It is going to be impossible for you to live in this town after Gladys's revelations." I was silent. My one thought was, how I long to hide from these prying eyes. The house is going to have to be sold, to cover Arthur's debts which are even more enormous than I feared. Philippa's brother, Hubert, is taking care of the sale. "Think of it as a holiday," urged Philippa. "Leave the children with Mrs Braithwaite – you said yourself she looked after them so well during the trial – and come to Paris, for a few weeks at least. See if you like it."

'And so it is arranged. Mrs Braithwaite is more than happy to have the children. Good old Nellie Braithwaite, she is the only one to have

stood by me. Carr handed in her notice the day after the murder. Baines simply stopped coming and there has been no sign of the boy, Joe Perkins, for weeks. Gladys stayed with us out of curiosity, I think, more than anything. She enjoyed the attention, being interviewed by the police and giving interviews to the newspapers. Now she has gone as well, no doubt to spend all that money the Daily Mail has given her.

'There is only Nellie Braithwaite left. We have been managing as best we can. Philippa has been a great help, revealing hidden talents with the duster. I haven't tried to engage any new servants. I know no one would want to work here, after all that has happened. The children and I will have to live in a very small way in the future. I am afraid Jessie is not adapting too well. She misses Carr and her piano lessons.

'Oh, I am so tired. Philippa is making the arrangements. I am content to leave everything to her. I couldn't have got through this dreadful time without her. She braved public opinion and visited me every day in prison.

'July 10th. The children went to Nellie Braithwaite's this afternoon. We are off to Paris tomorrow. Whatever happens, this will be my last night in St Anne's. It was a great wrench to part with the children. Little John clung to me at the end. Jessie, being older, hung back. She has doubts about me, I can see it in her eyes. I wonder how much she knows? I tried to shield her, but people would talk in her presence and she was questioned twice by the police. I hope that, in time, little Jessie will learn to trust me again. The plan is that I will send for them both when we get settled.

'I feel the wings of happiness beating around me. I am on the threshold, about to launch into the future. What will it hold?'

Kate put down the diary. 'I wonder why she never did send for her children?'

'Perhaps she never got settled?'

'How could she bear not to see them again?' began Kate, then stopped abruptly. The two sisters contemplated this sentence in silence. They had come up against one of their innumerable checks. It would not do to let the conversation develop further.

Soon after this, they went to bed.

Chapter Eight

The next day they finished packing the clothes and ornaments in their mother's bedroom. That left four other rooms to be cleared, not counting the bathroom.

'It takes longer than you'd think, even with the few things Mum owned,' Kate said dejectedly. She tore off a strip of masking tape and began sealing the cardboard boxes.

'You know, I've been thinking.' Liz sat on the edge of the bed swinging her legs. 'We ought to try to get Laura's stories published.'

Kate sat back on her heels and nudged her hair off her forehead with her wrist. 'I've been wondering about that ever since we found them, but would anyone be interested?'

'I should think so, don't you? An undiscovered woman writer. A contemporary of Virginia Woolf. You could edit the stories and write an introduction. It would give your career a hell of a boost.'

'Yes, well, it could certainly do with that,' Kate admitted. 'I don't know though, Liz. Do you think Laura would have wanted them to be published? They seem so autobiographical.'

By now she had read through them all. Nine heart-rending stories which told, in a wry tone echoing the diaries, of women in unhappy marriages, women stifled by social convention, looking back with nostalgia to their carefree childhoods.

'All writers want to be published,' said Liz firmly. 'Even those who say they don't. Especially those who say they don't.'

'I can't help feeling publishers would be more interested if we could find out what happened to Laura after she left Whitby. Did she write any more stories, for instance? I suppose I could make a trip to the British Library at Boston Spa and have a trawl through the journals there. But I would like to know what happened to Laura in Paris. Did she stay with Philippa, I wonder? Or did she marry again?'

'I hope not!' Liz reached for her cigarettes and lit one.

The phone rang. Kate picked up the receiver. It was Roger.

'It's not much to go on but my mother thinks she remembers Dad saying Philippa lived somewhere in the Latin Quarter. That would have been some time in the late 1960s. Dad died in 1970. I know it's a bit vague but –'

'It's more than we've managed to dig up anyway. Thanks, Roger. Would you like to speak to Liz? She's right here.'

'No.' He rang off.

Kate replaced the receiver. 'What have you done to Roger?' Without waiting for an answer, she told Liz what Roger had said about Philippa.

'I have an idea. Why don't I go over to Paris and see if I can find anything out?'

'What? Now?' said Kate, startled.

'Why not? You're going back to Hull tomorrow. I'd be at a loose end here, by myself. I'd planned to do some travelling while I'm over. Why not Paris?' A trip to France, she was thinking, might cure this restlessness that had plagued her ever since leaving Boston. It would certainly get her out of having to meet Perdita just yet – or Duncan, for that matter. 'And listen, why don't you come too?'

Kate shook her head. 'I'd love to, but Perdita will be back in a couple of days.' And she didn't, at the moment, want to go too far away from Duncan. She gazed at her sister. 'Well, look, if you're serious about this, there are daily flights to Paris from Humberside airport. Come back with me to Hull tomorrow and we'll book you on a plane.'

I shall see their house, thought Liz, with a kind of terror. I shall see where Duncan lives. She got up off the bed and wandered over to the window. 'All right,' she said finally.

The next day they drove over to Hull, across purple moorland, then down towards green fields and Pickering, where Perdita was staying with her godmother.

'We won't call on her,' declared Kate, skirting the edge of the town. 'She's supposed to be catching up on her school work.'

'Which school does she go to?'

'East Riding High. It's private,' she added. 'I've given up apologising for that.'

'No reason why you should. In America you wouldn't have to apologise.'

'Oh well, you know it's against my beliefs, but what can you do, with class sizes the way they are in the state sector?' She changed gear as they went down into Malton and on towards the Wolds. To Liz it seemed as if the road was downhill all the way to Hull.

Kate's house was in a long, wide avenue lined with chestnut trees and bisected by an elaborate stone fountain.

'A turning point for carriages in the old days,' Kate explained.

'It *is* like being in the country,' Liz remarked, getting out of the car and looking around.

Although Kate had told her they were only five minutes away from the city centre, the Avenues seemed like a leafy backwater. Huge old chestnut trees blocked off the noise of the traffic. Liz looked up and down the road. Solid two- and three-storey houses, Victorian or Edwardian mostly with, here and there, a modern infill.

'I saw a fox once.' Kate led the way up the path to the two-storey, semi-detached Edwardian villa. 'And there's rumoured to be a deer living somewhere about.'

She unlocked the front door. Inside it smelled of jasmine and turpentine. Walking through the rooms, Liz had an impression of space, after the cramped house in Whitby, of high ceilings and lots of light. Rugs in warm colours were scattered over the bare wooden floorboards.

'This is the sitting room, here, at the front of the house,' said Kate. 'And this,' she went on, leading the way down the spacious tiled hall to the back of the house, 'is Duncan's studio.'

The room was square and sunny, with a French window running the length of one wall and leading directly into the garden. Drawings, sketches, dirty rags and odds and ends of paint littered the old wooden table in the centre of the room. Canvases, framed and unframed, were stacked up against the walls. Liz's eye was caught by a large portrait of a girl hanging on the wall above the fireplace. She drew in her breath sharply and took a step forward.

'Is that . . .?'

'Yes, that's Perdita. It's my favourite picture of her,' Kate added.

Liz studied the portrait. Perdita, aged eleven or twelve, sat on the arm of a chair staring boldly out of the canvas. She was wearing jeans and trainers and her long red hair streamed down her back.

'She has spirit,' declared Liz.

'Oh yes, she has plenty of that,' Kate agreed.

Liz's eye moved towards the easel in the centre of the room. It held a large, unfinished painting of a naked young man standing in front of a window. Behind him was an unmade bed.

'Chris,' said Kate briefly.

Out of an obscure sense of loyalty to her sister, Liz didn't allow herself to linger on the picture. She had a fleeting impression of a tall, rather gangling youth with grey, pockmarked skin and a shaven head. The profile showed five studs in his left ear and one through his nose. He had tattoos down his arm. Did Chris really look like this, she wondered, and if so, what did Duncan see in him? Or was it artistic licence? A statement about Chris's position in society? The unwanted, the outsider. Suddenly she began to feel unnerved at being in Duncan's studio at all and started to edge towards the door. Kate led the way back across the hall, into the dining room, kitchen and conservatory. There was a piano in the dining room.

'Does Perdita play?'

'She used to.' Kate inspected the plants in the conservatory. 'Mm, these don't look too bad. Mrs Black's been doing her stuff.'

They went upstairs. Liz had the impression of lots of doors leading off the large, square landing. There must be at least six or seven bedrooms.

'You have so much space, Kate.'

'There are always people staying. Friends of Duncan or friends of Perdita. People come and go the whole time when those two are here. If it wasn't for Mrs Black, who comes twice a week and more if I need her, I don't know how I'd manage.'

Liz thought of the frigidly elegant apartment she had shared with Louise on Beacon Hill.

'Your life seems so rich,' she said.

'That's one way of looking at it.' Kate flung open a door. 'Perdita's room. Do you want to have a look inside?'

'I'm not sure.' Liz hovered uncertainly on the threshold.

'I won't come in myself,' said Kate. 'I never do unless I'm invited. Even Mrs Black is banned. I don't want to go in when Perdita's not here. I'm frightened of what I might find.' She gave a rueful smile.

'Perhaps I shouldn't.' Liz took a step back.

'Oh, she wouldn't mind you looking. You're the object of some awe and curiosity.'

Kate tried hard, but Liz picked up the edge of bitterness in her tone.

'I suppose I would be,' she replied lightly. 'The black sheep of the family. The wanderer. The exile. That kind of thing is an absolute magnet for adolescent girls.' She stepped into the room, as much to get away from Kate as anything else, and gazed in silence at the tiny TV set, the compact disc player, the Apple Mac. How expensive teenagers were these days! The untidy, lumpy bed had an Indian coverlet drawn haphazardly over it. Books and papers lay scattered across the desk. On the dusty chest of drawers stood a photograph of Duncan but none of Kate, and a flower drawing, perhaps by Duncan. The mirror above the dressing table was draped with a black cloth.

'Perdita's going through a Gothic phase,' Kate explained, from the doorway.

'What does that entail?'

'Lots of white face powder and dressing from head to toe in black.'

'I used to dress in black.'

'Yes, but black suits you. The effect on Perdita is rather corpse-like.'

Liz bent down to examine the books in the bookcase, a temporary-looking structure consisting of a couple of planks resting on bricks. There were some trendy American sex and drugs novels which Liz wondered whether Perdita should be reading then, rather reassuringly, tattered copies of Jane Austen, the Brontës, even a couple of schoolgirl stories by Elinor Brent-Dyer.

She straightened up. The room was haunted by an absent presence. Liz felt it looking back at her, judging her, possibly condemning her. She shivered, turned her back on it and rejoined Kate.

'Shall we go downstairs? I've seen enough.'

An hour later, Kate drove her sister to the airport.

PART TWO

Chapter Nine

Arriving at Charles de Gaulle, vast and chaotic after friendly little Humberside airport, Liz felt her neck stiffen and her shoulders tense up. It was always like this in Paris. During her few days in Whitby, she had slowed down. Now she was surrounded by people who walked faster, spoke more abruptly, were altogether more forceful than the slow-moving, placid inhabitants of Yorkshire.

In Paris she had always been on her guard. It was so much more violent, at least on the surface, than any of the other cities she had lived in. In the old days, living here, she had become tough. In French she never littered her sentences as she did in English with 'sort of', 'kind of' or 'perhaps'. In French she was definite, dramatic, she overstated. It was a necessity, otherwise you were ignored.

It occurred to her that they were waiting rather a long time for their luggage.

'Excuse me,' she said to a woman on her left whom she recognised from the plane, 'have any of our lot got their luggage yet?'

'Apparently not. My husband's gone to see about it.'

A stout middle-aged man with a red face returned at that moment. 'It should have come up ages ago, the woman said. Looks like they've lost it.'

'Lost it!' His wife went into a flat spin. 'They can't have! My new suit! The earrings you gave me for our anniversary, my bracelet, my –'

'Get a grip, Ethel,' her husband advised. 'She says we've got to fill in forms.' Clearly a man who liked to be in charge, he began rounding up the other passengers. 'They'll deliver our luggage to our hotels, when they find it.'

'When will that be?'

'Where is our luggage?'

'I'm leaving for Toulouse in an hour.'

'I'm supposed to be at a wedding this afternoon. I can't turn up in jeans.'

They crowded round the Frenchwoman at the baggage enquiries desk, turning their warm, open Yorkshire faces to her, eager for some answers to their questions. The woman made a phone call.

'They forgot to put your luggage on,' she told them, 'at – where are you from? – at Humberside airport. It's nothing to do with us.'

'I don't believe that for a moment!' exclaimed a woman in a Marks & Spencer cardigan. 'How could they lose a whole planeful of luggage in a small airport like Humberside? It's somewhere here, I'll be bound.' She gazed at the intricate network of moving staircases. 'Anything would get lost in this place.'

'That's right,' agreed another woman.

'Yes, yes,' muttered other voices.

Their English hackles rose. They were prepared to defend to the death English airports, English beef, sterling, the monarchy and anything else they could think of.

Behind the desk the Frenchwoman's thin lips tightened.

'Fill in the forms and the luggage will be delivered to your hotels when it arrives from Humberside.'

'A likely story,' sniffed the woman in the M & S cardigan.

Nevertheless she took a form. They all took one. There was nothing else they could do. They were powerless and in the hands of foreigners. They helped each other master the intricacies of the questions. They felt brave and defiant, linked together by a bond thicker than blood. More than one of them thought of Dunkirk.

'We'll laugh about this when we get home,' said Ethel's husband, in a misguided attempt to lighten the atmosphere.

'At least it saves carrying our luggage across Paris.' Liz backed him up, then regretted it as several people stared coldly at her.

'*I* had not intended carrying my luggage anywhere,' said the woman in the M & S cardigan. 'My son is meeting me in his car.'

'I'm going to look awfully funny at this wedding,' a young man said dismally, staring down at his scruffy pair of jeans.

They handed in their completed forms and made their way, a valiant band of brothers and sisters, to board the coach which was to take them to the train terminal.

'Of course it may have gone on to Amsterdam,' mused the young man in jeans. 'A flight to Amsterdam left Humberside at the same time as ours. Our luggage may have got mixed in with theirs.'

No one seemed to find this remark helpful. They digested it in silence, except Ethel who shrieked 'Amsterdam!' and collapsed into her husband's arms. 'I shall never see my earrings again,' she whimpered.

'For God's sake, wear them next time,' muttered her husband, shaking her off, 'instead of packing them.'

'How was I to know our suitcase would get lost, eh? Tell me that. How was I to know?'

'It's a contingency, Ethel. Always a contingency.'

Ethel and her husband kept this up all the way to the terminal.

In comparison with Boston's antiquated system, the Paris Metro was high tech, its hiss and roar startling. Liz took the RER to St-Michel, travelling through some of the dreariest suburbs in the world, row after row of grey apartment blocks. Nearing the centre, they rattled past the familiar sewer smell at Châtelet. On the Boulevard St-Michel she pushed her way through the crowds of milling students and tourists. After the quiet Whitby streets, Liz felt stunned by the noise and the bustle, the wail of police sirens, the insistent klaxons and screeching brakes of the Parisian drivers. Even Boston was more sedate than this. She wondered how Ethel would cope with Paris.

A pigeon flapped its wings against her cheek, making her jump. Paris pigeons were bolder and even more confident than the London ones. They flew low over the crowds, skimming people's heads. There was a smell of onions in the air, and *pommes frites* and something sickly, possibly *crêpes*. She turned off the Boul' Mich towards her hotel. It was one she had stayed in several times before. In the heart of the Latin Quarter, it had the advantage of being both cheap and central. She didn't expect to be remembered and she wasn't. Paris had always been a place where one could sink easily into anonymity.

She filled in the registration form and the immaculately coiffured woman behind the desk handed over her keys.

'*Quatrième, à gauche. Prenez l'ascenseur là bas,*' she instructed. '*Vous voulez manger le petit déjeuner dans votre chambre ou dans la salle à manger?*'

'Dans la salle à manger, s'il vous plaît.'

Liz stumbled to get her tongue round the once familiar language. It was eight years since she had last lived in Paris. Working in a *boîte* on the rue de la Huchette she had met Louise. Shortly after that, she'd given up her job and flown to Boston with her. And never looked back, until now.

She mentioned that her luggage was lost. For a moment the receptionist's face took on a chilly hauteur as if to say, I hope you don't expect me to get involved in any of this. When Liz calmly explained that the airport would deliver her luggage when they found it, the woman's facial muscles relaxed a tinge. She wasn't, after all, going to have to deal with a hysterical foreigner.

'Très bien.'

The receptionist gave Liz a curt nod. There was an endless stream of visitors to Paris. She couldn't afford to be charming to them all, especially not to a slightly louche-looking Englishwoman in jeans and T-shirt. She reserved her charm for Americans. They tended to make it worth her while.

Feeling down at heel and dowdy, Liz walked along to the lift and pressed the button. Frenchwomen were immaculate, they were forced to be, and Liz had often thought the strain showed in their faces. She remembered those endless and detailed dissections Frenchmen would make on any passing female – *'Une jolie blonde.'* *'Non, une fausse blonde.'* *'Celle là a les hanches trop minces.'* *'Et un jean pas chouette.'* They were impossible to please. She stepped into the lift and pressed the button for the fourth floor. Whereas an Englishman gave you a vague look over, taking in only the general effect, indifferent to details.

She opened the door to her room with a certain degree of wariness. It was not too much of a disappointment, however. A seasoned inmate of the cheaper Parisian hotels, by now Liz knew what to expect. The room was long and narrow. A lumpy-looking bed was pressed against one wall, a small table with a battered lamp squeezed against the other. A placard built into the wall, a stained and threadbare red carpet, dirty paintwork, made this room a paradigm of all the rooms she had ever stayed in in Paris. The tall, narrow slit of a window gave on to an exiguous balcony, from which it was possible to look down on to the street and across into a bedroom of the hotel opposite, where a woman stood in front of a mirror brushing her hair. By dint of craning her neck, Liz could just spy the tops of the twin towers of Notre Dame. After the red roofs of Whitby, the blue-grey of the Parisian rooftops seemed to her elegant, but cold.

Having no luggage to unpack, she scrutinised the notices on the back of the door. They informed her that the hotel had no fire exit and only one staircase. The fire instructions provided her with the helpful hint that, should this staircase become blocked off by smoke and fumes, a closed door kept wet, with material stuffed into the cracks, would protect her for a certain time. She found this less than reassuring. In this very city a friend of hers, renting a cheap apartment with dodgy wiring, had had to jump for his life from the third floor.

She leafed through the local telephone directory but could find no Philippa Hamley. This was a disappointment but not entirely surprising. It was a long time ago. Laura's friend had probably moved on, to a different district, or out of the city altogether; if she was still alive, that was. Liz sat down at the rickety table and began to compose an ad in French about looking for someone who might have news of Mlle Philippa Hamley, an Englishwoman living in Paris, last heard of in the late 1960s. It took her a long time. She thought there should be a subjunctive in it somewhere. And should she offer a reward? She looked up 'reward' in her pocket dictionary. Ah yes – *récompense*.

Liz went down in the lift again and passed the receptionist who gave her a tight little smile and reminded her she should leave her key behind every time she went out. She took her ad along to the newspaper offices. 'Every day for a week, please,' she said to the man in charge of the *petites annonces*. He corrected the wording of her ad, took her phone number and told her there was a reduced price for two weeks – would *Madame* care to take advantage of this offer? No, *Madame* wouldn't. A week in Paris was the limit Liz had set herself. Irrational, perhaps – looking for someone in Paris was like looking for the proverbial needle – but she couldn't afford to stay longer. Paris had always been an expensive city and she supposed it hadn't got any cheaper during the past eight years.

She went along to the main post office and hunted through some more telephone directories. No Mlle Hamley featured in any of them. There was nothing for it but to sit back and wait. If I had Louise's money, she thought, I'd hire a private detective. She purchased a baguette and a bottle of Vichy and went back to her hotel. Her holdall turned up at ten o'clock in the evening, just as she was beginning to regret not having invested in a toothbrush. She pictured Ethel's joy at being reunited with her earrings.

Liz slept badly that night. Her narrow little room was hot and stuffy and the slightest sneeze, cough or grunt from her neighbours penetrated her skull like a knife.

The next morning she was out early, walking the streets in an effort to clear the pain and muzziness in her head. The early morning had always been her favourite time of day in Paris, when the streets smelled fresh from their sweeping and watering, the café owners set out their chairs and tables on the pavements, and the tall grey buildings opened their shutters to the new day. She walked through a flower market towards the Seine and smelled a moment of countryside in the heart of the city. She leaned against the quay wall and gazed across the Île de la Cité, hearing church bells ring for mid-week mass. Somewhere out there lived a woman called Philippa Hamley, Liz was certain of it. She would use all her strength to wrest the secret from the city. *A nous, Paris!* she thought, echoing Rastignac's cry at the end of Balzac's novel.

She spent her days wandering around Paris, doing everything that was free. She walked in the Jardin des Tuileries and under the arcades of the rue de Rivoli. On Sunday she went to the busy Jewish quarter in the Marais and ate cheaply and well on falafel and pitta bread. Afterwards she strolled beneath the arcades of the Place des Vosges where the Parisian bourgeoisie came to spend two or three hours eating and drinking. She stopped to listen to a group of young people play scraps of Mozart and Bach. Another day she walked between the tall cool white and cream houses of the Île St-Louis, where every balcony was decorated with window boxes. She sat drinking coffee and listening to Vivaldi in an elegant wood-panelled café overlooking the flying buttresses of Notre Dame. It cost her the price of her dinner, but the view alone was worth it.

Usually she skipped lunch or ate a *pain au chocolat* or a *millefeuille* from the patisserie counter of a supermarket. Or she bought a *crêpe* and ate it walking along the street. In the evening, when she could afford it, she ate in the cheapest restaurants, taking always the menu *prix fixe*, eating pâté, noodles and *crème caramel*, accompanied by a *quart de rouge*. Execrable food. You could eat well in Paris, but only if you had money. A *salade Niçoise* she ate in a café in St-Germain-des-Prés blew her budget for two days. Paris was a good place to lose weight, she had always found. She began to long for a filling New England clam chowder or a Ben and Jerry hot fudge sundae.

All in all, though, she was happy. One evening she wandered by the Seine watching a brilliant sunset from the direction of the Tuileries shed a pinky-blue glow over Notre Dame and the Île St-Louis. A pleasure boat slid past, decorated with gaily coloured lights. People were dining on the deck. Bottles of wine stood open on every table. Forgetting her hunger, Liz was lost for a moment in the sheer pleasure of being alive. Out of these random images of the city she hoped a poem might finally come. And what if Laura were still alive, in this very city? No, she dare not think of it.

She didn't mind being on her own. It was difficult, she had always found, to be in Paris with somebody else. The city exacted a certain rhythm from her which never seemed to match other people's. The number of quarrels she'd had here! Quarrels, uneasy compromises, the final rupture, it had always been the same. Until she met Louise. Then there hadn't been any problem, at least at first. How she would have liked, though, to have visited Paris just once with someone who knew about art – with Duncan, for instance. She winced to herself at the absurdity and, she had to face it, the immorality of this thought and hastily tucked it away in the recesses of her mind.

The city had scarcely changed in the eight years she'd been away. Only the fire-eaters, jugglers and mime artists were gone from the Beaubourg, to be replaced by bulldozers and diggers. She walked past the *boîte* in the Latin Quarter where she had first met Louise. It was still there, but the name was different.

On the whole Liz thought she had changed more than the city.

She had grown older. She no longer automatically attracted the glances of young men in the street.

Some older ones, yes, but she didn't fear them. She was entering the years when a woman starts to become invisible except to those who know her. At first she felt nothing but relief about this. She was becoming *une femme d'un certain âge*. She could stop being afraid that every man who sat down at the table next to hers was going to strike up a conversation with a view to getting her into bed. Yes, it was definitely a relief.

Then, as she walked about the city, she began to remember those unhappy heroines in the Jean Rhys novels she'd devoured when she had first come to Paris. Sad, sick women, she had thought, obsessed with their fading looks, imagining everyone was staring at them and criticising their appearance. Nevertheless, as the days crept by, Liz began to think there might be something in it after all. She too had become old, older in fact than some of Rhys's heroines. Not old enough to attract sympathy and courteous attention, but old enough to be thought a little past it, a little frayed at the edges, suspected, perhaps, of trying to dress younger than her age. She wondered whether Duncan had aged. No, it wasn't possible. Not Duncan. He would look boyish at any age. He must do. How else would he be able to attract young men like Chris?

Liz spent longer and longer in front of the mirror in her hotel room before venturing out in the evening. She wished she could afford to buy some new clothes. Louise's designer jeans were beginning to look distinctly scruffy, at least by Parisian standards. When she had to walk past the terrace of a café, she made her expression deliberately hard and forbidding, imagining hundreds of eyes following her. The way some waiters looked at you would make you wonder whether you'd got spots or suddenly sprouted black hairs on your chin. If Kate was here, Liz thought, I wouldn't feel like this. We would laugh at the waiters instead of feeling laughed at by them. Perhaps it was a mistake to have come on her own. She had forgotten how neurotic you could get alone in a city where you no longer knew anyone. When a tourist stopped her to ask the way, she nearly jumped out of her skin.

The best times were sitting in some café in the narrow backstreets between the Boulevard St-Germain and the Seine, a *café noir* in front of her, smoking cigarette after cigarette, with no one casting her filthy looks because they were all smoking too. As she sat with a notebook in front of her, trying to coax the lines to come after the years of barrenness, Liz caught snippets of the conversations around her. *'Acheter'* – the verb seem to figure in every other sentence. *'Maigrir'* was another common word, at least among the women. *'Acheter'* and *'maigrir'*, they summed up the city.

Memories of her years in France surfaced from time to time. That prostitute in Montmartre who had been so friendly about keeping an eye on her bike. Eating mutton and vegetable soup in a steamy workmen's café with friends. The Frenchman who had left a gift for her at the *boîte* where she worked, with a note that said, 'I've watched you sitting on the terrace with your friends. You have a face like a Botticelli angel. I send you this.' It was a record. Bach, Pachelbel, Telemann. She had never discovered his name. She had led a random life, made up of unpredictable encounters in cafés. She'd thought she was happy. Then Louise had come and her life had changed. She had given up her job at the *boîte*. Together, they had toured the Dordogne staying, at Louise's expense, in various splendid châteaux. By the end of the holiday, Liz had known she wanted to be with Louise for ever.

But she didn't want to think of Louise. Not now, not here, alone in this city where her nerves were on edge through loneliness (was it really possible that Philippa Hamley was still alive?). She started to look for boltholes. The café where the waiters were friendly and attempted to joke with their customers. The bookshop, Shakespeare and Co, with its back room and the sofa where she could rest her aching feet. The bookshop still attracted groups of young people, interchangeable with those who had been here eight years ago. Tanned and fit, in shorts and carrying backpacks, they exchanged information about the city, where to eat, where to live, where to go dancing. As Liz sat on the sofa watching them, she felt the confused, formless beginning of a poem in her head. She went over her images and memories of the city. She waited, hoping the poem would gradually take shape by itself. But nothing more came to her.

After the first eager few days, Paris began to pall. Beggars waving their stumps at her in the Metro no longer seemed picturesque but menacing. One evening, as Liz walked back to her hotel, she became aware of footsteps coming after her. She darted down a side street, then ran all the way back to her hotel. She was sick of the noise and the snappy French shopkeepers. She was tired of the pedestrian crossings and the cars that nearly ran her down on them. She was fed up of having to dodge rollerbladers and skateboarders in the street.

Walking back to her hotel one afternoon, she saw a young woman in flowered leggings snatch a handbag from a Chinese tourist. A man caught hold of the woman's arm but she wriggled out of his grasp and ran away. What shocked Liz was not the theft – that was common enough in Paris – but the fact that the woman had been carrying in a harness a baby who could only have been a few weeks old. Sickened, Liz walked on feeling the air in the city had suddenly become infected.

The money she'd budgeted for these days in Paris was running low. If she was to keep some for her return to Whitby, she must be careful. To save money, she lived on cheese sandwiches and when she used up the last ticket of her carnet for the Metro she didn't buy another. Her sandals and the bottom of her jeans became dusty from tramping the streets. Waiters in cafés eyed her suspiciously as she lingered for hours over a *café noir*. One afternoon, she found herself in the Musée d'Orsay staring at a painting by Monet of a sunlit garden and hallucinating that she was walking down the sandy path in the picture towards the bottle of wine and the broken pieces of baguette on the table. She was hungry and depressed. It had all been a waste of time. She'd written no poetry, no one had replied to her ad and she couldn't afford to run it another week. She would stay a couple of days longer and then leave.

Late that night, she received a phone call.

'Hello?' she said, thinking it would be Kate.

But it wasn't Kate. Instead a brisk voice said, *'Allo.'*

'Allo,' returned Liz.

'Qui êtes-vous? Pourquoi avez-vous placé cette annonce dans le journal?'

'Qui est-ce qui parle?'

'Je m'appelle Philippa Hamley.'

Was this a hoax? The voice sounded so strong, so alive. Yet if it was Philippa Hamley she must be an old woman by now.

Haltingly, in the French she had got out of the way of using, having spoken only to waiters and shop assistants in the past few days, Liz explained that she was trying to find out about her grandmother.

'*Votre grandmère?*' The voice on the other end became a little impatient. '*Et qui est votre grandmère et qu'est-ce qu'elle a à faire avec moi?*'

'*Ma grandmère s'appellait Laura Chapman. Je crois que vous la connaissiez?*'

There was silence on the other end. Then the voice came, less sure of itself now and speaking in English.

'Laura Chapman? You are Laura Chapman's granddaughter?'

'Yes.'

'*Vraiment?* It's not a hoax?'

'No hoax. I am Liz Miller, Laura's granddaughter. My mother was Jessica Chapman.'

There was a long pause.

'*Eh bien.* Come for tea tomorrow afternoon, Laura's grand-daughter. Twenty-four rue Jacob.'

Liz put down the phone, threw back her head and laughed. Rue Jacob was just around the corner from her hotel, she had walked up and down it several times in the past few days. It was true that in Paris, unlike Whitby, you could live next door to someone for years without knowing who they were.

She went to bed in a turmoil of excitement, wondering what revelations the next day would bring. Was there a chance that her grandmother was still alive, that she might see Laura?

Chapter Ten

Liz spent the morning trying to decide what was the right gift to bring a very old lady who had invited you to tea. Chocolates? Flowers? In the end she invested in a small, expensive box of handmade chocolates. At five to four, she made her way round to the rue Jacob. Number 24 was a tall, square building divided into apartments on the first and second floors. The ground floor was occupied by a classy soft-furnishing shop. The rue Jacob was full of classy soft-furnishing shops, classy art galleries and classy publishing houses. Above the shop, however, the paint on the window frames was greyish and peeling.

Liz pressed the button marked Hamley/Dupuy, spoke her name into the intercom and, as the buzzer sounded, pushed open the heavy wooden door and stepped into a paved courtyard. Someone was hurrying down the stone stairs in the far right-hand corner of the courtyard. Liz stared as the stout, grey-haired woman in her fifties approached her. This couldn't be Philippa Hamley. She was too young. A terrible mistake had been made.

'*Madame Miller?*' enquired the woman.

'*Mademoiselle.*'

'*Suivez-moi.*'

On her guard, Liz followed the woman up the stone stairs. Was she about to have some kind of con trick played on her? Was she about to be kidnapped, perhaps? This advertising business was risky. She should have used a box number. The woman came to a halt outside a wooden door on the second floor.

'*Je m'appelle Marie-Noëlle Depuy,*' she said, in low tones. '*Mlle Hamley vous attend avec impatience mais je vous prie de ne pas rester trop longtemps. Malgré les apparences, elle se fatigue vite.* You understand?'

Liz nodded. 'I understand. I won't stay long.'

Marie-Noëlle opened the door and ushered her into a dark, narrow hallway, then into a room on her right. It was square and high-ceilinged, filled with heavy dark furniture. A Japanese screen stood in one corner. Shawls were draped over the sofas and chairs. A pair of glass chandeliers hung from the ceiling. A gilt-edged mirror dominated one wall. There were paintings everywhere. Flower paintings. Abstracts. A sketch by Matisse caught Liz's eye and made her draw in her breath sharply. It must be worth a fortune.

In a corner of the room, almost dwarfed by her surroundings, sat a small, white-haired woman. She half rose from her chair as Liz came forward. 'Ah!' She nodded. 'Laura.'

For a moment Liz thought Philippa Hamley must be wandering in her mind. then she added, *'Vous la ressemblez, ma petite. Venez, asseyez-vous.'*

She indicated one of the tapestry-covered chairs by the fireplace. Liz sat down. She was aware of Philippa's sharp blue eyes observing her. Laura was right, she thought, she misses nothing.

'Here, these are for you.' She thrust the box of chocolates rather clumsily towards Philippa.

'Ah! Comme c'est gentil!' Philippa looked at the box with an air of regret. 'I am afraid I can no longer eat chocolates, however. I have become *diabétique*.' She spoke English hesitantly, with a slight French accent. 'Here, Marie-Noëlle, these are for you.'

Marie-Noëlle came forward to receive the box then, with a stern glance at Liz, left the room.

Philippa Hamley stood up stiffly, grasping the stick leaning against her chair. She moved slowly over to a gas ring, half concealed behind the Japanese screen, and lifted off a small pan of boiling water.

'Une petite tisane? Ça fait du bien au milieu de l'après-midi, n'est-ce pas? Oh pardon, you don't like speaking French?'

'Oui. Si, I mean. But I don't speak it very well.'

'Ça viendra. It took your grandmother a long time to learn.'

'My grandmother – Mlle Hamley, I have to ask,' said Liz, unable to contain herself any longer, 'is Laura still alive?'

Philippa glanced over at her. *'Non, ma petite. Il y a longtemps que votre grandmère est morte.'*

There was a silence. Slowly and carefully, Philippa poured boiling water from the pan into the teapot. A smell of peppermint invaded the room, like the smell of loss. Laura was no longer alive.

'You have been to France before, *ma petite*?'

'Yes, I lived here some years ago. I was a waitress in a nightclub.'

'*Tiens!*' Philippa paused and looked at her again. 'I had a friend who owned a nightclub – Le Boeuf sur le Toit. You have heard of it?'

Liz shook her head.

'And yet it was so celebrated in its time. It was Cocteau's club.' Philippa sighed and turned back to preparing the tisane.

Liz felt she had somehow disappointed her. She studied the slight woman bending over the teapot, her back turned towards Liz. She wore a long plum-coloured skirt and matching velvet jacket. On her feet were a pair of elegant suede boots and jet earrings dangled from her ears. In her nineties (she must be that, surely), Philippa Hamley spoke and moved more like a woman in her seventies. She was a striking figure. Despite the slightness of her physique, one was immediately made aware of the forceful character who inhabited it.

'*Voilà votre tisane, Madame – pardon, Mademoiselle – Miller.*' Glancing at Liz's hands, bare of rings, she handed her the cup.

'Please, call me Liz.'

'Liz? *Mais pourquoi pas Elisabeth? C'est plus joli.*'

Liz shrugged. 'I don't know. Except for my parents, everyone's always called me Liz.' Apart from Duncan, who called me Lizzie. Would he still, if we were to meet?

'I shall call you Elisabeth,' declared Philippa, returning to her seat opposite Liz. 'Do you mind? It is more *convenable*, more dignified, for Laura's granddaughter. Are you the only one?'

'The only one? Oh, I see. No, I have a sister, an elder sister, Kate.'

'*Elle vous ressemble?*'

'A bit. She has red hair like me.'

'Yes, the red hair. I thought your grandmother the most beautiful thing I had ever seen. You have seen pictures?'

'Only photographs. Black and white.'

'Ah then, they wouldn't do justice. Her beauty lay in her colouring. That hair, her white skin, the long white Rossetti neck, her grey eyes . . .' She was silent for a moment. 'So you are little Jessie's daughter, the little Jessie who frightened her mother so.'

'Frightened her?'

'Laura felt that Jessie disapproved of her, condemned her, after the trial.' Philippa stopped suddenly. 'But perhaps you don't know about that? Tell me, Elisabeth, why have you decided to visit me, after all these years?'

'We thought – we were told – that Laura died in 1925. We have only just found out – about the murder and the trial. You see, Mother died recently and in a trunk in the attic we found these cuttings about the trial, some short stories and a diary which mentions your name. I – I know your nephew, Roger. He is selling Mother's house for us. He told us you went away to Paris. We thought you must have come with Laura.'

'Yes.' Philippa reflected a moment. 'Roger. *Tiens!* I have never even seen him. So he has taken over the family business that my brother Hubert used to run?'

'Yes. Roger's father, Hubert's son I suppose, died when Roger was twelve. It was always assumed Roger would take over the business as soon as he was old enough.'

'But you mentioned some stories?' The great-nephew Philippa had never seen was quickly dismissed as of no possible interest.

'Short stories, yes, written by Laura. They're very good. Kate and I would like to get them published. We'd do it properly,' she added hastily, noticing Philippa's expression change. 'Kate's a university lecturer. The 1920s and 30s are her special field. She'll know how to edit them, maybe even write an introduction for them. But we need to find out more about Laura's life after she left Whitby. What she did, whether she ever got anything published –'

'So that is why you have come,' Philippa interrupted her. She set down her cup, leaned forward and rapped the arm of Liz's chair with her knuckles. 'I am so glad, *tellement heureuse vous ne pouvez pas savoir*, that you have found more stories. Please publish them. Laura was such a good writer and perhaps the world has not yet tired of good writing, despite what people say.' She shook her head. 'Everyone remembers the men, yes – Joyce, Pound, Hemingway, Fitzgerald, they are remembered. But what has happened to the women? Djuna, Mina, Hilda, Mary Butts – who remembers them these days? Only Gertrude is still read – and then mainly by American postgraduates. I sometimes get letters from them, wanting me to write their theses for them.'

'Gertrude? Gertrude Stein?' said Liz, excitedly thinking, Kate should have been here, she would have loved this.

Philippa smiled. '*Oui, ma petite, Gertrude Stein – ça vous dit quelque chose?* We used to visit her apartment on the rue de Fleurus. At first we went to see her pictures and then, little by little, we got to know her – or at least Laura did. Laura was the one who talked to Gertrude. I, because I was a "wife" and not a writer, talked to Alice. Ah, their marvellous atelier filled with Picasso and Braque and Matisse. Gertrude gave me that when Laura died.' She waved a hand at the Matisse drawing Liz had noticed earlier. 'I could sell it. I could sell all of these paintings and move into one of those residential homes for the elderly in the suburbs. Join the living dead. But these are the work of my friends. I need them around me, they keep me alive.'

Liz became aware that Marie-Noëlle had slipped back into the room and was staring fiercely at her. She set down her cup.

'You must be tired?' she suggested. And, as Philippa didn't deny it, she rose.

'Come again tomorrow, *ma petite*.' Philippa's blue eyes gazed up at Liz. 'Tomorrow I will have had time to organise my thoughts. I will tell you about our life together.'

Liz hesitated. 'May I bring a tape recorder? You see, it would help Kate. I may forget things.'

'*Bien sûr.* I will see you tomorrow at three, Elisabeth, with your tape recorder.'

She was hurried away by Marie-Noëlle. At the door of the courtyard, Liz paused.

'Something that puzzles me. Why could I not find Philippa's name in the phone book?'

'She isn't in. Only I am,' replied Marie-Noëlle. 'Those who are our friends know this. She had some trouble years ago. A man who fell in love with her. People were always falling in love with Philippa.'

'I can see why.' Liz stepped through the doorway. 'Till tomorrow then.'

'*Très bien.*'

Marie-Noëlle closed the door firmly behind her.

Liz celebrated with a couscous in the Latin Quarter. Then she went back to her hotel room and made a list of questions for the following day. Kate would be pleased with her efficiency.

Chapter Eleven

The next day brought a letter from Kate.

Dear Liz,

Have you managed to find Philippa Hamley yet? Perdita is home. We went over together to Whitby to see whether there was anything she wanted from her grandmother's house before I get rid of any more stuff. We stayed three days and had a good time on the whole. Perdita was in a remarkably good mood for once. Roger was in and out a lot, measuring rooms.

Was he indeed? Liz fingered the letter. Had Roger taken a fancy to Kate? There was no mention of Duncan, but she hadn't expected that. He would still be in Teesside with Chris. She folded up the letter and put it in the inside pocket of her jacket. What with this letter and meeting Philippa, she began to feel less alone in Paris.

This time she brought flowers, a small bunch of freesias. Marie-Noëlle hurried away to put them in a vase.

Philippa was dressed in green today. A long green skirt, black silk shirt and a green shawl draped elegantly over her shoulders. On her feet she wore green buckled shoes. She had a Frenchwoman's attention to dress. No wonder they had been suspicious of her in Whitby.

They drank tisane again. Camomile. Liz placed her small tape recorder unobtrusively on the three-legged table beside Philippa's chair.

'I fell in love with your grandmother the moment I saw her. I was just nineteen. I had come about a post as governess. I hoped she might help me find one.'

'Yes, it's in the diaries.'

'Is it?' Philippa leaned forward in her chair. 'You know, to my knowledge, Laura never kept a diary all the time she was with me.'

'She was happy, perhaps? The diaries are not happy. Until you came, Laura had no one to confide in.'

Philippa's expression softened. 'I should like to read them.'

'I'll photocopy them and send them over.' Liz hesitated. 'You had quite an effect on Laura, too. She said in her diaries that there was no one like you in Whitby.'

'Whitby! Laura was wasted in that town. She was beautiful, she was talented. She reminded me of the friends I had made in Paris. But she had no *confiance*, confidence, in herself. It had been battered away by that brute of a husband of hers. One can speak freely of such things now, one couldn't then. But I knew what was going on. I'd lived in Paris. I'd heard of such things. I knew I had to get Laura away from that man. I was determined to from the day I realised why she always wore high collars and long sleeves, even in the hottest weather.'

As she spoke, Philippa beat one clenched hand into the palm of the other, giving off an air of steely determination. Liz wondered whether determination like that might lead someone to plan a murder.

'Then, after the terrible time of the trial, everyone in Whitby thought your grandmother was crazy. Crazy and guilty. I had to get her out of there. I knew she wasn't crazy, but she would have been if she'd stayed, especially after they found the bottle under the stairs. That treacherous *bonne*.'

'Gladys?'

'Gladys. Always such a sulky look and then to do something like that . . . She made a small fortune out of that newspaper, enough to set up business as a haberdasher. Nellie Braithwaite mentioned it in one of her letters to Laura.'

'My mother worked in a haberdasher's,' remarked Liz.

'Heaven help little Jessie if it was the same one.'

'It must have been,' said Liz, suddenly seeing how it all fitted together. 'It was called Simpson's. That was Gladys's surname, wasn't it? I remember it from the newspaper cuttings.'

No wonder her mother had been badly treated. For Gladys, employing Jessica Chapman must have been a heaven-sent opportunity to bully the daughter of her former employer, to exact revenge for all the imagined slights over the years. Why, though, knowing what Gladys had done, had her mother gone to work in her shop? Perhaps she had hoped to recapture something of her early childhood? Or perhaps Jessie had always been on Gladys's side, against Laura?

Hesitantly, Liz asked, 'You didn't think my grandmother was crazy; did you think she was guilty?'

Philippa's eyebrows rose. 'Laura? Never. People who thought that were foolish. She wouldn't have been capable *malgré*, despite, his bestial behaviour.'

Liz hesitated again, then asked quickly, 'Mlle Hamley –'

'Call me Philippa, please. Laura's granddaughter should call me Philippa.'

'Thank you. Philippa, have you any idea who might have killed Arthur Chapman?'

Philippa's blue eyes rested on Liz for a long time, for so long in fact that Liz wondered whether she was about to make a confession. Then she shook her head. 'I have no idea. *Aucune*. But I know it wasn't your grandmother. No one knew Laura better than I did.' She paused. 'I always thought it was one of your grandfather's debtors. You know that he gambled? Do you gamble, Elisabeth?'

Liz laughed. 'Only with words.'

'*Tiens!* You are a writer too? Like Laura.'

'Not a very successful one, I'm afraid. I'm a poet. I occasionally manage to get a poem printed in some obscure literary magazine. I've had only one collection published and even that didn't pay.'

'Also like your grandmother.' Philippa smiled. 'In the beginning Laura made no money at all from her writing. When we arrived in this city we lived from hand to mouth. I had always lived like that, but it was difficult for Laura at first. We had the fourth-floor rear flat up a dark and narrow spiral staircase.' She sighed. 'Oh, those stairs, those stairs! Everyone we knew in Paris lived up steep narrow staircases. There was a shared toilet on each landing. No *douche*. We had to make do with the public baths. Oh yes, Paris was filthy in those days. It took Laura a long time to get used to it. She'd been accustomed to having so much and we had no servants, we did all the cooking ourselves. She was a terrible, terrible cook, your grandmother. Couldn't even make a decent tisane. It was cold as well. So cold in the winter. We would burn our little bundle of twigs or our *boulets* of coal dust that gave out lots of smoke but no heat and we would huddle together in bed with Laura's fur coat over us. When we first came to Paris, we lived off the boulevard St-Germain. And here I am,' she added, seventy years later, still in the same *quartier*, still living in two rooms. It is possible to survive on very little, you know.'

'I know,' agreed Liz, reflecting that this evening she would very likely dine off half a baguette and a yoghurt smuggled up to her hotel room.

'In the beginning I gave English lessons to spoilt rich children, just so that we could eat. Then, bit by bit, your grandmother's talent began to get noticed. People started to take an interest in her. She was published in the small magazines – *The Egoist, The Little Review, transition*. It was what I had always hoped for her. They didn't pay very much but she was given money from time to time by Hilda Doolittle's friend, Winifred Bryher. Winifred helped so many artists. And there was Sylvia, of course.'

'Sylvia? Sylvia Beach? I visited her bookshop the other day.'

'Did you? I never go there now. It's not what it was. In those days it was a lending library as well as a shop. Sylvia permitted your grandmother to borrow as many books as she wanted without charge. Dear Sylvia, always so kind and generous. I don't know what we would have done without her.'

Liz, making an effort, dredged up her scanty knowledge of the period. 'Did you ever meet Ezra Pound?'

'No, he was gone to Rapallo by then. People remembered him though, striding through the streets in his flapping cloak and wide-brimmed hat. No, he was gone so he couldn't help us, as I'm sure he would have if he'd been here. He helped so many struggling writers. What do they do nowadays, I wonder, impoverished artists, now that the age of the patrons has gone? So we got by. No one we knew was rich. If we had money we helped each other out, and it was always possible to get credit at restaurants. Some of us didn't pay our bills for years. And what fun we had. Such fun! Paris in the Twenties, there's never been anything like it. We sang, we danced. we drank, we went to nightclubs. On Friday afternoons we attended Natalie Barney's salon right here, in the rue Jacob. Natalie had a tree growing in the centre of her salon and the ceiling was decorated with pictures of naked women. In her garden she had built a Temple of Love. Natalie herself, dressed in white from head to toe, her hair piled up, a long white fox skin draped around her shoulders, would introduce us to her monocled women companions in their tweeds and stiff collars. We drank coffee at the Flore or the Dingo or the Dôme, sitting among writers and painters and painters' models and characters and drinkers. Then we would end up at Le Train Bleu for some late-night dancing. Ah! The intrigues that went on, the petty jealousies, you can't imagine! Djuna chasing Thelma Wood all about the city and hitting over the head anyone who tried to come between them. Live fast, die young, and make a beautiful corpse – that was our motto.'

'Tell me about a typical day,' suggested Liz, with an eye to Kate's introduction.

Philippa leaned forward, clasping her knees. '*Eh bien*. In the mornings your grandmother wrote, sitting up in bed with a jug of coffee by her elbow, while I went off to teach my brats. We'd meet for lunch in some cheap café, sauntering past Michaud's on the corner and seeing Joyce dining with his family, little tragic Lucia by his side. Afterwards, *pour digérer*, we would stroll along the banks of the Seine and gossip with the *bouquinistes*. Then we'd go back home and take a nap. You see, Elisabeth?' She broke off suddenly. 'I remember it perfectly. It was an important time of my life, perhaps the most important time,' she added quietly. 'Well, when we awoke from our nap, I would make a tisane and Laura would read aloud what she'd written that morning and I would offer suggestions. Not very many.' Philippa smiled. 'As her happiness returned, she became more sure of herself as a writer. She didn't need my suggestions. Come six o'clock, we were ready to go out on the town. We went from café to café, gathering more people as we went. We'd dine somewhere and then go on to a club to listen to jazz and to dance. At some stage of the evening, either Scott or Zelda, or both, would pass out and have to be bundled into a taxi. The rest of us would go off to dance among the cabbages in Les Halles. We would walk home as the dawn came up over the city. It is very beautiful the dawn over Paris. Have you ever seen it, Elisabeth?'

Liz shook her head.

Philippa sighed. 'If the youth of today only knew how we enjoyed ourselves! They have lost the art. Always so serious about their studies, their careers, their computers. They have lost the art of conversation and their dancing is execrable.' She paused. 'I have never loved anyone as much as I loved Laura and she – she learned eventually to love me back. We were very, very happy for twelve years.'

'And then?' asked Liz softly.

'Then she caught TB. It was rife in Paris at that time, in our *quartier* especially. For six long months she lay coughing and choking. I nursed her myself. But it was no good.' She shook her head. 'She died and a year later the war came. I was glad, in a way, that Laura didn't have to live through that terrible time. Nazis tramping through the centre of our beloved city. And when ordinary life returned, it wasn't the same. The gaiety had gone.' She fell silent.

Liz hesitated. 'Did she never . . .? Why did she never send for her children?'

'Laura had lost confidence in herself as a mother. During the trial, the newspapers called her all sorts of names – witch, poisoner, painted Jezebel. It – what would you say nowadays? – it damaged her self-esteem. She worked herself up into a hysterical state over Jessie. The child had always been fond of her father. He had indulged her. Laura was convinced she had seen accusation and suspicion in her daughter's eyes.'

Yes, thought Liz, Mother's eyes which sent shivers down my back as a child.

'You see, Elisabeth, it may be difficult for you to understand but there were many mothers here who had left their children behind for the sake of their art – Mina, Hilda, Mary Butts. It wasn't uncommon. Besides, they were Arthur's children too and that she never could forget. Especially *le petit*, he resembled Arthur.'

'Did he?' Liz thought of her quiet, shy uncle. 'But Uncle John's not like my grandfather. He's gentle.'

'He has his mother's nature then.'

Philippa began to move restlessly in her chair. Liz saw that her time was running out. Marie-Noëlle would be putting in an appearance shortly and there was so much more she wanted to find out.

'Didn't Laura talk about her children? Didn't she miss them?'

A strange and sudden sense of loyalty to her mother made Liz pursue her questioning possibly beyond the limits of tactfulness. After all, it had been Philippa who had taken Laura away from her children.

'I don't know. I can't tell whether she missed them. I have never been a mother, *Dieu merci*, have you, Elisabeth?'

'No.' Liz glanced down at her lap. 'I have never been a mother.'

'Then neither of us know. But I don't want to give you the impression that your grandmother had no heart. Laura used to cry sometimes, at night, when she thought I was asleep.' Philippa was silent for a moment. 'But she couldn't have gone back. It would have killed her.' Again, she beat her fist into her palm.

Liz looked up. 'Because of everyone thinking she was a murderess?'

'That and . . .' Philippa hesitated, 'other horrors. Whitby had become a nightmare place for her. Years afterwards, she would wake up in the night screaming and cling to me sobbing. She had dreamed Arthur was still alive, you see.'

'Yes, the beatings. They're mentioned in the diaries.'

'Not only that.' She hesitated again. 'When I first saw Laura naked – it took a long time, she had to learn to trust me – as I say, when I first saw her naked, I ran to the bathroom and vomited. There were scars, terrible scars, all over her body. Cigarette burns on her stomach and her back. And one of her nipples had been cut off.' She clenched both hands. 'Then I regretted Arthur Chapman was dead. I would have loved to have had the pleasure of killing him myself.'

'My God!' said Liz in horror, turning white.

Philippa glanced at her. 'Yes, one can speak of such things now and be believed. One couldn't then. Forgive me, my dear. I shouldn't have told you. Only I wanted to make you see what Laura's life had been. Why she could never go back, why I couldn't even let her think of it. You are not married, I think? You have *un petit ami*, perhaps?'

126

'*Une petite amie*,' corrected Liz. At least, I used to have.

Philippa stared at her. 'So history repeats itself, *hein*? Perhaps you too understand the brutality of men?'

Liz thought of her two years with the Stars in Your Eyes escort agency in London and how, after that, she had fled in gratitude to the protection of women. She nodded. 'Yes, I know about men.' She paused, thinking over what Philippa had just said. 'But why did Laura never tell anyone? Even in her diary she talks only of being hit. Never of – of the other things.'

'Who could have helped her? She couldn't tell her mother, it would have broken her heart. She did once try to say something to the doctor, but he refused to believe such things could happen. I think it was he who later started the rumour that Laura was a little crazy. With no one to help her escape, she tried to play down Arthur's violence in her mind. She pretended to herself that her situation wasn't so bad, no worse than what other wives had to endure.'

'Yes, she does that in her diaries.'

'You see, Elisabeth, people lacked the words for such things. You are a poet, you know that when the words don't exist, neither do the acts. They have to be named in order to be recognised.' She paused and looked at Liz. 'Perhaps you should consider publishing Laura's diaries as well as her stories. They would be a valuable record of women's lives in that period.'

'They're so private,' Liz objected. 'Would Laura have wanted anyone else to read them?'

Philippa thought for a moment. 'If she believed it might help other women in her situation then, yes, I think Laura would have agreed to them being published. She didn't speak much about her life with Arthur but she did once say she hoped no other woman would ever have to endure what she had endured. She felt so alone.'

'Until you came along,' said Liz softly. 'You saved her.'

She became aware of Marie-Noëlle's presence in the room. Switching off the tape recorder, she rose.

'I mustn't tire you.'

Philippa smiled. 'It has been a great pleasure, Elisabeth, to speak of the past and of Laura. A great and unexpected pleasure, at the end of my life. I had thought I would never be able to speak of her to anyone again.'

Liz hesitated, aware of Marie-Noëlle's steely gaze. 'The stories Laura had published, in those magazines you mentioned – they should be easy enough for my sister to track down, shouldn't they?'

Philippa spread out her hands. 'I don't know. I am not a scholar. I don't know how easy it would be to find them. Such a long time ago.'

'Do you have copies of them?' Liz asked, suddenly struck by an idea.

Philippa visibly hesitated. 'I will look and see.'

She doesn't trust me, thought Liz. She must know whether she has any stories belonging to my grandmother. She can't need to look.

'How long are you staying in Paris, Elisabeth?'

'Two or three days. Not longer. I have to get back.'

'Then I will let you know if I find anything.' She rose stiffly from her chair and shook hands with Liz. 'Goodbye for now, Laura's granddaughter. I am so glad to have met you.'

As Liz was escorted out by Marie-Noëlle, she turned to gaze once more on the small, frail woman standing by the fireplace. This is the woman Laura loved, she thought, the woman who loved my grandmother. Will there be anyone to guard my memory with such loyalty after my death?

'Thank you for observing my little rule,' whispered Marie-Noëlle as she showed her out.

Liz was glad she had won Marie-Noëlle's approval. She had a feeling that it was not easily earned. It was good to know that in old age Philippa Hamley, who had cared for Laura, now had someone to care for her.

Three days passed without a word from the rue Jacob. Waiting for Philippa to call, Liz walked up and down the street several times but the windows of the old woman's apartment remained firmly shuttered. Had Philippa gone away? Surely not at her age and given her frailty? Wandering around thinking of Philippa, Liz saw Paris as suddenly full of old ladies. They were everywhere, smartly costumed, heavily rouged, carrying little dogs under their arms. The Parisian bourgeoisie. Philippa was nothing like them.

On the third day, for something to do, Liz strolled through the Jardin du Luxembourg where a band was playing and students sat on iron chairs around the fountain, talking or eating or scribbling or flirting. She walked out of the Jardin in the direction of the rue de Fleurus where Gertrude Stein had lived, with Alice Toklas.

It was a rather grand six-storey apartment block with wrought-iron balconies and the inevitable geraniums in window boxes. Built in 1894, so the plaque above the door told her, it must have been newish when Gertrude moved there in 1903 with her brother, Leo. Liz stood and gazed at the door through which so many writers and painters had passed – Hemingway, Picasso, Scott Fitzgerald, Matisse and, she now knew, her grandmother. Gertrude and Alice – that had been a relationship between women that had endured. The trouble was, she thought, turning away, neither Louise nor I would have been content with Alice's role. We both wanted to be Gertrude. We both wanted to dominate.

On the fourth day, just as she was thinking of packing up and going back to Whitby, Liz came down to breakfast to find a large, hand-delivered parcel awaiting her and a note in unfamiliar writing. The note was from Marie-Noëlle. She wrote in French. Translated it read: 'Philippa was taken into hospital yesterday afternoon with suspected pneumonia. I am on my way there now. She wanted you to have these. Best wishes, Marie-Noëlle.' There was no mention of the name of the hospital. Probably this was deliberate. Marie-Noëlle was discouraging visitors.

Liz sat in her room all day, reading through Laura's stories. Some had been published, others were still in manuscript. The stories continued the theme, begun in Whitby, of women's lives but the writing was more assured now, more experimental too. Some were set in Paris. There were descriptions of Gertrude's rooms, of Picasso glimpsed there once, of Natalie Barney's lesbian salon and the writer, Radclyffe Hall. There was even a description of a young American, who could only have been Hemingway, writing with intense concentration in a café, a pile of unpaid saucers at his elbow. These are priceless, thought Liz. She decided she couldn't possibly leave Paris till she heard further news of Philippa.

Two days later, she received a black-edged note from Marie-

Noëlle. 'Philippa died at three this morning, quite peacefully and without pain, as she would have wished to go. The funeral will be at the Père-Lachaise cemetery on Thursday at ten o'clock. Please come, if you can. Philippa would have wanted Laura's granddaughter to be there.'

Philippa's funeral was attended mainly by women. Mostly elderly, but some young ones as well. About one hundred and fifty mourners stood by the grave in the drizzle listening to the words of the priest. Only as she was standing there did it occur to Liz to wonder whether she should have informed Roger of the death of his great-aunt. Then she thought how out of place Roger would have felt among this gathering of women, artists, literary folk and bohemians. Their clothes alone – shabby silks, fringed scarves, tattered boots – would have scandalised him.

Several of the elderly women came up to Liz afterwards, pressing her hand and asking if it was true she was Laura's granddaughter and was going to publish her stories. They told her their names but Liz recognised none of them. Kate should have been here, she thought, at this event, this monument to Paris's literary past. She took down the name and address of each one who had known her grandmother. Kate would want to come over and interview them. Surrounded by a throng of women, Marie-Noëlle smiled tiredly across at Liz, then was borne away by her friends.

In the afternoon, Liz caught the plane back to England. Sitting with Laura's stories on her knee, thinking for the first time in days about Hull, Liz was suddenly filled with nervousness at the thought of what lay ahead of her. For what lay ahead, undoubtedly, was a meeting with Perdita.

PART THREE

PART THREE

Chapter Twelve

The restaurant was designed to resemble an American aircraft hangar. The decor appeared to have been imported from Seattle – the neon street map on the wall, the cigarette and beer advertisements, the 1920s plane, made of canvas and wood, suspended above their heads. Liz wondered if it had been in such a plane that Philippa and Laura made their escape from England. Or had they travelled, more prosaically, by train and boat?

Liz, Kate and Perdita were seated at a table by the window, waiting to order. The menu offered them 'an authentic American experience' and consisted of things like chilli and barbecued ribs and chicken wings. Liz felt that she might as well have been back in Boston. The cocktail list was a mile long and everything non-alcoholic had Virgin in front of it – Virgin Pina Colada, Virgin Mary, Virgin Screwdriver. The main part of the restaurant had been taken over by a cheerful and very noisy office party. Somewhere in the background a trio played jazz. Liz watched the lights twinkling over the Humber for a moment, then turned to look at Perdita.

Kate had been right about the Gothic phase. Perdita's face was dead white, the result of having been plastered with some kind of powder or paint. There were four gold studs climbing up her left ear and one through her nose. A heavy black cross hung around her neck for decoration, Liz was sure, rather than to convey any statement about her religious beliefs. She wore a black T-shirt and a long black skirt that was dusty around the hem from trailing along the ground as she walked. Her lips were the colour of bruised cherries. Kohl-rimmed eyes stared out of her white face. Her hair was short and black. That the black had come out of a bottle would have been obvious to Liz even if she hadn't seen Duncan's portrait of the red-haired young girl or remembered the few wisps of red hair on the newborn Perdita's head.

As Liz studied her she saw that Kate had been right about another thing – beneath the warpaint, Perdita was a taller, more slender version of their mother. She had the same delicate oval face, the same sharp dark eyes. This was the first opportunity Liz had had to really look at Perdita. She had been met by Kate at the airport and driven back to the house in Hull. Perdita would be there, Kate had informed her, but Duncan wouldn't. By the time the car pulled up in the Avenues, Liz's voice had dried up and her hands resting in her lap were damp with fear. She had followed her sister into the house, heard a light step in the hallway and there was Perdita. Slowly, Liz raised her eyes to meet this stranger's gaze.

'Hello, Perdita,' she said softly. She made no move to come closer. A handshake seemed too formal, a kiss over-familiar, in view of the circumstances.

Perdita said nothing for a moment, simply stood there staring at Liz, her thoughts a mystery to the watching sisters.

'So you're Aunt Liz,' she said eventually.

'Let's drop the aunt part, shall we?' Liz responded, hardly knowing what she was saying, but desperate to break the ice. 'I'm far too young to have a niece your age.' She laughed nervously.

'OK, Liz,' Perdita replied coolly, to disguise the fact she was flattered to have been put so soon on an equal footing.

'Well!' Kate turned and fiddled with some letters on the hall table.

Liz cast a nervous glance in her sister's direction. Should she have discussed with Kate beforehand the problem of what Perdita was to call her? But perhaps she'd been worrying needlessly for, after a few seconds of fiddling, Kate swung round and said quite cheerfully, 'Now you two have met up at last shall we go out to celebrate? My treat. Or don't you feel up to it?' She turned to Liz.

'No, I'm fine. It's only a hop over from Paris and in fact I'm starving. It was orange juice and a biscuit on the plane.' And three days since I've had a proper meal, she added to herself.

'Where shall we go? Perdita, where shall we go? You eat out more often than I do.'

'I never eat anywhere nice. There's nowhere cool to eat in this dump of a city,' Perdita added, determined to put on a sophisticated front for this relative of hers who lived in the States.

Kate, looking at Liz, rolled her eyes. 'We'd better stay in then.'

Faced with this threat, Perdita pulled herself together. 'Let's go to the American Diner. It's neat. Dad took me there once.'

Dad, Dad, Dad. The word echoed like a hammer blow through Liz's skull till she was afraid she would scream. Dad. Mum. Aunt. No wonder she had been scared all her life of labels.

So here the three of them were, sitting waiting for their food in a restaurant bizarrely transplanted from the States, where Duncan had once taken his daughter. Liz wondered whether Perdita and Duncan often went out alone together and what Kate felt about this.

She became aware that the other two members of her table were having an argument.

'Mum! You can't wrap me up in cotton wool for ever. I'm not going to break, you know! Break, darling!' Perdita banged her chest in the manner of Edina in *Absolutely Fabulous*. Then, dropping that manner, she said rather flatly, 'Everyone else is going.'

Kate looked at her with a wry expression on her face. 'That clinches it, does it? What everyone else does, you've got to do too?'

'You're determined to ruin my social life, aren't you?'

Kate flinched. She was nervous of Perdita, that was clear, and inclined to give in to her, out of some obscure sense of guilt perhaps.

'Darling, I don't want to stop you going out with your friends. I'm just thinking of the school work you have to catch up on.'

Kate stopped. They had made a pact, more for her own sake than Perdita's, that Liz would not be told of her exclusion from school. She was due back on Monday.

'No problem. Amy said I could borrow her notes.'

Kate sighed. 'I don't like the sound of these raves, Perdita. People seem to die at them. What if someone offers you an Ecstasy tablet?'

'I can always say no.'

'Can you? Will you?' Kate stared pointedly at her.

'Of course.' Perdita glanced casually out to sea.

To Liz, it sounded like a rerun of all the arguments she'd ever had with her own mother; only then it had been discos and alcohol and getting back by midnight, which was probably just about the time Perdita's raves got going.

'What does Duncan say? Did you mention this to him when you were speaking on the phone?'

'Dad said he'd leave the decision up to you.'

'Oh God!' Kate groaned. 'I'm going to the restroom, as Liz calls it.'

She stood up as the cheery young waitress brought their enchiladas and rice.

As soon as Kate had left them Perdita dropped the carefully studied nonchalance, leaned across the table and said to Liz, 'I've been longing to meet you for years. You've led such an interesting life.'

Careful, thought Liz. If she let this hero worship develop, she would have Kate's hostility to deal with.

'I've moved about a bit,' she agreed cautiously. She helped herself to rice and passed the dish over to Perdita. 'Lived in four different cities and done lots of different jobs. But it hasn't been a bed of roses, you know.' She sighed. 'I had such high hopes when I left Whitby but one book of poems doesn't seem much to show for all these years away, does it? I sometimes wonder whether I wouldn't have done better to have stayed put and followed some definite career, like Kate. Suddenly our lives don't seem that different any more, except that Kate's has more stability,' she added, forgetting that stability means nothing to an eighteen-year-old.

'Think of what you've seen.'

'Kate's travelled. She was telling me about your trip to Russia.'

'Holidays,' responded Perdita dismissively. 'She hasn't lived abroad, like you.'

Liz crumbled a piece of bread on her plate. 'You go abroad to escape your problems and find you've brought them along with you. I know a lot of things I didn't know when I left Whitby. Of the two of us, perhaps Kate made the wisest choice – stay and face up to yourself.'

'Oh yes, Mum's always *wise*,' responded Perdita bitterly, then broke off as Kate returned to their table.

Kate looked from one to the other. For a moment her expression was unfathomable.

'We were talking about how wise you are,' put in Liz, suddenly nervous.

A muscle relaxed in Kate's face.

'Were you?' She sat down. 'Surely not. I find that hard to believe.' She smiled at them both and helped herself to rice.

Liz felt a palpable sense of relief. She started to eat.

'What do you think about these raves, Liz?' asked her sister. 'Have you ever been to one?'

'Goodness me, no! The life we – the life I – lead in Boston is extremely staid,' she added, for Perdita's benefit. 'The most I get up to is becoming slight tipsy in bars.' She wondered whether Perdita had been told she lived – had lived – with a woman. Perhaps not. 'Anything I know about raves has been gleaned from newspapers.' She glanced across at Perdita. 'I do know I wouldn't touch Ecstasy with a bargepole. No one has worked out yet what the long-term effects of it are and you seem to die whether you drink too much or too little water. Dangerous stuff.'

'I agree.' Kate looked at her sister in surprise. Obviously she hadn't expected Liz to take this line. I do have some sense of responsibility, thought Liz crossly.

Perdita looked disappointed, then sullen.

'I'm going,' she muttered. 'You can't stop me.'

Kate raised her eyebrows at Liz in mock despair. 'Let's drop the subject, shall we?' she suggested. 'We don't want to spend the whole of Liz's first evening back rowing. We'll discuss it later.'

Perdita shrugged. 'All right. So long as you realise I'm going anyway.'

Ignoring her, the two sisters began talking about Liz's meetings with Philippa in Paris.

'She was wonderful. And she knew so many writers and artists. Oh, Kate, I wish you could have met her. You would have loved her and you'd have known what to ask her.'

'I'd like to have met her, it would have been like encountering a piece of history. There are people alive who knew some of the writers of that period but they're getting fewer and fewer. Still, at least one of us was able to talk to her before she died – and you have the tape and the stories.'

Kate had pounced on Laura's stories the minute Liz had unpacked them, and spirited them up to her room. She was excited by the project of editing her grandmother's work and already had one or two ideas for the introduction. In the end, even Perdita became infected by their enthusiasm and was drawn into the conversation, asking a couple of quite intelligent questions, Liz thought. She would do well at university. Watching her lean forward to ask Kate a question about Laura's writing, Liz saw for a moment herself reflected in Perdita's face, as if in a mirror. It was the strangest sensation, like spying on a younger version of herself. Then Perdita sat back in her chair and the mirage, or echo, or whatever it had been, vanished.

'So, what do you think of her?' enquired Kate later that evening when they had returned to the house in the Avenues and the two sisters were sitting in Kate's flower-filled conservatory, drinking coffee. Perdita had gone to bed, or at least retreated to her room.

'She's wonderful, Kate,' said Liz. Her voice softened. 'You've done a marvellous job.'

'Oh. Well. Do you think so?' An involuntary smile appeared on Kate's face. To hide it, she leaned forward and plucked a dead leaf off a plant. Then she sat back, recomposed her features and said, 'Of course, she can be quite bolshie. As you saw this evening.'

'Aren't all teenagers? No, I think Perdita's great. She has so much self-confidence and, underneath the warpaint, intelligence. As I remember it, a girl's adolescence was a terrible time. Like entering a dark tunnel. Suddenly, if you wanted to retain any individuality, there were no road maps any more. Society was telling you to be one thing, but if you wanted to be something different you were on your own, groping in the dark for a friendly hand from someone who would see you as more than marriage fodder.' She turned to look at Kate. 'Or perhaps it's not like that any longer?'

'I don't think it is. Young women these days are much more in control of their lives than we were. They don't sit in, like we did, waiting for the phone to ring. Perdita sailed through the early years of adolescence without a hitch. It's only the last part that has been difficult.'

'Well, that's one change for the better.'

'Yes, I've always been glad Perdita is female. It's the girls who have the confidence nowadays. They know they're better, fitter, smarter than the boys. The boys round here, they haven't much hope. They see their fathers made redundant and their mothers and sisters getting all the jobs. And the funny thing is, as their employment prospects worsen, the men are taking on a more decorative role. My male students turn up to classes with rings through their noses, ponytails, necklaces, dyed hair, the works. They struggle to make their mark in the only ways available to them.'

'How strange that in just a few years everything should have changed so much.' Liz looked at her sister. 'This isn't what we meant, is it? That young men should become despised, un-employed, demoralised? What we wanted was some balance between the sexes.'

'I wouldn't feel too sorry for them,' Kate said tartly, tweaking off another leaf. 'There are three professors in my department and none of them is a woman. We have some way to go yet.' She changed the subject. 'Are Laura's Paris stories as good as the ones she wrote in Whitby?'

'Better, I think.'

'I can't wait to read them. When we've got the arrangements about Mum's house sorted out, I'd like to spend a few days drafting an introduction, while everything is still fresh in my mind and while you're still here to check things with.'

'Yes, I can't stay here for ever. I'll have to think soon about going back to the States and earning some money. I went over my budget in Paris.'

'I could –'

'No, Kate, don't start lending me money. I've got enough for another few weeks.'

'In that case we'd better get a move on with Mum's house. Perdita and I did some more clearing out those days we were over but there's still some left to do. Shall we go to Whitby tomorrow, the two of us, finish the clearing and discuss arrangements with Roger? How does that sound?'

'Fine by me.' Liz glanced surreptitiously at her sister. Had there been a special note in Kate's voice when she mentioned Roger's name? Or was that her imagination? She paused for a moment, then, summoning up her courage, she put the question she had been longing to ask ever since she had stepped off the plane at Humberside airport. 'How's Duncan?'

'Staying where he is for the moment,' answered Kate. Liz felt relief wash over her. 'Chris needs a lot of cheering up. He got a three-year conditional discharge for a community work sentence.'

'Just for stealing some bread to eat?'

'Yes, it's not the first time he's done it and apparently you can't plead necessity as a defence if you've offended more than once. It was buns from a bakery last time. Evidently, in the eyes of the law, your situation is considered less desperate if you are starving on more than one occasion.'

'How ridiculous.'

'It is,' agreed Kate. 'Added to which, Chris has been ordered to pay one hundred and fifty pounds compensation for damage done to the shop. He broke a window.'

'Where on earth will he find that kind of money?'

'Duncan,' she said briefly. 'Or rather me, via Duncan.'

'Oh, Kate,' breathed Liz.

'Don't pity me. I'm not a hero,' her sister responded sharply. 'I knew what I was getting into when I married Duncan. I knew he had affairs with men.'

'Did you? I didn't. Not for years.'

'Mad, bad and dangerous to know. And simply the most gorgeous man around. Oh yes, I went into it with my eyes open. I had to have him, whatever the drawbacks. And I do feel rather sorry for Chris. He follows Duncan around like a lapdog. He once told me Duncan is the only human being who has ever shown any interest in him.'

'But what's in it for Duncan?' asked Liz, tilting back her chair. 'If that portrait of Chris in his studio is anything to go by, I can't see the attraction.'

Kate rested her eyes on her sister for a moment, then she said quietly, 'Duncan likes rescuing people. Especially young people. And my God did Chris need rescuing! He's cleaned himself up a bit now. He had scabies when Duncan first brought him home. I made Duncan take him to the doctor.'

I couldn't have done it, thought Liz, I couldn't have taken that much care of him. It's better he went back to Kate. Aloud she said, 'Does Perdita know about Duncan? I mean about his affairs with men?'

'She does now. She was about fifteen when she began to guess. Till then we had tried to hide it from her.' Kate glanced across at her sister. 'It hasn't been the perfect upbringing, I'm afraid.' There was a defensive note in her voice. 'But we tried to do our best.'

We all tried our best, thought Liz later, as she undressed for bed. I went away. I left you with Duncan and Perdita. We all did our very, very best.

There'd only been one lapse. Five years after she left Whitby, alone in London and in a panic, she had sent a note to Duncan up in Hull.

'I feel like I've lost part of myself. Since leaving you, my life has been all on the surface. I have found no one who has touched me in the way you did. I dream of you at night. I wake up every morning with your name on my lips. My whole body screams out in need of you. Please, if I ever meant anything to you, come and see me now. I need to see you one last time. That's all I ask. I'm older now.' (All of twenty-four! thought Liz, lying in bed, recalling every word of that note.) 'I can bear to see you and let you go again. I know your real life is with Kate. It has to be.'

Duncan had answered in the most loving, reassuring way. But he hadn't come to see her.

She had kept the letter with her for years. It was lost now, mislaid somewhere during that time which was simply a blur. That time when she'd cared very little what happened to her; when she'd drifted in and out of affairs with men, not even affairs, one-night stands more like, moving between Paris and London in a drug-filled haze, learning all about the perversions, the tawdry longings, the secret obsessions of men, selling herself short at every available opportunity. There'd been weeks when she'd woken up in a different bed every day, unable to remember the name of the man lying beside her, or where she'd met him.

Years and years of missing you in strange rooms, in strange cities, the body lying next to me or on top of me never the right one. Trying to fuck myself into life, fucking my way out of despair.

141

Standard manic-depressive stuff. And then, little by little, being reborn. It hadn't been sudden. She hadn't suddenly woken up one morning thinking life was, after all, worth living. It had come upon her in small ways – sitting in the Jardin du Luxembourg watching the sunlight fall through the chestnut trees, walking through rain-soaked bluebells in a wood in southern England. Gradually, she had edged herself back into life, eased off the drugs, eaten more healthily. Her weight had crept up from an anorexic seven stones to seven and a half, then eight. She had learned to allow herself small pleasures – strawberries in season, good music, films. She had become fit for a relationship again.

Moving to Dublin for the summer – she'd been told it was a good place to be for a writer, but all the work she had managed to find was waitressing – she'd met Caro. Liz had begun to see that the love of women, a different sort of thing from the love of men, might, astonishingly, be where her salvation lay. Still broken and bruised, she had spent two wonderful years in Ireland, soothed by Caro who worked as a nursery nurse in one of the roughest areas of the city and knew all about battered and damaged children. She had grown up with Caro, been given the chance to be dependent for a while. Then, in a mad dash for a cheap kind of freedom, she'd gone and spoiled it all by a one-night fling with – some woman whose name she couldn't even remember now. Maire? Mairead? Morag? Something like that. Caro had lost patience with her and thrown her out.

Back in London, working in a wine bar in Kensington, she had met Sarah. A calm, settled time. She was less dependent on Sarah than she had been on Caro. Her first, and so far only, collection of poetry came out. Lyrical poems of unrequited love; for Duncan, of course, though he was never named. For a while, she was much in demand at poetry readings. She was getting stronger now, getting ready for the second great passion of her life. Only, after Duncan, she had never expected anything to be permanent. She had always expected to be walked out on and now she had been. Call it wish-fulfilment.

She switched off the light and lay awake in the darkness, her hands clasped across her chest. Louise, where are you? Is it working out with Annie? She could only wait. She had done everything in her power to make Louise stay. Dragged her out of bars, run down the street after her sobbing, rolled around on the floor in agony crying 'Please, please don't leave me!' while Louise had sat impassively on the sofa, smoking cigarette after cigarette. She couldn't do any of that any more. She felt completely exhausted.

She could write to her, as she had written so often in the past, one of her begging letters. 'I need you, Louise. You're the only one who can keep me together. Doesn't that count for anything with you? I'm going to pieces here without you. Please forgive me for all those times we've quarrelled. I've been terribly, terribly stupid. I can't bear to lose you.'

She could write all that, she had written it before. It would still be true, more or less. But it wouldn't do any good. She was alone in the world, she had to face it. Pray God Duncan wouldn't come anywhere near her. Pray God Kate would protect her if he did.

Chapter Thirteen

'Perdita, Liz and I thought we would go over to Whitby today to finalise arrangements with Roger about Grandma's house. Do you want to stay here for the weekend, or shall we drop you off at Jenny's in Pickering on our way?'

'I'll come to Whitby with you.'

Perdita lolled in a chair in the kitchen munching an apple. She hadn't yet put on her white facepaint and was looking less Gothic this morning. She was still dressed in black, though – black T-shirt, black jeans, expensive black trainers.

Kate raised an eyebrow. 'Are you sure you want to, darling? You know how bored you always get, away from your friends.'

And what about that rave you made such a fuss over last night? Kate kept the question to herself. If Perdita had forgotten about it, she wasn't going to remind her. In fact, suggesting they drop her off at her godmother's had been a ploy to get her out of Hull for the weekend. It now seemed as if that had been unnecessary.

'I'm coming, Mum,' Perdita said firmly, finishing up her apple.

'Then you'd better go and pack what you need for the weekend. We're leaving in half an hour.'

Perdita slouched out of the kitchen. Kate stood up and began clearing away the breakfast things. Liz gave her a hand.

'Really she's unaccountable,' said Kate in a low voice, standing at the sink. 'All that fuss last night about how she must go to that rave or the rest of her life would be blighted and today she seems to have forgotten about it.'

'Perhaps she's trying to please you.' Liz dried a plate. 'She's decided not to go to the rave in deference to your wishes but she can't quite bring herself to say so.'

Kate considered this for a moment, then shook her head and resumed her washing up. 'The thing you have to remember about Perdita is that she never, ever, considers anyone but herself. Perdita and unselfishness is an oxymoron. Like Yorkshire water. Sorry,' she glanced at Liz, 'local joke. Our reservoirs have run dry.'

'I suppose, being beautiful, she gets lots of invitations?'

'Oh yes.' Kate sighed. 'Young men swarm around her like flies. She doesn't seem to take much notice of them though. Says they're immature and silly. She goes round in a gang of young women.'

'Beauty never made you selfish, did it?'

'I suppose I never thought of myself as beautiful.'

'Oh but you were!' exclaimed Liz. 'All that luscious red hair –'

'Rather faded now,' put in Kate ruefully.

'You got noticed everywhere,' Liz went on. 'My glamorous, clever elder sister. No wonder I had such trouble getting through adolescence. I was small, shy and underdeveloped. I always knew I was in the halfpenny place compared to you.'

'How crazy!' exclaimed Kate. 'Considering . . .'

She stopped. They both knew that what she had been about to say was, considering Duncan left me for you. Ah but, thought Liz, completing the argument in her head, he came back to you. Kate pulled out the plug. The sisters watched the water drain away. Liz went upstairs to fling a few things into her holdall.

They drove over the moors to Whitby. The sky was grey today, the hills dark greens and purples. The two sisters in the front, Perdita in the back of the car, were silent for most of the way, each concentrating on her own private thoughts. Kate was going over Laura's stories in her mind.

'You know I think I may have found out something about Arthur Chapman's murder.' She changed gear as they began the descent into Whitby.

'Really?' exclaimed Liz, jolted out of the past.

'I was reading Laura's stories last night. Do you remember the one set in the West Indies?'

'Vaguely.'

'Well, I think it may contain a clue to the identity of Arthur's murderer.'

'Does it? How?'

'Let me read you it when we get to the house. See if anything occurs to you.'

'OK.'

'I've arranged that Roger will meet us there at four. Do you want to be dropped off in town, Perdita?' Kate asked over her shoulder, as they neared Whitby.

'No thanks. I'll come up to the house with you.'

'What are we going to do about Mum's house, Liz? Roger still thinks we should rent it out. I'm not in favour. It could be messy and take up a lot of time and energy. Do you really want to keep it on?'

'I'm not sure.' Liz stared out of the car window.

'We'll have to come to some decision soon,' Kate said impatiently, finding her sister's last remark unhelpful.

'I know. I'm sorry.' Liz glanced down at her lap. 'I suppose the sensible thing would be to sell it and not have to think about it any more.'

'Can't we keep it on, Mum?' Perdita piped up from the back. 'I could live in it.'

'You will be away at university, we hope, for most of the year. I can't keep two homes going for you up here.'

'I was thinking of taking a year out.'

'What!' Kate's head swivelled round dangerously for a second. The traffic was building up as they approached the outskirts of Whitby. She turned her attention back to the road. 'This is rather sudden, Perdita, isn't it? I've nothing against taking a gap year, in fact I think it's a good idea, but most people plan these things well in advance. What do you intend doing?'

'I don't know. See life, I suppose. Take a break from the books. I could stay in Grandma's house and find work in Whitby. I'd pay you rent.'

'Work? What as?'

'A waitress, or something.'

'Sounds rather unambitious. Wouldn't you prefer to go abroad for the year and teach English? I might be able to arrange something for you.'

'I don't *want* to go abroad. Besides, you shouldn't be so insulting about waitressing. It's what Liz does.'

Kate flushed. 'Liz does other things as well. She writes poetry, she –'

'It's all right, Kate,' said Liz calmly. 'It *is* unambitious work and I certainly wouldn't recommend it.'

'Even supposing you could find work like that,' added Kate. 'Do you realise what unemployment is like in this town? Local businesses are closing down every week.'

'Whenever I try to think of something positive to do, you always pour cold water on it, Mum.'

'I don't, darling.' Kate negotiated the car past the crowds of tourists and turned into Henrietta Street. 'I just want you to do something interesting with your life.'

'Staying in Whitby interests me.'

Kate pulled up on the patch of waste ground at the top of the street and twisted round in her seat to look at Perdita.

'Darling, I can't believe that. The number of times I used to bring you over to see Grandma and you would complain of being utterly bored!'

'That was different. I was younger then.'

'Well, I just don't think spending the year in Whitby waitressing is the best use you could make of your life.'

Kate switched off the engine and got out of the car. Perdita followed in sullen silence. Arriving at the house, she ran up to the tiny boxroom which had been reserved for her ever since she was a child and slammed the door behind her.

'Honestly, she's so inconsistent!' Kate exploded in the sitting room. 'Sometimes she makes me want to wring her neck!'

Liz, whose sympathies in the car had partly lain with Perdita, felt it would be wise to refrain from comment.

'The wretched child's given me a headache.' Kate fumbled in her bag for some Anadin and swallowed two. 'That's better. Now what I need is a strong cup of coffee. Fancy a sandwich for lunch, Liz? I've brought over some bread and cheese from Hull.'

'You think of everything. Yes, I'd love a sandwich.'

'We'll leave Perdita to get her own lunch.'

'You've done well with the sorting out, Kate,' Liz said, wanting to cheer her sister up. She looked around. Only carpets, curtains and the larger furniture remained. The room looked more spacious, now that their mother's many china ornaments had been removed.

147

'It would have taken me ages to cope with all this. You always were the practical one.'

I didn't have much choice, thought Kate, turning away and going into the kitchen to make sandwiches. It was forced on me. Given the choice, I might have preferred to have been something else. To have glided through life, for instance, like you and Duncan. She was determined Perdita wasn't going to be like that, however many arguments it might involve. Carefully, she sliced the bread and began to spread butter on it. She wanted Perdita to learn to face up to things, to plan, to take responsibility. It led to more happiness in the end, Kate was convinced of it. Or if not happiness, then stability and security, which were perhaps the most that could be hoped for in life. Stability, she thought suddenly, what stability have I got, in spite of all my planning? Duncan is about to leave me for Chris. Standing at the kitchen table, breadknife in hand, Kate wept silently and secretively, as she had wept all those years ago when she first found out about Liz. Then she dried her eyes, finished buttering the bread and brought sandwiches and coffee into the front room.

'Read me that story of Laura's,' said Liz. 'I've been turning it over in my mind ever since you mentioned it in the car. I can't for the life of me think what the clue to Arthur's murder might be, but then I haven't your training in literary analysis. Also, I can't remember it very clearly.'

'I'll go and fetch it.'

Kate went upstairs. Liz heard her asking Perdita if she wanted a sandwich and Perdita's refusal.

'I don't know what's the matter with her.' Kate came back into the room with Laura's manuscript in her hand. 'She's behaving most unlike herself. Wanting to live in Whitby, of all places, and now not eating. Perdita's not normally one to let a row get in the way of her lunch. Well, here it is.' She sat down on the sofa. 'Laura's story. It doesn't have a title. It was never published and I think I know why. It's written in the first person and the heroine's name is Dorothy.

I came from far away over the seas to marry my husband. The seas seemed tranquil enough but I was told later that beneath them lurked sharks and barracoutas.

148

'I came out from Southampton on a French ship in the year 1921 to marry a man twenty years older than myself. William's family has owned plantations on this island for generations, as far back as the time of the slave owners. His great-grandfather owned over two hundred slaves; among them many were his mistresses and his children. I knew nothing of this when I sailed out to marry William.

'We had met the year before in Bath, not entirely by chance. Disdaining to marry a Creole, William had come to England to find a suitable wife. He had written to his aunt to this effect. His aunt was one of my mother's closest friends; as children, they had shared a governess. William's aunt immediately thought of me, her friend's eldest daughter. I was twenty-four and still unmarried. Mother was getting anxious. When she received Emily's letter she thought she had found the solution to the problem of what to do with me. Poor Mother!

'Together the two women planned our "surprise" encounter in the Pump Room. After that, William and I were thrown together as often as possible. We were frequently unchaperoned, in view of William's age and my mother's desperation. He was tall and distinguished. He brought an air of the outside world with him, a welcome change after stuffy old Bath. His stories about his island and the coffee plantations his family owned there fascinated me. I had always wanted to travel but so far, despite having had a French governess, I had never been further than London. When, the day before he was due to leave England, William took me to tea and asked me to share his life in Dominica, I scarcely hesitated for a second. There is nothing for an unmarried daughter in Bath.

'Our engagement delighted my mother and William's aunt. It was agreed that I would wait six months and sail out to join him. I suppose there are women who know as little about their husbands as I did and yet go on to have happy marriages. I wonder.

'William was waiting for me at the port. We were married that same day in the English church in Roseau, the capital of Dominica, a shabby little town. Any delay in the marriage ceremony would have been frowned upon and would certainly have led to me being excluded from the society of the three hundred or so white inhabitants of the island. They are very old-fashioned here. The ladies wear long white gloves when they call on each other in the afternoons. For the ceremony

I wore my grey travelling suit. At the last minute, someone thrust a bunch of orchid-lilies into my hands. I scarcely remember anything of my wedding, except that I wished my mother could have been there. When I came out of the church, I was William's wife and it was time to meet his family.

'*We ate at a long table. Strange food that I had never tasted before and I didn't know the names of. Yams and sliced avocados. Even the food I did recognise – the crayfish, the stuffed crab – tasted different from at home. I scarcely touched anything. A servant brought me some rum punch to drink. What with the heat and the strangeness of my surroundings, it went straight to my head. I sat watching William make the rounds of his relations, chatting and gossiping with them, paying no attention to me. Then I think I must have fainted for the next thing I remember is lying down in a cool room with the shutters drawn and someone fanning my face. After a while, William came in and the servant girl left. This was the hotel where it had been arranged we would spend our first night before going on in the morning up into the mountains to William's estate.*

'*I don't remember much of my wedding night, only that it was not as I expected it would be. It was altogether wilder, more brutal than I had imagined.*

'*The next morning, we rose early in order to make progress before the heat of the day set in. I have never been skilled on horseback and William's lovemaking had left me sore and bruised. I thought that journey would never end. Up and up we went through the lush green vegetation, accompanied by two porters carrying my luggage. My head began to ache. The colours were brighter, the smells stronger than anywhere else I had ever been. I didn't think such a place existed on earth. It was overpowering: The mountains seemed to crowd in on us. Eventually, when I thought I could bear it no longer, we stopped to rest the horses beside a shady pool fed by a mountain spring. William broke off a green leaf as big as a bowl, held it under the spring and handed it to me. "Mountain water," he said. "Taste. It will do you good." I could not decide whether he was kind or not. The memory of the previous night was still with me. Perhaps I shall get used to it, I thought, in time. I never got used to it.*

'*Eventually we arrived at William's estate and I caught my first* glimpse of the long, low, one-storey building that was to be my home. The servants were lined up to greet us on the lawn, standing under the shade of a flamboyant tree. An old man, a young man, a woman and a young girl. The first to step forward was the woman, Lila. She was dressed in a brightly flowered creole dress, with a striped head handkerchief. Heavy gold earrings dangled from her ears. She curtsied, then fixed me with her gaze. I remember thinking that she looked sorry for me. She pushed forward the little serving girl who gave a shy curtsy and fled. I was introduced to the overseer, Baptiste, and to the old man whose name I have now forgotten. The servants lived in the outhouses next to the kitchen, across the muddy yard from the main house.

'I was not prepared for the shabbiness of William's house. It was not at all as I had been led to expect. The rooms were bare and unpainted and what furniture there was seemed to be falling apart. An effect of the damp, I learned later. Here, chairs become unstuck, books rot, ants and mice gnaw away at everything. No wonder they call this island the "Cinderella of the West Indies".

'We ate dinner in the uncarpeted dining room hung with portraits of William's ancestors and views of Westminster Abbey and the Tower of London. We ate at a huge old table lit by candlelight and decorated with trailing yellow flowers. Cornélie, the little servant girl, brought in the food. Mountain chicken, followed by curry and stewed guavas. Again I hardly touched any of it, but I drank two glasses of the ice-cold champagne Cornélie brought us. William spoke little. Only when we went out on to the veranda to finish our champagne did he come to life and told me the names of the plants and trees we could see on the lawn by the light of the moon that was brighter than any moon I had ever seen in England. Strange names – hisbiscus, frangipani, oleanders, madonna orchids, two breadfruit trees, lobster claw ginger and trailing lianas. The vegetation runs riot on this island. I have often had dreams of being strangled by a giant tree fern. Nature is not on man's side here. It is not gentle and tamed, as in England, but violent and menacing, bringing disease and death.

'We sat conversing like any well-brought up lady and gentleman, but when we went inside, it was a repetition of the night before. William flung me down on the bed half undressed, ripped my chemise and seized hold of my breasts. Then he plunged his fingers inside me, working them furiously in and out, in and out, till I thought I would scream with pain.

'"Come on," he grunted. "There's no need to behave like an English lady out here."

'Then he turned me over and took me in a way I would not have thought possible.

'"Now you know what I like," he said.

'He woke me three more times in the night. Once he made me kneel on the bed and took me from behind like the dogs I used to watch in the park when I was a child, till my governess told me sharply to look the other way.

'In the morning when I awoke, he had already left, gone over to the other side of the island, his note said, to inspect some land he was thinking of buying. Cornélie brought me breakfast in bed, coffee and cassava cakes and guava jelly. She cast a curious glance at my torn chemise and the rumpled and stained bedsheets. Now you know what men are like, I thought, and now I know. But I didn't. Not all men are like William. It has taken me a long time to realise this.

'I spent the day wandering round the house and the garden, waiting for him to come back. The servants left me alone, except for Cornélie who silently brought me my meals. I didn't know then how much the old Creole families are hated on this island. "White cockroaches," they call us. They never forget that we were once slave owners.

'Darkness began to fall and still William had not returned. I lay in a hammock on the veranda. The noise of the crickets and the frogs grew deafening. The scent of the flowers opening at night made me feel giddy. I fell into a sort of a swoon. The next thing I knew, William was standing over me. I could smell the rum on his breath. I started to rise. "No, please!" I exclaimed. "Please don't!" Paying no attention, he lifted me out of the hammock and carried me into the sitting room. He laid me down on the floor and took me then and there. I tried to resist. What if one of the servants walked in?

'"Damn you," he said. "I'll show you how to love. I'll make a passionate woman of you yet."

'I am a passionate woman, but women need a little tenderness too. This strange wild lovemaking is not at all what I expected. William is not the man I took him to be in England, so polite and restrained and distinguished. Out here he is fiercer, angrier, more despairing. The estate is gradually falling into disrepair. Even the money I brought him on my marriage won't be enough to save it. He drinks to forget his troubles. And his drinking makes him wild. There are bruises on my arms after his lovemaking. The things he asks of me in bed are strange, often perverse, but the strangest thing is, my body cannot refuse him. It has learned to grow hungry for his ways of making love. In bed I am a different woman from the English lady I am in daylight and I wonder how that has happened. Then I remember that William's family were once slave owners. Brutality is in his blood. It has been easy for him to turn me into his slave. I was brought up to please gentlemen.

'I have found out something else about William – he has a mistress, or perhaps several. Well, I must turn a blind eye. What else can I do? I am alone here, without friends or family, alone in this alien, frightening country. I cannot go back home. They would not want me, without a husband. I must endure everything . . .

'I have lived here now for five years, on this beautiful, violent, disease-ridden island. I have two children – four-year-old Sophie and two-year-old Edward. Since Edward's birth, William no longer comes near me. He has what he wanted from me, he has his heir of pure English blood. He no longer needs me, except to bring up his children. He takes his pleasure elsewhere and I must learn to live in this hot climate without love.

'We have new servants. The old man died and Baptiste went to work for some wealthy whites down in Roseau. He has been replaced by Pierre and his helper, a boy called Emile. When Cornélie turned fourteen, she became William's mistress for a short time. Then he tired of her and she had to go. I gave her money and she sailed to Jamaica to seek her fortune but I fear her life will not turn out well, now that she has been corrupted by William. She is no longer a shy little Catholic serving girl. I shall always wonder whether her fate turned on that moment when she came into our bedroom and saw the debris of our lovemaking.

'Lila is still here. She has become a good friend and my children have become her life almost as much as they are mine. They play every day with her little daughter (father unknown even to Lila, I think). The parish priest paid us a visit when little Dorothy was born (she is named after me) and said I should dismiss Lila as a punishment for her immorality. Of course I refused. I am not a Catholic; I do not have to do what he says. The men in Whitehall think they rule this country, but in reality it is run by the coloured merchants and the Catholic priests.

'Despite a bad hurricane which nearly destroyed our coffee plantations, the estate is beginning to prosper, in a mild way. I sometimes think that if only William would stop drinking, we might be able to give our children a proper future. I am beginning to get used to this island. I am beginning to understand the patois. I have grown used to the cockroaches and the stinging ants. I have learned to love the humming birds and the hibiscus flaring in the hedges; the fireflies and the sweet-scented frangipani. England seems a grey faraway place where, compared to Dominica, the people live like shadows or ghosts of human beings. I can barely remember what my life there was like. My mother died a year ago, so there is nothing to go back for, even if it was likely we could raise the fare. It's a strange thought that my children may never see England.

'Edward has had a touch of malaria. I have been sitting for hours on the veranda, looking out towards the dark blue sea in the distance and rocking him in his little wicker cot covered with mosquito netting. Occasionally one of the servants crosses the lawn and we nod to one another. If it is Lila, she brings a piece of sewing and comes and sits by me. Unless William is in the house, that is. He disapproves of my making friends with servants. On the other hand, he dislikes it when ladies from the town come to call on me. Not that they do that very often. We are so isolated up here. I think William wants me to have no friends. I know too much about him and he is afraid of what I might say.

'Sometimes Emile comes to tend the flowers, as Pierre has showed him. I sit and watch him and occasionally he looks up and our eyes meet. We are two of a kind, that boy and I. We watch and wait, with cold English calculation, my husband would say. But the boy is not English, though he is certainly of mixed parentage. I know what I am watching out for – the safety of my children, that is my one concern in life. But what is the boy watching for?

'William came back drunk last night as I was sitting here on the veranda. I hadn't seen him for five days. "Englishwoman!" he sneered as he went past, then turned and dragged me inside by the hair. He pulled me into his bedroom (we have long since given up sleeping in the same room) and beat and punched me. Then, thank God, he collapsed in a stupor on the floor. The noise had woken the children who were screaming in their beds. My face bleeding and my dress torn, I crawled on my hands and knees to their room where Lila was trying to calm them. "Hush up, child. Hush up," she was saying, rocking little Sophie in her arms. She took one look at me, uttered an exclamation and helped me from the room. "No good see children like that." She bathed my face, put some herb on it and fetched me a clean nightgown. "White men no good husbands." "Some of them are, Lila," I replied. "I was just unlucky." Then we said no more. She stayed with me till I fell asleep. When I woke the next morning, someone had placed a branch of sweet-smelling jasmine on my quilt. I thought it must have been Lila but she said it wasn't. Could it have been William?

'I have found out about the boy, Emile. His mother, it appears, was William's mistress. One of his mistresses. When he discarded her, she starved to death on the streets of Roseau. The boy went barefoot and lived by scavenging until some nuns took him in. A strange coincidence that he has ended up here. Or is it a coincidence? It is William he watches, I have discovered. He looks at my husband sometimes as if he wished him at the bottom of the boiling lake. Does William know that Emile is his son? I somehow think not, or he would hardly have employed him. It has always been William's policy to deny paternity. He claims none of these women can be trusted to tell the truth about the fathers of their children. Whether it is true or not, I think Emile is convinced William is his father. I wonder what he intends to do about it?

'A week later, the whole household is aroused from their beds by a bloodcurdling scream coming from my husband's room. I grab my nightgown and dash down the corridor. A white and quaking William stands in the doorway of his room, pointing at the floor. Someone has left a trail of chicken feathers and a basin of blood, chicken's blood probably, outside his room.

'"Get it away! Get it out of my sight!" he screams.

'I have to do it myself. None of the servants will touch it.

'"Obeah," he mutters when I return, having removed the offending articles to the bottom of the garden. "It is obeah."

'"Surely you don't believe in that?" I say.

'But he does. His da, his nurse, brought him up on stories of zombies and loups-garoux and soucriants who come in the night and suck your blood. William is as superstitious as anyone on the island. Also, the drink has demoralised him and weakened his faculty for rational thought. And of course, the fear that someone may be practising black magic against him makes him race out of the house to the nearest bar. He returns around midnight, dead drunk. Too drunk, thank God, to give me more than a token slap in the face. As he is doing this on the veranda, Emile materialises out of nowhere. William looks at him, lets go of me and shuffles off, shielding his face with his arm, as if trying to ward off danger.

'"I bring you this, mistress," says Emile, holding out a branch of sweet-scented jasmine. So it is he who has been making my room smell so beautiful in the mornings. I accept the jasmine and on impulse take his face in my hands and kiss his forehead. "Thank you, Emile," I say and wonder if he has appointed himself my protector. I smile to myself. He is so young. Just a boy. He looks in need of protection himself.

'All is calm for the next few days. Then William finds white powder scattered over the floor of his dressing room. I try to persuade him one of the servants must have done it, to ward off the cockroaches, but he will have none of it. Pushing me aside, he mutters, "This house is haunted," and sets off down the mountain. I was never to see him alive again.

'According to reports, William spent the day drinking in town. At night, on his way home, he slipped and lost his footing on the old swing bridge. His body was washed up two days later. The locals said it was obeah. The whites said the bridge must be mended. I know that, drunk and in a state of terror, it would have been easy for William to slip in the dark. There had been a downpour and the bridge would have been treacherous and the river full. Sometimes, though, when I look at Emile and his eyes meet mine, I wonder what exactly did happen on that bridge and whether one young boy took revenge on his father for treating his mother the way the whites used to treat the slaves?

'All I know is there has been no more obeah. We have all of us,

Lila, Pierre, Emile, myself and the children, lived here peacefully and, yes, happily for the past two years. I never thought I would ever be happy on this island, but I am. The townspeople think I am a witch. They think I put a spell on William that led him to his death. They make their way up here sometimes, bringing me gifts of ginger cakes and tamarinds in syrup, wanting me to put a curse on someone. I have to send them away. But I make sure they never go away empty-handed. I am treated with respect now, with more respect than a woman would have in England. I shall stay here and work the estate until the forest swallows it up again, as I know it eventually will. Nature always wins here. I have kept Emily's secret, whatever it is. I owe him a great debt. His revenge has set me free.

'That's the end.' Kate fell silent for a moment. 'Now do you see?' she said.

'It's a lovely story,' Liz replied. 'But what on earth has it to do with Arthur's death?'

'Do you remember the gardener's boy employed by the Chapmans? He's mentioned in Laura's diaries. I looked up his name. Joe Perkins. Remember him? The sullen boy who hardly opened his mouth when Laura interviewed him.'

'Yes, I remember now. It was one of the earliest entries. So?'

'So what if he, like Emile in the story, was really Arthur's illegitimate son? We know Arthur had at least one mistress. What if this son, Joe, killed his father out of revenge, like the boy in the story? What if Laura gradually pieced all this together in Paris and wrote it out in this story? The story contained the clue to Arthur's murder and that's why she never tried to get it published, never even gave it a title.'

'It's a long shot.'

'Have you a better idea?'

'No.'

'Well then.'

Liz pondered this for a moment then said, 'But where did Laura get her information from about Dominica?'

'In her diaries, she says that C told her about Dominica.'

'C?'

'Do you remember she mentions her brother Charles who ran away to join the Navy? Perhaps he visited Dominica and came back and told Laura all about it. We know she was always longing to hear about other countries. She wrestled with this Dominican material for quite a while, first writing the story of Delia and the sick sailor, Captain James Lockhart, who came from Dominica and then, in Paris, making up this story. I suppose she thought, by setting the story so far away from Whitby, she was covering her tracks.'

'Mm. I can see why you're a literary critic, Kate. You're much better at this sort of thing than I am.'

'Years of practice, my dear,' retorted Kate. She was feeling rather pleased with herself. For once, being an academic rather than a poet had come in useful.

Chapter Fourteen

Just before four, Perdita came downstairs. Liz had gone out to smoke her second cigarette of the afternoon, nervous, presumably, at the idea of meeting Roger again. Perdita was almost as bad, thought Kate, refusing all offers of food and prowling around the sitting room like an animal in a cage.

'If you're bored, darling, why don't you go out for a walk?'

'I'm not bored,' growled Perdita.

Feeling a headache coming on again, Kate left her alone. What on earth was the matter with Perdita today? Liz came back into the sitting room smelling of stale tobacco.

The doorbell rang. Perdita froze. Liz gave a sharp intake of breath. With a glance at them both, Kate went to answer the door.

'Hello, Roger. I appreciate you coming. Come into the sitting room,' said Kate, in what Liz recognised as her social voice. I must have been mistaken, she thought, there can't be anything between them. Unless Kate is putting on an act for our benefit.

'Liz is here.' Kate ushered Roger into the room. 'And Perdita. Quite a family gathering,' she added.

'Hello, Liz,' said Roger, looking more relaxed than he had done at their last meeting when he'd stormed off and left her standing on the pavement.

From her perch on the windowsill, Liz cautiously waved a hand at him.

He turned. 'Hello, Perdita.'

'Hi,' mumbled Perdita, seeming to squash herself further into the wall.

She doesn't like him, thought Liz, with a certain satisfaction. I never liked any of my mother's friends. Old witches who thought they were entitled to make comments about you in your presence, comments such as 'Hasn't she grown?' or 'She's lost that nice smile she had as a little girl' or, when she slammed out of the room in exasperation, 'She never used to behave like that, did she?'

'Sit down.' Kate pulled out an armchair. 'We still haven't decided what to do about the house, I'm afraid. We were discussing it in the car on the way over.'

Roger sat down, opened his briefcase and took out a sheaf of papers. 'I could put it on the market for fifty thousand,' he said. 'But I don't think you'd get that much. You'll probably have to be prepared to come down to forty thousand.'

'It sounds a lot,' said Kate, 'but it won't come to very much once we've paid all the expenses.

Liz sighed. The average price of a one-bedroom condo on Beacon Hill was two hundred thousand dollars. Once again she saw doors closing in front of her.

'Whereas,' Roger consulted his papers, 'if you rent it out, you could get three hundred and fifty a week in the tourist season.'

'Less upkeep and maintenance and advertising,' Kate pointed out.

'Still, Mum, in the long run you would make more money that way. It could be a real money spinner.'

Kate gave a mild tut-tut. 'You certainly wouldn't be able to afford to pay me three hundred pounds a week.' She turned to Roger. 'Perdita has this mad idea that she's going to take a year off and come and live here.'

'Oh?' He glanced across at Perdita.

'If she is to have a gap year, I'd like her to do something more worthwhile,' Kate went on. 'You wouldn't allow your daughters to mooch around here for a year, would you?'

'I'm not sure.' An indecipherable expression crossed Roger's face. His gaze shifted to his papers. When he looked up again, he had resumed his professional manner. 'Well, as I said before, there's no hurry about this. I'll take a few more measurements while I'm here and draft a description of the house and the fittings and you can let me know what you decide. Are you staying long?'

'Till Sunday afternoon.'

'Evening, Mum.'

'Afternoon,' said Kate firmly. 'You have to be back at school on Monday, darling. There'll be things to sort out.'

Roger took up his measuring tape, calculator and notebook. 'Are you leaving the carpets and curtains?'

'Yes. You don't want them, do you, Liz?'

Liz shook her head. What use were carpets and curtains in rented rooms? As far as she could see, she would never own her own home. She would always lead a rackety, gipsy life. She remembered what Philippa had said, 'It is possible to survive on very little.'

'I met your great-aunt in Paris, Roger.'

'So you managed to track her down. What was she like?'

'Wonderful.'

Liz described Philippa Hamley and the kind of life she had led. Roger listened politely but didn't seem much interested in this bohemian relative of his and even looked quite relieved when he heard she had died, as if that absolved him of any further responsibility in the matter.

'That's very interesting,' he said, when Liz had finished her tale. 'I'm glad you enjoyed your stay in Paris. Now I'll get on with my measuring, if I may.'

'I'll make you a cup of tea,' offered Perdita. 'Does anyone else want one?'

'Darling! That would be lovely!' said Kate, surprised. 'Since when has she ever offered to make tea?' she whispered to Liz when Perdita was out of the room. 'You must be having a good effect on her.'

Liz smiled. 'Doesn't sound like me.'

'No, it doesn't, does it?' agreed her sister.

'Watch it, you!' Liz reached out a hand and playfully rumpled Kate's hair. She grinned over at Roger who was looking faintly embarrassed at this scene of sisterly affection. 'Roger, we've something else to ask you. Have you ever heard of a Joe Perkins? He's mentioned in our grandmother's diary and we were wondering whether he still lived in the town. He would be quite elderly by now, well into his eighties, I should think.'

'Joe Perkins.' Roger considered for a moment. 'The name rings a bell. I'll ask around.'

'Thanks.'

'Here's your tea, Roger.'

Perdita presented him with a cup from the tray she had brought in. A cup, thought Kate, not even a mug.

'Thank you.' Roger rose from his kneeling position on the carpet and took the cup from her rather awkwardly.

'Do you take sugar?' she called, over her shoulder.

'No, thank you, Perdita, I don't.' He smiled down at his shoes.

What is going on, wondered Liz, watching them.

'Well, Roger,' Kate set down her cup. 'we'll get out of your way and let you continue with your measuring.' She glanced over at the other two women. 'I thought we might stroll down into town to do some shopping and maybe have tea out. There's absolutely nothing to eat in the house.'

'Good idea,' said Liz.

'I'm not hungry,' replied Perdita. 'I'll stay here. I've a book to read.'

'All right, darling. We'll bring back some food for you,' said Kate. 'Goodbye for now, Roger. We will try to make up our minds as quickly as we can.'

'No hurry,' he repeated, smiling over at her.

The sisters walked down the cobbled streets, past the tourist shops and picked up some things from the supermarket near the station. Then Kate said, 'What do you fancy for tea?'

'Fish and chips.'

'You don't!'

'I do.'

Kate groaned. 'I hope you're going back to America soon. I shall put on pounds while you're here.'

They went to a café down by the harbour. Liz could have sworn it was one she had been to with Duncan. The decor had changed, moved more upmarket, but the view across the harbour to the cliffs opposite was exactly the same. How strange if it really is the same place, she thought, and I was last here with Duncan. She took up the menu. And yet if she couldn't be here again with Duncan (and how could she be?), who more fitting to return with than Kate?

'Cod and chips,' she said, as the waitress came up to them, notepad in hand.

'Prawn salad,' said Kate firmly.

'Coward!' murmured Liz.

'Prawns are off today, I'm afraid,' replied the waitress. 'Crab's off, prawns are off. Anything else is all right.'

'You see?' said Liz. 'It's fated.'

'Oh, what the hell! Cod and chips for two,' Kate ordered, closing up the menu and handing it to the waitress.

'Good for you!' responded her sister.

'I'll pay for it later when I get on the scales.'

'Throw them away.'

'It's all very well for you to talk. I've reached the age when every meal I eat seems to go straight to my hips. *You* still haven't got any hips to speak of.'

Liz glanced out of the window. Your boyish hips, he had said. Your schoolboy figure. It was true she had often worn boys' clothes, preferring them to girls'. Even at the age of thirty she had been able to get into boys' shorts. Not any longer.

'Roger seemed more at ease today.' Kate's voice broke into Liz's thoughts.

'Yes, thank God. Last time I saw him he was distinctly crabby.'

'So you said.' Kate's eyes narrowed. 'What had you done to him?'

'Nothing – at least . . .'

'Yes?' Kate's glance was ironic.

'He suggested going out together one evening and I asked if I could bring you along.'

Kate burst out laughing. 'Liz, you didn't! No wonder he turned crabby on you. There he was, trying to pick you up again after all these years, and you ask if you can bring along your aged sister as chaperone!'

Liz shrugged. 'I wasn't going to go out and leave you sitting in on your own.'

'You can if you want to, you know.'

Liz shook her head. 'I don't want to in the least, thank you very much. That was one right decision I made in my life.' She broke off as the waitress brought their food.

'I hope Perdita makes some right decisions.' Kate shook vinegar vigorously over her chips. 'I've always believed this stuff breaks down the fat, that's why East End kids are so skinny. What do you think of this latest scheme of hers to take a year out?'

'I don't know. It could be a good idea. Depends how she uses it. I agree waitressing would be a waste of her time.'

Kate reddened. 'Sorry about that. I didn't –'

'It's all right. There are many more opportunities for kids these days. Only you'll have to be sure that after a year away she will still want to go to university.'

'That's the trouble. She changes so quickly. Overnight, practically. God knows what she'll want in a year's time. I'd hate her not to have the experience of university life.'

'Yes,' said Liz shortly. 'You don't want her to miss out on that.' She carefully speared a pea.

Kate glanced at her sister. 'Do you regret it?' she asked softly.

'Not really. I doubt if I'd have stuck it out for three years.'

'It was still a possibility for you to go. You had a grant, a place waiting for you –'

'I know. My choice. I just couldn't see it. Not after all . . . all that had happened.'

Kate looked away, out of the window. 'You grew up too quickly.'

'I didn't grow up at all,' retorted her sister. 'That was the trouble. It took me years and years to grow up.'

'I wish Perdita would – sort of – I don't know – find herself. She doesn't seem to know who she is.'

The words swirled round in Liz's mind. 'I don't know who I am.' Words spoken in a different context years ago. After that wonderful first afternoon with Duncan in rooms borrowed from a friend of his. Making love on the carpet and then on the bed. The first time for me. He so gentle. I so impatient. Increasing the excitement, the many taboos being broken. The consciousness of being outside the law. Illegal, irreligious, immoral – all of that. Not caring about any of that, only caring about the feel of this man, whom I'd hero worshipped for so long, moving inside me, actually desiring me, wanting me, *me*, the disappointing, rebellious, sulky younger sister.

Then the day after, the let-clown. Creeping about, eyes lowered, skirting the wall, feeling dirty, tawdry, cheap. A shabby trick to play on your sister, a shabby, sluttish trick. Meeting Duncan two days later in a café, which might very well have been the same café she is sitting in now with his wife – was that why she had remembered? Coming into the café in a rush, dumping her satchel on the table, saying crossly as he tried to take her hand, 'Since we made love, I don't know who I am any more. I can't be Kate's sister because sisters don't do this kind of thing. Duncan, who am I?'

And he took me back to his friend's rooms and made it all right again. For a while, at any rate.

Sitting opposite his wife, her sister, Liz wondered how she could ever have thought it all right. Oh, there were plenty of explanations. Her father had died in the middle of her adolescence. She was looking for a father figure. Duncan fitted the bill perfectly. The funniest, cleverest man she knew. He was coaching her for her exams. There were plenty of things to look up to him for. And he was married to her glamorous elder sister. Perhaps I wanted to catch some of your radiance, Kate? Show I could compete in your world. Was that the reason? Mother always encouraged us to be rivals. She never wanted us to be close. Didn't like the thought of us ganging up on her, I suppose. She wanted us to relate to her separately (the sensible elder daughter who could be relied upon, the scatty younger one who needed looking after) and to each other only through her. Added to which, growing up in this small, stuffy town, everyone knowing everyone else, I wanted something of my own. And Duncan was that, my own delicious, thrilling secret.

On his side, perhaps, the younger sister had simply been more fun. Kate, so grim and closed up after her second miscarriage and the doctor saying it would be dangerous now to try again and Kate trying anyway for the baby that wouldn't come. Liz a younger, more cheerful version of Kate.

Yes, there were plenty of explanations, but in the end none of them explained anything. How could she have done it? And to Kate, of all people?

'I shouldn't worry about Perdita,' she said slowly. 'She will find herself in the end.'

When they returned to the house, Roger had gone and there was no sign of Perdita either.

'I expect she's mooching about somewhere.' Kate shrugged. 'I'm going to make myself a cup of coffee and settle down to the rest of Laura's stories. That's if Uncle John doesn't call round. I told him we would be here. What about you?'

'I'll sit with you.'

Kate read Laura's stories in the sitting room while Liz sat endlessly replaying scenes from the past in her head and occasionally slipped out to smoke a cigarette.

At half past eleven, just as Kate was getting anxious, the front door banged. Perdita stood in the doorway of the sitting room, surveying them.

'He's found your man.'

Kate looked up from Laura's manuscript, momentarily confused. 'What man? Who?'

'He's found your Joe Perkins for you. A retired landscape gardener living in Robin Hood's Bay. Here's the address.'

Perdita came into the room and handed her mother a slip of paper.

Kate's brow cleared. 'I see. You mean Roger.' She looked up at Perdita. 'How did you come by this?'

Perdita wandered over to the windowsill where Liz had sat earlier, perched on it and began drumming her fingers. 'After he'd finished his measuring, Roger invited me out to supper. We went to that posh wine bar on the West Cliff,' she added smugly.

While Liz and I were slumming it down by the harbour, thought Kate, while Liz forbore to mention that she, also, had been to this bar with Roger.

'That was kind of him. Wasn't that kind of him, Liz?'

'Mm.' Liz was watching Perdita. For some reason there was a small smile playing around those cherry-coloured lips. 'And then what did you do?' she asked deliberately.

'We . . . we went back to Roger's office and he looked through some old files on his computer and found Joe Perkins's name. Roger acted for him a few years back when he sold his house in Whitby and moved to Robin Hood's Bay. That's why he remembered the name. Of course, it may not be the same Joe Perkins. But he'd be about the right age, Roger says.'

'It's something to go on,' agreed Kate. She fingered the slip of paper in her hands. 'Fancy a trip over to Robin Hood's Bay tomorrow, Liz?'

'Certainly,' replied Liz, keeping her eyes fixed on Perdita.

Under Liz's persistent gaze, Perdita blushed, looked down at the floor and slouched off out of the room.

'There's some food in the fridge, darling, if you're still hungry,' Kate called after her. She glanced across at Liz. 'Rather a turn up for the books, old Roger inviting Perdita to supper and Perdita accepting. She normally runs a mile from my friends. Perhaps Roger will have a civilising influence on her?'

'Perhaps,' replied her sister.

'Anyway, it's a stroke of luck about this Joe Perkins. I'm really quite excited about that. He might be able to tell us all sorts of things about Laura,' Kate added, her eyes shining with excitement.

She looked so happy that Liz didn't have the heart to voice her suspicions about Perdita. She said good night and went up to bed, hoping that her guess would turn out to be wrong. God knows, things were complicated enough already without Perdita adding to them. And what on earth did Roger think he was up to?

Chapter Fifteen

The next morning Kate and Liz went over to Robin Hood's Bay. As Kate drove along the narrow country road, Liz looked out of the window. The storm-tossed clouds had turned the tops of the hills olive green with, here and there, patches of brighter colour where the sun shone through. In the distance, a couple of fields of oilseed rape glowed yellow, matching the yellow of the huge dandelions lining the grass verge. If only she could capture this in words, as Duncan captured it on canvas (she had noticed one or two landscapes very like this in his studio). His gift had always seemed to put her meagre talent for poetry in the shade. He was the creative one in the family. She had needed to find some other identity. Sometimes she thought she was still looking for it.

They parked in the car park at the top of the hill. Cars, except for those belonging to residents, were no longer allowed down into the town.

'We can stay two, three or four hours,' declared Liz, studying the ticket machine.

'Two hours should be quite long enough,' said Kate firmly. She'd seen the prices.

'You extravagant thing, you.'

Liz put in the money and waited for the machine to spew out the ticket. As Kate went to fix it on her windscreen, Liz stood staring over the bay. It had lost none of its beauty. Beyond the cluster of red-roofed fishermen's cottages, the arm of the shore curved round as if in protection, providing miles of unspoilt sandy beach. On the cliff above lay green fields, half in shadow, half in sunlight. She glanced to her left at the row of prosperous Victorian houses built, like Laura's house in Whitby, to overlook the bay and escape the infections of the town below.

'It hasn't changed a bit,' she remarked, as Kate joined her.

'Did you expect it to?' responded Kate drily. 'Its livelihood, i.e. tourism, depends upon it never changing. Soon England will be one big theme park, frozen into its past.'

Liz laughed. 'Everywhere's the same. Cape Cod makes the most of its Pilgrims.'

The sisters began their descent of the steep hill.

'Let's hope we don't have to go *all* the way down,' Kate said breathlessly. 'I'm thinking of the climb back up again.'

They were about halfway down when Liz exclaimed, 'Here it is! This is the street.'

They stopped and gazed down the terrace of elegant sandstone cottages.

'I've always admired these,' said Kate.

They walked along the narrow cobbled street and stopped outside the number indicated on Roger's slip of paper.

'He's probably not in,' murmured Kate, rapping the door-knocker.

'A man in his eighties? I don't suppose he gets about much.'

They stood back and gazed at the house. It had three floors, with two windows on the ground floor, three on the first and an attic room in the roof. The date over the door was 1732. Behind them, separated from the house by the narrow lane in which they were standing, was a small patio garden filled with flowers. It looked directly on to the road below.

'This place gives me vertigo,' whispered Liz. 'I've always felt claustrophobic in Robin Hood's Bay. All these houses crowded in on one another and the way the sea hems in the town at high tide. Don't you find it menacing, Kate?'

'Not at all,' said her sister briskly.

The white painted front door opened. A lean, elderly, slightly stooping man with glasses looked surprised to see them.

'Mr Perkins?' Kate enquired. 'Mr Joe Perkins?'

'Yes. What is it? I never buy anything.'

'We're not selling anything,' retorted Liz.

Kate gave her a nudge.

'Are you lost? Are you tourists?'

'No. I'm sorry to disturb you, Mr Perkins, but we wanted to see you because we think you might be able to help us. We think you may have worked for our grandfather,' Kate explained, carefully and loudly, in case he was deaf. 'Arthur Chapman was his name.'

Mr Perkins flinched slightly. 'Yes, I worked for the Chapman family. A long time ago. Who are you?'

'We're his granddaughters,' said Kate. 'You see, we recently discovered a diary written by our grandmother, Laura, and . . .'

'Laura.' His face softened. 'So you're her granddaughters.' His eyes rested on Liz's red hair. 'I might have known. Well, you'd better come in.' He opened the door wider and stood back. 'And there's no need to shout. I may be eighty-four but I am still in full possession of my faculties.'

'Sorry.' Kate stepped meekly over his doorstep.

He pushed open a door to his left. 'In here.'

They entered a small room exquisitely furnished with delicately carved chairs and a pale cream chaise longue. In one corner stood a walnut writing desk.

'Oh!' Involuntarily, Liz took a step towards it.

Mr Perkins followed the direction of her gaze. 'Yes, that was Laura's. She used to write at it every morning. I would see her through the window as I raked the gravel or weeded the flowerbeds or did any other job Sidney Baines didn't fancy doing himself. I spotted it in a local auction a few years back and snapped it up. I knew at once that it was hers. As you can see, the hinge is slightly bent.' He went over and demonstrated it to them. 'Laura asked Baines to fix it but he never got round to it.'

'Were you fond of our grandmother?' asked Liz softly.

'I was. We all were, all except that Gladys Simpson. Spiteful creature, thick as two thieves with her master. The rest of us who worked at St Anne's didn't have much time for Arthur Chapman. We kept out of his way as much as we could. He had a filthy temper and he treated his wife very badly.' He looked at them. 'But perhaps you know that.'

'We do now,' replied Kate. 'We knew nothing about our grandmother until recently. Our mother died and we were going through her things and we found Laura's diary.'

'And some newspaper cuttings,' added Liz, earning herself another sharp nudge from Kate.

'Your mother? Ah yes, I remember seeing the notice of her death in the *Gazette*. Little Jessie, who was always getting into trouble for running on to the flowerbeds. She grew up to be a formidable woman. I used to see her around town occasionally. I don't think she remembered who I was. Well, sit down, Laura's granddaughters, and tell me your names.'

'I'm Kate and this is Liz.' Obediently, they sat on the curved chairs.

He looked at them. 'This isn't just a social call, is it? You said you thought I might be able to help you. Help you with what?'

'Well,' began Kate, 'there's something we were hoping you might be able to clear up for us.'

'Yes?' He glanced sharply at them.

'You see . . .' Kate hesitated. How on earth was she to broach the question of whether or not he was Arthur's illegitimate son?

'We read about Arthur Chapman's murder and Laura's trial in the newspaper cuttings we found and we wondered if you knew who poisoned our grandfather?' burst out Liz. Kate heaved a sigh of despair. 'Also,' Liz rushed on, 'we found this story, written by Laura, which suggested to us that our grandfather may have had a son who was, well, not Laura's.'

Joe Perkins stood up. 'I can tell,' he said drily, 'that this is going to be a lengthy conversation. Would you like a cup of tea?'

'That would be very nice,' said Kate. 'Can we help?'

'No thank you. My kitchen is small and I have become used to doing things for myself.'

Walking rather stiffly, though without a stick, he left the room.

'Did you have to blurt out everything like that?' hissed Kate to her sister. 'Here was I trying to be tactful and you go and blow it.'

'It was the only way. And it's worked, hasn't it? He's gone off to the kitchen to give himself time to think.'

'What if he did murder Arthur? What are we going to do then?'

'Haven't a clue. Let's play it by ear.'

Liz broke off as the rattle of spoons in saucers warned them Mr Perkins was coming back. Kate sprang to open the door.

'Thank you. Now then. It's Earl Grey. I hope that's all right?'

He handed them each a fragile china cup and sat down again.

'Since you want to know, let me tell you about my life –'

'Please, Mr Perkins,' Kate interrupted, 'if it disturbs you in any way, don't. We had no right to ask, no right to intrude.'

Liz rolled her eyes. Sometimes Kate carried tact too far.

'No, you do have a right. I owe Laura's granddaughters something.' He paused and took a sip of tea. 'Besides,' he looked at them, his eyes twinkling, 'going over the past is one of the few pleasures that remain to an old man like myself. Well then, I was brought up by my mother in Whitby. We lived in two rooms in a boarding house on the West Cliff. We were desperately poor. At night we slept in the same bed to keep warm. My mother often went without food so that I could eat. When her health permitted, she did odd cleaning jobs around the town. We had no friends. No one called to see us. No one wrote. When I grow old enough to ask questions, my mother told me that my father had been a fisherman and he had drowned at sea before I was born. She told me my grandparents were dead too. I found out later that wasn't true. They were alive and living in Staithes. They had disowned her – and me, come to that.

'From time to time, late at night, we would be visited by a man in a dark coat, with a hat pulled down over his face. He never stayed long; a few moments at most. I used to hear him and my mother murmuring together in the other room. It was Arthur Chapman, but I didn't know that till many years later. He brought my mother odd bits of money, whenever he'd won something at the card table, I suppose, or on the horses. My mother accepted his money, for my sake, though by then she hated the sight of him and wanted nothing more to do with him.

'As I grew older and went to school, the boys used to shout out "Bastard!" at me in the street. Everyone knew my mother had had me out of wedlock, as the term then was. What they didn't know was the identity of my father. We had no friends in the town, no one to help us. Children were told by their parents not to play with me. At school, the teachers placed me at the back of the classroom and ignored me.' He clasped his hands in his lap. 'You can see that I have a lot to thank Arthur Chapman for. When I was twelve, my mother died. She got flu and, half starved as she was, it went straight to her lungs and became pleurisy. Except for leaving me, she wasn't sad to go, hers had been a wretched life. As she lay dying she told me, finally, the name of my father. She told me where he lived and to ask him for help. I did go to have a look at his house. I couldn't believe that my father lived anywhere so grand. But I didn't want his help. I wanted to survive on my own. I had nothing but hatred for Arthur Chapman, for what he had put my mother through. Without my mother's restraining influence – she was a gentle person, broken but never made bitter by her experiences – that hatred grew.'

He was silent for a moment, then he resumed his narrative.

'After my mother's death, I left school and found work down at the docks, fetching and carrying for the fishermen. It wasn't work that interested me. I had never been attracted to the sea, despite growing up beside it. Gradually, a plan began to form in my head. I wasn't making out very well on my own. I didn't want to stay dogsbodying for the rest of my life. I would put my pride in my pocket, get to know Arthur Chapman and force him to recognise me as his son. I had learned that he was well-respected in the town. I thought he might at least help me find a decent job. Fate played into my hands. One day, I overheard Sidney Baines complaining that he had too much work in the Chapmans' garden. I turned up the next afternoon and offered to give him a hand with what he was doing. Planting potatoes, I think it was. It became obvious during the course of the afternoon that Sidney Baines wasn't a man who was keen on hard work. I persuaded him that I was energetic and eager and that I could take a lot of chores off his hands. He took me to your grandmother to ask her to employ me. I was so nervous during the interview that I hardly opened my mouth.'

'I know,' said Kate softly. 'It's in Laura's diary.'

'Is it? Fancy that.' He looked pleased. 'And that's the story of my life. I started gardening on a whim, almost, and it became my life's work. Times changed. The fact that I was illegitimate hardly bothered people any more. I built up a reputation in the town as a gardener and eventually I started my own landscaping business. I married. A happy marriage. When I retired we moved to this house. My wife died five years ago. I have one son. Unfortunately he didn't take to the business. He's ranching out in Australia.'

'And Laura?' prompted Liz. 'You got to like her?'

'She was the first woman I fell in love with. I was just a lad. Fourteen. She was the only real lady, apart from my mother, I had come across. I used to watch her through the window as I gardened, writing at her desk or playing with her children, my little half brother and sister. Sometimes she would come into the garden to pick roses for the house and she'd say a few words to me. Ask me if I was enjoying the job, remark on how nice the flowers were looking. She was always very kind to me. Poor lady, married to that brute . . . The more I learned about Arthur Chapman, the more I grew to despise him. All the servants knew he beat her and kept a mistress in town.'

'So you planned revenge on him?' said Liz, undeterred by Kate's warning glance.

He was silent for a moment.

'I decided to confront him. I was determined he should make amends for leaving my mother to die in poverty and shame. I waited in the street one evening and waylaid him as he walked home from his card game. "Good evening, Mr Chapman," I said, stepping out of the shadows, in front of him. He looked a bit startled at first, then, leaning closer till I could smell the whisky on his breath, he said, "Good evening, Joe." "Do you remember May Perkins?" I said. He blanched a bit at that. "I might," he said. "Well, I'm her son." "What of it?" He shoved me aside and walked on. "I'm your son too," I said.

'He stopped on the pavement. "Don't be ridiculous. I have a son. John. He's tucked up in bed at home. Now enough of this nonsense or I'll have the police on to you." "I am your son, just as much as little John is," I said. I ran after him and grabbed his sleeve. "And you owe me something. I'll keep your secret but I want you to lend me some money and help me find a proper job."

'He sneered at that, threatened to get his wife to dismiss me, then on second thoughts, sacked me himself, then and there. I wasn't having that. I told him I'd spread it round town that he was my father. I remember his reply as if it was yesterday. "If you want to dabble in blackmail, you've got to do better than that, you young scoundrel," he said. "Who would believe you? With my reputation

I could have you drummed out of town and by heaven I will if you give me any more trouble." He turned on his heel. "Good night. Good riddance!" he shouted back at me.

'I stood on the pavement, clenching and unclenching my fists in anger. He was a brute. He had mistreated two women, ruined my mother's life and was ruining your grandmother's. He deserved to die.' He looked at them. 'I remembered that Baines had recently bought some cyanide to get rid of a wasps' nest. I knew where he kept it in one of the greenhouses. It was a simple matter to slip into the breakfast room early the next morning and mix a small quantity into the sugar. I knew I was taking no risks. The servants had their own bowl and Laura never took sugar. Just as I was finishing the job, I heard someone come along the passage from the servants' quarters. I ran away and hid in the first place I could think of – the cupboard under the stairs. I left the empty cyanide bottle there intending to go back and retrieve it later. Events overtook me.' He paused. 'Afterwards I was frightened. I thought that either Baines or myself was sure to be the chief suspect and that Baines would find a way of putting all the suspicion on to me. But when the police questioned me, it was clear they had only one suspect in mind. I ran away and prayed to God that your grandmother wouldn't be hanged.'

'And years later, in Paris,' said Liz, 'she guessed who had done it and why.'

'Perhaps she knew all along,' he replied. 'I wouldn't be surprised. But she never gave me away.'

'No, she wouldn't,' said Liz. 'You see, you gave her her freedom.'

'What a risk, though,' Kate put in. 'She risked her life to save yours.'

'I know.' He bent his head. 'All these years it's not the murder of Arthur Chapman that has been on my conscience but the fact that my cowardice put your grandmother's life in danger. I owe everything to Laura Chapman. Without her example, I would never have got on and made something of my life. I couldn't waste it, could I, after what she had done for me?'

'No, indeed,' said Kate.

'I have never told anyone about this, not even my wife. To tell

175

you the truth, it's been preying on my mind rather, these past few years. In some ways, it's been a relief to talk about it, and appropriate that it's Laura's granddaughters I have told.' He glanced sharply at them. 'So what are you going to do now? Haul me off to the police station and say, look, here's one unsolved murder off your list?'

'Of course not!' burst out Liz.

'It was a long time ago,' said Kate, more soberly. 'I don't suppose you've made a habit of murder, have you? Or have you?'

He shook his head. The question seemed to amuse him.

'And you needn't have told us,' Liz pointed out. 'Why did you tell us?'

'I knew, if you were truly Laura's granddaughters, you would understand and not judge me. I haven't been disappointed.'

'I suppose we are some sort of relatives of yours?' said Liz.

He smiled. 'Some sort. Close enough at any rate for me to invite you to call again if you are ever this way.'

'Thanks. We'd like to.'

He sat back in his chair and shut his eyes for a moment, as if overcome by fatigue.

Time to go, Kate mouthed at Liz. Her sister nodded.

'Thank you for telling us this, Mr Perkins.' Kate waited for him to open his eyes, then rose from her chair. 'We're hoping to publish our grandmother's stories. I'm writing an introduction. I shall be touching on her life and the trial but I won't mention anything of what you have told us.'

'Thank you.' He smiled up at them. 'I'm an old man. If anything should happen to me, then you may tell the world the truth, in the interests of setting the record straight. If anyone is interested, that is.'

'Oh, I'm sure people will be interested,' put in Liz. 'We are hoping Laura's stories will create a bit of a stir in the literary world.'

'Good. I'm glad people will be able to read them at last. She was always scribbling away when she thought no one was looking.'

'I'll send you a copy,' Kate promised. 'You come out rather well in one of the stories.'

'I suppose we did the right thing?' she said, as they drove back to Whitby.

'He's eighty-four. What possible threat can he be to anyone now?' replied her sister.

'I suppose you're right.'

'And because of his action, Laura was able to escape from Whitby and start a new life in Paris. I don't think we need leap to defend Arthur Chapman's rights.'

'No, indeed,' agreed Kate. 'Look, do you mind if we drop in on Uncle John on the way home? I've heard nothing from him for ages. I'm getting a bit worried about him.'

'Shall we tell him we've found out who murdered his father?'

'I think not. He might want revenge. Or at least insist on telling the police.'

'Uncle John? I don't think so. He's not the type.'

'You never know how people are going to react,' said Kate firmly. 'Besides, we promised Mr Perkins we would keep it a secret until after his death.'

'Uncle John might like to know he has a half-brother,' Liz pointed out. 'I should like to know.'

'Would you? Why? What possible difference could it make to Uncle John's life now?'

'They could keep each other company, two elderly men on their own. They might go drinking together.'

Kate laughed. 'You *are* sentimental. Well, we'll see.'

She parked the car down by the harbour and they climbed up the litter-strewn steps to their uncle's flat. Kate knocked on the door. After a short delay, he opened it. He looked smarter than when they had last seen him, wearing a spotless white shirt, an olive-green cardigan and what looked like a new pair of trousers. Kate wondered whether he had found someone to do his laundry.

'Oh,' he said when he saw them. There was an odd expression on his face, as if he had been caught out in something.

'We were worried about you,' Kate explained. 'We came to see if you are all right.'

'I'm all right, pet. Never better. Come inside.' He let the door swing open.

Kate stepped into his sitting room, followed by Liz. The room was not unoccupied. Sitting upright on the edge of their Uncle

John's sofa, her legs tucked primly to one side, was a woman of about sixty. She had dyed blonde hair, cut short and permed in tight little curls all over her head, strawberry-pink lipstick, strawberry-pink nails, mascara, bright blue eyeshadow, the works. Liz stared, fascinated. Her figure had that sort of firm, trim look to it that Liz associated with women in her childhood who'd worn girdles. Between the strawberry-pink nails dangled a cigarette on a filter.

'This is – um – Ursula,' mumbled Uncle John, gesturing vaguely towards her. 'Ursula, love, these are my nieces.'

Ursula's eyes widened. Hastily stubbing out her cigarette, she got up off the sofa and smoothed down her tight-fitting dress.

'Pleased to meet you. I have heard a lot about you.' She shook hands with them both. 'Sit yourselves down, pets, while I make us all a nice cup of tea.'

'Please don't bother –' began Kate.

'It's no bother, love. Me and your uncle generally have a cuppa around this time.'

They sat down. Ursula bustled off into the kitchen. Liz reflected that she seemed to know her way around the flat pretty well.

'That's my Ursula.' Uncle John looked at them with a mixture of shamefacedness and pride. 'What do you think of her? Grand lass, isn't she?' He paused. 'As a matter of fact, we're thinking of tying the knot.'

Liz opened her mouth and then closed it again.

Kate, always more skilled socially than her sister, said, 'This is sudden, isn't it, Uncle John?'

She wondered whether Ursula was some kind of gold digger, not that there's much gold to dig for here, she thought to herself, looking around the tiny sitting room.

'In one way it is.' Their uncle leaned forward, his hands resting on his knees, and stared at the fire. 'And in another way it isn't. You see, Ursula and me, we knew each other years back, when she war nobbut a lass. We thought of making a go of it then but Jessie – your mother – was dead set agin it. Thought Ursula warn't good enough for me, or summat like that. Any road, the thing petered out and we lost touch. She's been living in Brid all these years. Been married and widowed and has three grown-up sons. She came on a day trip back here a couple of weeks ago. We ran into each other in the

178

town centre. I'd have known her anywhere –'

He broke off as Ursula came back into the sitting room carrying a tray.

'I was just telling them the news, love.'

'Were you?' Ursula glanced at Kate and Liz, then busied herself setting out the cups. 'Then you'll know your mother was against this match.'

'That war years ago, love!' protested her husband-to-be.

'That's by the by. Jessie Miller wasn't one to change her mind. She was agin it then and she'd be agin it now.' She poured out the tea. 'And you may be agin it, but it's goin' to happen. I'm not goin' to let him slip through my fingers a second time, however long or short the time we've got left together.' She handed Kate a cup.

'I'm not against –' Kate began.

'I'm not takin' any chances. Your uncle's not as young as he was. If anything untoward happens I'd like to be on hand. So we're getting married. I don't approve of this living together. I know all you young ones do it, but it's not for people our age.'

'I'm moving,' added their uncle. 'Ursula's got a flat in Brid. Bigger than this, better for the two of us. You can't swing a cat in this place. It's her own flat,' he said proudly, 'with the mortgage paid off.'

'It sounds lovely,' said Kate.

Charlotte Brontë, Liz remembered irrelevantly, had burst into tears on first seeing Bridlington. As anyone would, she thought, though of course the amusement arcades and souvenir shops, for which the word tawdry would seem to have been especially invented, had not been in existence in Charlotte's day to spoil the beautiful sweep of the bay. Charlotte Brontë had cried because it was the first time she had seen the sea . . . Liz became aware she was expected to say something.

'I'm very pleased for both of you,' she said lamely.

Ursula brightened up. 'I'll make a comfortable home for him, my dears. I did it for Reg, my first husband, and I can do it for your uncle. At the end of the day, that's what matters, isn't it?'

'Yes,' agreed Kate, demurely sipping her tea and trying not to catch Liz's eye.

'I'm not taking much with me,' their uncle said. 'Ursula's flat is fully furnished. We were wondering whether you'd like that, Kate?' He pointed to the walnut dining table. 'Seeing as you were so interested in it.'

'I'd love to have it.'

Kate glanced at Liz. This didn't seem the moment to go into details of how Arthur Chapman had been murdered. Uncle John probably wouldn't thank them for raking up old family history in front of his wife-to-be. Liz must have been thinking the same for she gave a little shake of her head.

'I don't think you need worry about him any more,' remarked Liz as they returned to the car, having promised to visit Ursula and their uncle in his new home.

'Yes, his life seems well and truly taken care of, doesn't it?' agreed Kate, swinging out along the harbour and up the hill.

'Mother was wrong.'

'She was. But remember it must have been hard on her, coming down in the world like that. Still, I'm glad they've got together in the end.'

'So am I.'

They turned into Henrietta Street. 'Oh,' said Kate, as a car flashed past them, 'wasn't that Roger?'

'Yes, it was,' replied Liz quietly.

'I wonder what he wanted? Something about the house, I suppose. What a pity he didn't wait a moment longer. He may have wanted us to sign something. Never mind, I expect Perdita will tell us what he came for.'

She pulled up on the patch of wasteland. Liz got out and looked over the harbour for a moment. A pleasure boat was chugging out and a party of schoolchildren was being hurried along the pier by a couple of harassed-looking schoolteachers. With a feeling of foreboding, she turned and followed Kate into the house.

Perdita was sitting in the kitchen, her feet on the table, munching crisps.

'How did you get on?' she asked. 'Did you find your Joe Perkins?'

'We did and he did it and we're not going to do anything about it because he's such a nice man. Darling, do you *have* to put your feet on Grandma's table?'

With a grunt, Perdita swung them off

'I've got another piece of news for you.' Kate sat down on a chair. 'We called in on Uncle John on our way home and – guess what? – he's getting married. Isn't that amazing?'

'At his age? I think that's obscene!'

Kate rolled her eyes at Liz.

'I hope he doesn't expect me to be bridesmaid,' Perdita muttered. 'I'm not wearing one of those dresses.'

'I expect it will be a very quiet affair in a register office. She's been married before.'

'Thank God for that,' drawled Perdita. 'At least one of them will know how to do it.'

'Do you have to be quite so crude?' Kate, seeing there was nothing to be gained by pursuing this subject, changed it. 'Darling, we passed Roger on our way up. What did he want?'

'Oh – er, he came to take measurements.'

'Again? I hadn't realised selling a house entailed such a lot of measuring.' Kate laughed.

Liz glanced at Perdita, who screwed up her empty crisp packet and threw it with unerring aim into the bin. Then she yawned and stood up. 'I think I'll go and have a lie-down.' She slouched out of the room.

'Do you want any lunch?' Kate called after her. The only response was a grunt on the stairs. 'I suppose that means no. Shall we have something to eat, Liz? Oh.' Kate spied two unwashed mugs in the sink. 'She must have made Roger tea again. That's a good sign. She is getting more thoughtful, don't you think?'

Liz muttered something non-committal. She went over to the window and drummed her fingers on the sill. 'I'm going upstairs to fetch a book,' she said suddenly.

'Right. Ham in your sandwich?'

'Anything. Yes.'

She went up the narrow stairs and tapped softly on Perdita's door. There was a grunt. Then a mumbled, 'Come in.'

Perdita lay on the bed where Liz had lain as a teenager listening

181

to Radio Caroline and counting the years till she would be free to leave home. Perdita, seeing who it was (she had expected Kate), sat up and switched off her Walkman. Liz wandered over to the window and leaned against the frame.

'It's probably none of my business, Perdita, but is there something going on between you and Roger Hamley?'

Perdita's eyes widened. 'You're right, it is none of your business.' Then, more sharply, 'Did Mum send you up here?'

Liz shook her head.

'You're not going to tell her, are you?'

'Tell her what, Perdita? What is there to tell?'

'Oh, nothing.' Perdita picked moodily at the fringe of the candlewick bedspread. After a moment, she said, 'Roger and I – we've been seeing each other. A bit. It started last time we were over here. I don't want Mum to know.'

'Why not?'

'I just don't. She wouldn't understand. She'd say he was too old for me.'

'He *is* too old for you.'

'I didn't think *you'd* say that. You sound like Mum,' remarked Perdita, disappointed.

'We are sisters, after all.' Liz came and sat on the edge of the bed. 'Perdita, where is all this leading?'

'I don't know.' Perdita shrugged. 'Why should it lead anywhere? Roger likes me and I like him. That's all there is to it.' Then, dropping her cool a fraction, 'You're not going to tell Mum, are you?'

'I don't suppose so.' Liz got up off the bed. 'But how long do you think you can keep it a secret from her?'

'I dunno. I guess we'll tell her sometime.'

Liz didn't like that 'we' – it sounded too established, too permanent.

'God! How I hate this bedspread!' exclaimed Perdita, who shared her generation's inability to concentrate on one subject for more than a few minutes at a time.

'I used to hate it too,' said Liz lightly. 'In my day this was the "guest" room, though there were never any guests. I used to come here sometimes and listen to music on my radio. It was my refuge. If you look carefully you'll find a patch worn bare where I used to pick at that bedspread just as you're doing now.'

Perdita stared at her. 'You used to get fed up too?'

'Oh yes, I got fed up.'

Liz went out of the room and back down the stairs.

'The sandwiches are ready,' called Kate. 'And I've put the kettle on for coffee. I don't know about you, but I've drunk enough tea today to last me a month. What happened to the book?'

'What?'

'I thought you went upstairs to fetch a book?'

'Oh, er, I got chatting to Perdita and forgot all about it.'

'I see.'

The atmosphere in the kitchen turned several degrees cooler. Kate was prepared to tolerate, even welcome, her younger sister's presence here, but not for her to have conversations in private with Perdita. Pride forbade Kate to ask what they had spoken about. Wordlessly, she set a ham sandwich and a mug of coffee in front of Liz. They sat side by side in the kitchen eating, the silence broken only by a few random remarks about the weather. It's going to be hell when she finds out, thought Liz.

Chapter Sixteen

The bust-up came sooner than Liz had expected. At eight o'clock that evening, Perdita appeared downstairs dressed in a black tank top that showed off her midriff, black tights, Doc Marten's and a wisp of a skirt that barely skimmed the top of her thighs.

Kate's eyebrows shot up.

'Where are you going?'

Liz noted she had omitted their mother's part of this sentence, 'dressed like that'. Probably parents couldn't get away with saying that kind of thing any more.

'Out.' The adolescent's eternal cry. 'Just out.'

Kate looked Perdita up and down. 'Um, are you going anywhere in particular, darling? I mean you look so nice. Are you meeting someone? I didn't know you knew anyone in Whitby.'

'Roger's taking me out to dinner.'

Liz heard Kate's sharp intake of breath. She shut her eyes.

'When did that get itself arranged?'

'When he came round this morning.'

'While we were out. Did he know we were going to be out? Did he, Perdita?'

Perdita's eyes dropped to the floor. 'Yes,' she mumbled.

'I see.' Kate's lips tightened. 'Is there anything else you want to tell me, Perdita?'

Liz opened her eyes. 'I . . .' she began, then shut up as the other two glared at her.

'I don't have to tell you anything, Mum. But since you ask – Roger and I are seeing each other and, yes, we are having an affair. Now are you satisfied?'

Perdita stormed out of the room.

'Wait, Perdita, come back –' began Kate.

They heard the front door slam.

Kate swung round, her face blazing with anger. 'This is all your fault!'

Liz shook her head. 'It has nothing to do with me, Kate. I didn't introduce Perdita to Roger. To tell you the truth,' she added quietly, 'I thought you and he . . .'

'Oh no, that's not my style. I don't go out with married men,' said Kate bitterly.

'Roger's a widower,' Liz reminded her.

'And old enough to be her father!'

'I know,' acknowledged Liz. 'And for that reason why not sit it out? This is bound to blow over eventually. Is it worth ruining your relationship with Perdita for?'

'You talk as if I'm the one to blame!'

'No, Kate, I –'

'*She*'s the one who started it. She's doing it deliberately to hurt me. She's calculating – like you. If you hadn't been so cruel to Roger all those years ago. If you hadn't used him as a shield to hide your affair with – with my husband, this would never have happened. Roger's doing it to get some sort of twisted revenge on us both. Oh God! I wish you'd never come back. If you hadn't rejected Roger, if he hadn't seen you again, this would never have happened.'

'If you didn't smother Perdita,' retorted Liz, her patience snapping, 'she wouldn't be so desperate to get away from you!'

The sisters stared at one another aghast as the old house rang once again to the sound of their raised voices.

'Well!' said Kate eventually. She turned away.

'Kate, I didn't mean . . .'

'Yes, you did.'

The floor began to tilt before Kate's eyes. The past was coming back to haunt her. Roger and Liz, Duncan and Liz, Perdita and Roger and Liz and Duncan, changing partners in some sort of crazy dance. The past hadn't gone away, it wasn't safely buried. It had been lying in wait all these years, to trap her. Wave upon wave of blackness whirled past her eyes. There was a roaring in her ears. She crashed to the floor.

'Kate!' Liz ran over, bent down and gently shook her. 'Kate!'

After a few moments, Kate opened her eyes. 'It's all right.' She smiled weakly. 'Silly thing to do. Sorry.'

'Here, take hold of my hand.'

Liz put an arm round her sister and helped her up off the floor and into a chair.

'Look, you ought to go to bed for a bit.'

'It's eight o'clock!' Kate protested. 'I'd never sleep.'

'Take one of my sleeping tablets. They're very mild.'

'I can't. I've got things to do. I want to wait up for Perdita. I want to sort things out. I want to . . .'

'I'll wait up for Perdita,' said Liz firmly.

'But . . .'

'Kate, you're in no fit state to argue. Go to bed and I'll bring you a hot drink and a sleeping tablet. Go on! Let me be in charge for once.'

When Liz brought up the mug of cocoa and the sleeping pill, she found her sister in bed, already half asleep.

'Here, drink this. You look as if you could do with sleeping right through till morning. Do you often do this sort of thing?'

'Only when my daughter starts sleeping with elderly men.' Kate smiled feebly and took the cup. 'Thanks. Look, I – I'm sorry for what I said downstairs. I went out of my head for a moment.'

'It's all right. I'm sorry too.'

'No, you were right. I probably am too protective of Perdita – after all, she's an adult now, she'll be living away from home next year. It's just that I've always been so afraid of her turning out like – like . . .'

'Like me?' finished Liz.

'Well, yes. Oh, I don't mean it the way it sounds. I'd like Perdita to have the chance of a settled happiness, that's all. Duncan hasn't been the most stabilising of influences.'

'So you've had to do it all.' Liz patted her hand. 'Poor Kate. Don't worry. I'm here now. I'll sort out this mess. Maybe I'll have a word with Roger myself.'

'Tactfully, Liz.'

'Tactfully, of course. Now drink your cocoa and get some sleep. Everything will seem different in the morning. These pills are miracle workers.'

Kate paused in the act of swallowing the tablet Liz had given her.

'They are legal, are they?'

Liz laughed. 'Yes!' She leaned across and kissed the top of her sister's head.

Kate sank back into the pillows and closed her eyes. It was good to let go for a bit. She seemed to have been struggling along on her own for years now, worrying about Perdita, worrying about Duncan. She hadn't been sleeping too well lately, it would be nice to wake up in the morning feeling really refreshed for once. She hoped Liz wouldn't go barging in, though. Roger was sensitive and would need careful handling. Liz always tended to treat him as if he had skin as thick as an ox's. Oh well . . . she closed her eyes and slept.

Liz tiptoed downstairs and sat alone in the front room. She began to reread some of Laura's stories, but she was too nervous and keyed up to concentrate. She paced the room, she made cups of coffee, she drank some wine; ignoring Kate's rules she smoked cigarette after cigarette. Just after two, she heard a car pull up outside. A few moments later there were footsteps on the pavement and the front door banged. Liz sprang out into the hall.

'Ssh! Kate's asleep upstairs.'

'Yes, she normally is at this hour,' said Perdita unconcernedly.

'I mean she needs to stay asleep. She fainted earlier this evening.'

'Christ!' Perdita went into the sitting room, flung her bag on to one chair and herself on to another, draping her legs over the arm. 'Mum gets so worked up about things.' She glanced across at Liz who had gone to stand by the window. 'I suppose she told you I was excluded from school?'

'No, she didn't,' said Liz, startled. 'What for?'

'Smoking a couple of joints on school premises.'

'Not a good idea.'

'What? Smoking, you mean?'

Perdita sniffed the air that reeked from Liz's cigarettes. Her eyes rested sarcastically for a moment on the half-empty bottle of wine standing in the hearth.

Goodness, thought Liz, if motherhood is this difficult . . . She tried a different tack.

'Kate's worried about this business with you and Roger.'

'I'd have thought she'd be pleased I'm going out with somebody so respectable,' retorted Perdita, smoothing down her fragment of a skirt.

Going out, thought Liz, or staying in? The fact that Perdita's hair was slightly damp at the ends hadn't escaped her notice. Had the evening involved showering, then? And where had that taken place? Roger could hardly have taken Perdita to his home, not with his three daughters and his mother about. Had he borrowed a friend's flat to take her to – as she and Duncan . . .?

'It's Roger's age,' she explained quickly. 'And the fact that you're still at school and have exams soon. And . . . and other things that happened in the past.'

'I wish people would keep out of my life!' growled Perdita. 'It's bad enough Mum interfering. It has nothing to do with you. You're only my aunt.'

Liz flinched. 'It has something to do with me,' she said quietly. 'You see long ago, before you were born, Roger and I had a relationship. Things didn't work out between us. I think that may have something to do with the way he's behaving now.'

'So that's it, is it?' Perdita's dark eyes blazed at her. 'You're jealous. It didn't work out for you and you can't bear to think it might work for me.'

Liz shook her head. 'No, that's not it. Perdita, think. Roger's old enough to be your father. You're not much older than his eldest daughter. The situation's absurd, don't you see?'

Perdita tilted her chin. 'I don't see that age matters a bit, so long as we love each other. You're so bloody conventional. Like Mum.'

'Well,' said Liz drily, 'I've never been called conventional before. Do you love each other?' she added.

'We're trying to find out,' replied Perdita, with more maturity than, going on the conversation so far, Liz would have given her credit for. 'Anyway,' she continued, 'if Roger is a father figure for me, so much the better. It's been obvious for a long time where Dad's priorities lie.'

'Your father loves you, I'm sure.'

'How do you know?'

'From what I remember of Duncan, from what Kate's told me.

He's going through a difficult time right now. You need to be patient.'

Perdita snorted. 'You're like Mum, finding excuses for him. Dad's always going through a difficult time. He's been going through a difficult time all the while I've been growing up. He's fifty-two! He shouldn't be having difficult times any more!'

'Life doesn't get any easier as you get older, you know. You'd think it would, but it doesn't.'

'Christ! You *do* sound like Mum! I'm off to bed.'

Perdita untangled her legs, picked up her bag and sauntered out of the door as nonchalantly as if they had been discussing the latest weather report. Liz was left to wonder whether her intervention had made the situation better, or worse.

The next morning Kate emerged from her room bleary-eyed but less fragile-looking than the night before. The two sisters sat in the kitchen over mugs of coffee discussing the situation in low voices.

'It could be worse.' Liz attempted to cheer her sister up. 'Roger's solvent, sober, he hasn't got a drug habit. And we know he must wash regularly. Charlotte Hamley would have been very strict about that.'

'Solvent, clean, sober and nearly forty,' said Kate wryly. 'The very last person I'd have expected Perdita to fall for . . .'

She broke off as Perdita slouched into the kitchen in her Snoopy T-shirt. Try as she might, Liz couldn't stop herself wondering what Roger would make of her nightgear, if things ever got as far as them moving in together. Ignoring them, Perdita made herself coffee, heaped slices of bread and jam on to her plate and retreated with this feast to the fastnesses of her own room.

Kate raised an eyebrow at her sister.

'I'm going to phone Roger,' Liz said decisively.

'Careful,' warned Kate. 'If you get his back up, he'll only dig his toes in further. If you see what I mean.'

'I shall be the soul of discretion.'

'Huh!'

Liz phoned Roger and arranged to meet him at one o'clock outside the museum in Pannett Park. It was an old haunt of theirs. In earlier years they'd often walked up and down the paths between the flowerbeds, arguing furiously over this and that.

He was already waiting as she climbed up the hill to the museum, a tall, distinguished-looking man dressed unexceptionally in grey cords and navy sweatshirt. Yes, she thought, I can understand what Perdita sees in him. He's reassuring. I used to feel the same.

'Hello, Roger,' she said awkwardly.

'Hello.'

'Shall we walk about a bit?'

'Fine.'

His manner was more composed than her own. They walked in silence as she struggled to find the words to express what she wanted to say.

'I suppose you've come about Perdita?' he said eventually.

'Well, yes, I have. Are you surprised?'

'Surprised that it's you who has come, yes. I expected Kate. Not surprised that Perdita's cared about. She deserves to be,' he added. 'She's had a rough time.'

'Duncan?'

He nodded, pressing his lips together as if willing himself not to speak. He gave the impression of someone who might have a lot to say on this subject, if he chose. Liz had never been sure how much Roger had guessed about the past. Certainly there had been times, as Kate had said, when she'd used the pretext of meeting Roger to see Duncan instead.

'You never liked him, did you?' she hazarded.

'Not much,' he admitted. 'Jealousy, I suppose. However,' he stopped to look at the view over the pantile-roofed houses, 'it's a moot point now which of us has made more of a success of his life. I hear his paintings don't sell too well.' He turned to her.

'Don't they?' she said lightly. 'But then when was commercial success ever a standard for anything?'

Anger sparked in his face, though he said nothing. Liz bit her lip. She mustn't antagonise him. Kate was right. She lacked tact. She began pulling leaves off a laurel tree.

'Must you do that?' he said, exasperated. 'This is a public park. You can get fined for that sort of thing.' He glanced nervously over his shoulder.

That was Roger all over, she thought, the law-abiding citizen. All the more surprising, then, that he was risking his reputation with Perdita. They walked on. She decided that directness was called for; they couldn't have another future ruined.

'Roger, I've come to ask you to break it off, at least until after Perdita's exams.'

'I have no intention of interfering with Perdita's exams. I'm not demanding in that way. I'm giving her support. I have two teenage daughters, I know how difficult exam times can be. Tell Kate I'll not let her get upset. Breaking off now *would* upset her,' he added.

'Kate's terribly worried.'

'Is she?' For a moment guilt appeared on his face. 'Tell her not to be. I know what it's like to be a single parent and from what I gather, Kate has been carrying the can for Perdita for a long time. She's got in with a wild crowd at school. Kate should see I'm helping to get her daughter away from all that.'

'You've always liked Kate, haven't you?'

'She reminds me of your mother – she's practical, responsible. Yes, I like her. I admire her.'

'Unlike me.' She glanced at him, half mischievously.

'Yes, I never *admired* you.'

There was a silence.

'Perdita's so young though,' Liz ventured.

'She's older than her years, with what she's been through. I hope you don't think,' he turned to look at her, 'that I seduced an inexperienced schoolgirl? Perdita is *not* inexperienced.'

'Oh,' Liz felt herself flushing.

'In fact she has probably slept with more people than I have.'

'Oh.' Did Kate know this?

'I'm not into seducing virgins. I have three daughters of my own.'

Liz felt the rug slowly being pulled from under her.

'Anyway,' Roger went on, driving home the fact that he was gaining the upper hand, 'I still don't understand what business this is of yours? You long ago relinquished any rights over my life. You did it quite willingly, as I seem to remember.'

It was faint but it was there, and Liz caught it, the trace of bitterness in his voice. She looked at him, remembering Kate's words.

'That's what this is all about, isn't it, Roger? Some kind of twisted revenge for the past?'

'You overestimate your importance,' he replied coldly.

She chewed on this in silence. At length she said, 'I'm not going to change your mind, am I?'

'No.'

There seemed nothing more to be said. After a few moments they parted, as they had parted so often in the past, in mutual irritation and misunderstanding.

'You were right, Kate,' she said when she got back to the house. 'I've only made things worse.'

'Never mind, I haven't done too well either. I had another row with Perdita while you were out. Her latest bright idea is to scrap doing her exams altogether, take a year off and sit them next year.'

Liz groaned. 'You can't let her.'

'She's a grown woman.' Kate sighed. 'I can't force her to sit behind a desk and take her exams. She claims she's been upset by this business with Duncan and Chris – well, I can understand that. It *is* upsetting, not knowing whether he's coming or going. And then there's her exclusion – I gather she told you about that?'

'Yes.'

'So you see,' Kate gave a wry smile, 'I haven't been doing such a good job after all.'

'You have, Kate, you have. This is not your fault.' It's the people around you – Duncan, Roger and a certain wilfulness, which I recognise only too well, in Perdita herself.

'Liz, this is beyond me. Perdita says she's not coming back with us.' Kate sat down on a chair and rested her head in her hands. 'I've got a splitting headache. I think the best thing we can do is go back to Hull this afternoon and phone Duncan. He's got to come home and help me with this.'

'Yes,' replied Liz, swallowing down her fear.

Chapter Seventeen

When they arrived back in the Avenues, Kate phoned Duncan. Liz prowled around the house, smoking a cigarette, feeling tense, irritable, hostile. She didn't want to meet him, she really did not want to meet him. For a brief moment she contemplated using her return ticket to Boston. Then she thought, why should I run away? Who is he anyway? A charmer who bewitched me when I was young and inexperienced. An incredibly selfish man who can't decide whether he's AC or DC and has messed up two women's lives – three, if you count Perdita.

'Kate, how long does it take to drive down from Middlesbrough?'

'About a couple of hours, I should think.' Kate glanced at her sister. 'You needn't be here if you don't want, only I guess Duncan will be staying the night. He sounded pretty angry on the phone. Talked about rushing over to Whitby and having it out with Roger. I managed to dissuade him from that,' she added.

'I'll be here.' Liz tilted her chin in a manner that was familiar to Kate. It was one of Perdita's tricks too. 'I'll go out for a walk.'

She wandered around the Avenues. There weren't many people about; she passed a white Rastafarian and a middle-aged man with a ponytail and bare sandalled feet. Some of the houses were almost derelict, with peeling woodwork and scraps of old curtains tacked across the windows. Some had wooden supports. Subsidence was a problem round here, Kate had said. Others had been done up and turned into nurseries or residential homes for the elderly. She peeped into living rooms as she went past. Untidy family rooms with books, music stands and toys scattered around; in one she saw a white panama hat tossed over the back of a sofa, like something out of a stage set; in others, desks and computers and fax machines dominated. All these houses, all these lives, she thought. Complicated lives, she supposed, as complicated as what had gone on in the Chapman household, as complicated as what went on in Kate's.

She sat in Pearson Park, watching families feed the ducks and children scamper about in the playground. She wandered in the clammy heat of the Victorian conservatory. She tried to locate Philip Larkin's house. Finally, knowing that all this activity was just so much displacement, she turned back in the direction of Kate's. An unfamiliar yellow Deux Chevaux was parked outside. Finding Kate in the kitchen, she raised her eyebrows. Kate nodded.

'Yes, he's arrived.'

Liz's throat went dry. She swallowed nervously. The palms of her hands began to sweat. She brushed them up and down her jeans. Then the door opened. Duncan came into the room.

'Kate, I can't find . . .' He stopped, seeing Liz. 'Oh. Hello,' he said.

Her first thought was – is this the man I broke my life in two for? Duncan seemed strangely shrunk. He stooped a little. His eyes had a watery, weary look about them. His chestnut hair was threaded with silver. Time and something else – was it suffering? – had eaten away those once boyish looks. He was wearing jeans, a black T-shirt and an old tweed jacket, exactly the same sort of clothes he had worn when she had last seen him.

'Hello, Duncan,' she said calmly.

They shook hands. Liz congratulated herself on feeling perfectly indifferent.

'Well, how do you find England after all these years?' he asked, sounding more like an elderly uncle than a former lover.

Liz replied in the same vein, keeping the conversation light and trivial and impersonal. To Kate watching, it was as if the past hardly mattered to them; they'd had so many relationships in the intervening years; it was only people like herself – loyal, tenacious, stubborn – to whom the past meant anything. Duncan and Liz lived lightly, shedding relationships as they went, in a way she could never do. There's something to be said for living like that, she thought. It causes less emotional upheaval in the end, at least to oneself.

Duncan's voice enquiring as to the whereabouts of his new brushes broke into her thoughts.

'I think I saw them in your bedroom, though what they were doing there . . .'

She went upstairs to look for them. Duncan, after a glance at Liz, followed his wife out of the room.

That's that then, thought Liz, with a feeling of relief. The first meeting over and everything remarkably civilised.

Half an hour later she was reeling around in such agony that she had to get out of the house. Pain was inside her, outside her, all around her, ringing in her ears, hitting the roof of her mouth, clenching her stomach. She was trapped in a cage of suffering. Feeling dizzy, she stood outside Kate's front door for a moment to steady herself, then stumbled blindly down the avenue, going first in one direction, then the other. She kept in the shadows close to the garden walls, avoiding people's eyes. Possibly they would think she was drunk. She felt drunk. Drunk on pain.

She ran back into the park, as if seeking a refuge, and sat down on a bench. The families were packing up their picnics ready to go home.

It had come back to her, everything she had felt about Duncan, all the pain and the longing and the love. Wanting to take care of him, yet knowing she would not be allowed to. Being convinced that she would never meet another man like him, realising that she would have been content to live for ever on the fringes of his life, except that he had said that would be no life for her.

Time had robbed him of some of his energy, but the charm was still there if you looked hard enough. That intensely masculine face. Those dark eyes. The lock of chestnut hair flopping over his forehead. The laugh lines at the edges of his eyes. His swarthy, almost Spanish complexion. The sensuous, rather cruel mouth. Caro, Sarah, even Louise, after all, they'd only been second best; not because they were women and he was a man, but simply because of who Duncan was, how he made her feel.

She remembered now how they had parted. In the café down by the harbour she had plucked at his sleeve wanting something from him, some gesture of tenderness, and he had shaken her off, yes, actually shaken her off, as you might shake off a troublesome young puppy who has played that trick once too often. He had been wearing a dark tweed jacket. She could remember clearly the feel of the heavy, rough material under her fingers. It was after this that she had stood up and through sheer will-power, forced herself to walk out the door of that café without looking back. Their final meeting. All these years she had blotted it out.

Was this how Perdita felt about Roger? If so, none of them stood a chance against her. She would go her own way, spoiling her opportunities as Liz had done, learning about life on the pulse rather than through books. But I wouldn't like her to have the life I've had, thought Liz, getting up from the bench and making her way slowly back to the house. Doing odd jobs here and there, struggling to survive, going from relationship to relationship (for Perdita would never stay with Roger, in the long run she would grow tired of his old-man ways). No. I wouldn't want that for her. Kate's right, we must do something to stop it. She quickened her steps towards the house.

She found Kate on her way up to bed.

'Sorry, Liz, I feel knackered. What on earth was in that sleeping pill? I'll have to lie down for a bit. There's food in the freezer. Help yourself to anything you like. Duncan's painting in his studio. He won't be out for hours.'

Liz wandered into the sitting room. The problem of what to do about Perdita had obviously been shelved for the time being. She picked up an out-of-date newspaper, glanced at it, then tossed it aside. The sound of a Bach concerto could be heard coming from Duncan's studio. She was wondering whether, if she put on the television very softly, it would disturb him, when the doorbell rang. Liz waited a moment then, as apparently nobody else was going to answer it, went to open the door herself.

Roger stood on the doorstep, dressed in his business suit and looking nervous.

'Roger! What on earth are you doing here?'

'I'm worried about P-Perdita. I've come to have a chat with Kate about her.'

'Kate's upstairs asleep. I don't want to wake her. She's been through a lot lately,' Liz added pointedly.

'I know.' Anxiously, he bit a nail. 'L-look, w-what about

Duncan? That's his c-car outside, isn't it?'

'Yes.'

'I'll t-talk to him then.'

'I wouldn't advise it. He's very angry.' But she stood back all the same to let him in.

'Where is he?'

'In his studio. Down there on the left.' She pointed. 'But I really don't think –'

'N-nonsense.' Roger shoved past her. 'We're both rational adults, aren't we? Surely we can talk this t-thing through in a c-civilised fashion.'

He set off down the corridor with an air of determination. Liz followed hoping, for Kate's sake, to contain whatever damage might result.

Roger tapped on the door. Getting no response, he pushed it open and stepped into the room. Duncan, his back to them, was painting away with a passion and absorption Liz remembered from the old days. He was working on Chris's portrait.

Roger cleared his throat. Duncan swung round.

'Bloody hell! You!' he exclaimed, and dropped his palette. 'You've got a nerve, coming here.'

'I want to talk to you about P-Perdita,' Roger began. 'She shouldn't be taking time off s-school. I'm worried about her.'

'You're worried about her!' Duncan exploded, his dark eyes blazing. 'My God! You're the one who seduced her. You're the one who's ruining her life.'

'I'm n-not . . .'

'My daughter has her whole life in front of her. Do you think she'll stay with an elderly jumped-up estate agent for the rest of her days?'

'No, I don't,' Roger said slowly. 'In fact I wouldn't encourage her to.'

'So you just wanted to take her virginity, was that it? Is that the sort of thing you're into?' Duncan took a step forward.

'Perdita wasn't a v—' began Roger, then stopped as Liz kicked him on the shin. He changed tack. 'I want to help Perdita. At this stage in her life, I believe I can give her the support she needs.'

'Some fucking support! You child molester! You bloody rapist!'

In his fury Duncan reached out blindly, grabbing the nearest thing to hand and crashing it down hard on Roger's head. It was the portrait of Perdita. Roger's face appeared through the canvas, looking surprised. A tin of paint followed the painting. It hit Roger on the cheek. He sank to the floor.

'My God! Duncan!' exclaimed Liz, bending down. 'What on earth have you done? He's out cold.' Blood streamed from the gash on Roger's cheek.

'He looks bad, doesn't he?' said Duncan, suddenly contrite. 'I'll call an ambulance.' He hurried away.

Liz picked up a cloth and began wiping some of the blood from Roger's cheek. He was still unconscious. There were cuts all over his face and his right eye was beginning to swell.

Duncan came back into the studio. 'They'll be here in five minutes, they said. How is he?' He bent over his victim.

Roger's eyelids began to flutter. 'I . . . I . . .' he moaned.

'It's all right, Roger,' Liz said. 'The ambulance will be here soon. Just lie still.'

He shut his eyes again.

'Can't we get that thing off him?' Duncan pointed to the torn canvas draped around Roger's neck. 'It looks damned uncomfortable.'

'I don't know,' replied Liz doubtfully, wishing Kate was here. 'We might cut him again. There's a lot of glass about.'

'Hell!' muttered Duncan angrily. 'Why the fuck did he turn up here anyway?' He began dabbing turps on to his hand. Paint was spattered over his clothes and on the floor as well. 'It would have to be sodding gloss,' he added under his breath.

'Roger's worried.' Liz glanced up at Duncan. 'I think he really does care about Perdita, you know.'

'Does he?' He paused in his dabbing. 'It's not just a dirty old man's fling then?'

Liz reflected that Duncan seemed to have forgotten that Roger was a good deal younger than himself and that he was having a relationship with a boy of – how old had Kate said Chris was? Seventeen?

'What's happening? I thought I heard voices . . .' Kate stood in the doorway in her dressing gown, blinking and rubbing her eyes. She spotted Roger lying on the floor, surrounded by fragments of canvas and glass. 'My God! What on earth have you done? He's not dead, is he? Liz, I thought you were in charge.'

'I was,' said Liz, crestfallen. 'Things got out of hand.'

Duncan stepped forward. 'Darling, I'm sorry. It was my fault. I lost my temper.'

Kate stared rather blankly at him, then stooped to inspect Roger.

'He needs an ice pack on that cheek,' she said, thinking of what neither of the other two had. 'You've phoned for an ambulance, I hope?'

'Of course,' replied Liz, relieved to be able to appear even vaguely efficient.

As Kate went to fetch the ice, the doorbell rang. It was the ambulancemen.

'Had a bit of a set-to then?' said the younger of the pair.

'A bit,' admitted Duncan, shamefaced.

The elder ambulanceman whistled when he saw Roger lying on the floor. 'Nasty old mess. By rights the police should be called. This gentleman may want to press charges.'

Roger opened his eyes and muttered something incomprehensible.

'Let's get him off to casualty first and worry about that later,' said his colleague. 'How are you feeling, sir?'

Roger moved his head an inch and winced. 'Terrible. I've got a splitting headache and I seem to have a hot brick on my cheek.'

'Oh God, I'm sorry,' muttered Duncan. With a grimace, he fled the room.

'Lie still, sir. We'll soon have you comfortable.'

Together they eased the painting over Roger's head and lifted him on to a stretcher.

'Where are you taking him?' asked Kate.

'Hull Royal.'

'One of us ought to go with him in the ambulance,' she said. 'He's a . . . a friend,' she explained to the elder of the two men.

'Really?' he said, clearly astonished at the fashion in which they treated their friends.

Kate flushed.

'I'll go,' put in Liz quickly. 'You're not dressed and anyway somebody needs to look after Duncan. I think he's cut himself. I'm sorry, Kate,' she added. 'Your favourite painting.'

Kate, with tears in her eyes, was picking up the torn fragments of Perdita's portrait. 'He was never violent before,' she said, softly. 'I never knew Duncan could be violent.'

Didn't you, wondered Liz. What the hell do you think he's made of then? She remembered the love bites, the bruises on her arms and thighs after their lovemaking. Was he like that with . . .? She closed the question down in her mind. There were some things she would never be able to allow herself to think. She followed the stretcher into the ambulance and held the ice pack against Roger's swelling cheek.

In casualty, they took one look at him and sent him down to the theatre to have stitches put in his face. Liz hung around. When Roger was back on the ward, stitched up and with the paint scraped from his hair, a police officer came to ask if he wanted to press charges.

'No.' Roger shook his head. 'Ow!' he groaned.

'I'll put it down as a domestic then.'

The policeman scribbled something in his notebook and went away.

'That was decent of you,' said Liz.

Roger glowered at her from beneath his bandages. 'I'm not doing it for you or for Duncan, not even for Kate. I'm doing it for Perdita. He is her father, after all. She's had enough to put up with from Duncan over the years. The last thing she needs is to see him up in court on a GBH charge.'

'How long are you going to be in here?'

'At least forty-eight hours, probably longer,' he replied glumly. 'They're talking of doing a scan.'

'Is there anything I can get you?'

'Yes there is, as a matter of fact, since I'm so unexpectedly stuck here.' He ticked the list off on his fingers in a gesture that reminded Liz of his mother, Charlotte Hamley. 'I need a phone to tell them at home what has happened. The girls will be all right, Mother will be with them. I need a toothbrush, toothpaste, a comb and some pyjamas. Also a newspaper, a small radio, a notepad and something to write with. Think you can manage all that?' He looked at Liz uncertainly, no doubt wishing she were Kate.

'Of course.' She rose from the chair by his bed.

It took her a while to organise everything but she managed to buy most of what Roger wanted in the hospital shop on the ground floor and she arranged for a phone to be brought to his bedside.

'I'll look in tomorrow.' She stood at the foot of his bed. 'See if there's anything else you need.'

'Don't bother. I'll be all right. Thank you.'

'Oh.' It was an unusual sensation, being rejected by Roger. Liz hesitated. 'What about getting home? You'll be in no fit state to drive.'

'I'll have someone from the office fetch me. And someone else pick up my car from Kate's house.'

'I could –'

He waved the suggestion away. 'It's all right. Someone will have to come over tomorrow anyway to bring my laptop. I feel useless without it. If I had known this was going to happen, I'd have brought it with me. I could be getting on with things.' His hands twitched restlessly over the hospital blanket.

'Are you sure there's nothing else I can do?'

'No. Thank you,' he replied firmly.

'Well, take care, Roger. I am – you know – sorry about this.' She lingered in the doorway.

'So am I. My head hurts like hell. Ouch! Shit!'

Liz fled down the corridor.

She caught the last bus back to Kate's house. The evening had been like some weird dream, like those dreams she'd had in the early days after leaving Whitby, in which she and Kate and Duncan and Roger had got muddled up together. How many times in them had she run from Roger to Duncan? And now it seemed as though she no longer had anything to give that Roger wanted. Ironic the way life turned out.

She found Kate anxiously waiting up. Liz told her the news about Roger and that he had decided not to press charges. An expression of relief crossed Kate's face.

'Thank heavens for that. To have Duncan in court is the last thing we need right now. God!' She went suddenly limp in her chair. 'I feel exhausted. I'll have to go to bed. Duncan's out on one of his midnight strolls. He'll be back in a moment if you want company.'

'I'm off to bed,' Liz said hastily.

Chapter Eighteen

'What I can't understand,' said Liz the following morning as she and Kate lingered over a late breakfast, 'is why Duncan got so angry? I know Roger and Perdita is not exactly an ideal situation, but it's not as if Duncan has led such a conventional life himself, is it? Why did he react like that?'

'Don't you see?' From behind the teapot, Kate looked at her sister, an odd expression in her eyes. 'Roger and Perdita. The age gap. Perdita's eighteen, exactly the age you were when –'

'Oh.'

'It awakened all the old guilt.'

'Did Duncan feel guilty?' Liz looked down at the table. 'I never knew.'

'Of course he felt guilty. Tortured himself for a while. He was on twenty milligrams of Valium a day for two years after you left. It smashed his memory to pieces and didn't do his painting much good either. That GP ought to have been shot.' Kate stood up briskly and began stacking pots in the sink. 'I told you Duncan likes rescuing young people,' she added over her shoulder. 'Now you see why.'

'Yes.' Liz stared at her plate for a moment, then roused herself and said, 'Leave those, Kate. I'll do them.'

'Will you? All right. Thanks. I've got to go into college this morning. I may be on sabbatical but there's a couple of admin jobs I need to finish off.'

'When will you be back?' asked Liz, alarm in her eyes.

'Around four. Don't worry,' Kate added, 'Duncan's likely to stay in his studio all day. He hasn't been doing much painting lately, what with one thing and another. He was itching to get started this morning.'

I know, thought Liz. Lying in bed, she had heard Duncan moving around in his studio directly beneath her room. He had put on some blues. Erma Franklin. 'Take another piece of my heart now, baby.' She had lain in bed, listening. It was a favourite of hers. They still had the same taste in music.

Liz sat alone in the kitchen, her hands round a half-warm mug of tea. After all these years, to have slotted back into their lives as the sister-in-law from abroad – it was too easy. And at the same time distinctly odd. That was Kate's way – bury the past, don't speak of it, hide it away as if it has never been, get on with life. But the past wasn't so easily buried. They ought to speak openly about it, clear the air, instead of living in this atmosphere of half-truths.

'Has anyone told Perdita about Roger?' she asked as Kate popped her head round the door on her way out.

'I did. I phoned her last night, while you were at the hospital.'

'How did she take it?'

'Oh, annoyed with us all for interfering with her life. Upset that Roger came to see us without telling her. Generally pissed off that we seemed to be treating her like a child. You know the kind of thing.'

'Yes. Do you – do you think she'll come back now?'

Kate shrugged. 'I don't know. What's going on in Perdita's head right now is anybody's guess. She's angry with Roger, refuses to come and visit him in hospital. I worry about her being alone over there. But she's grown up. I have to learn to let her make her own decisions.'

She went out abruptly, shutting the door behind her. She still doesn't like discussing Perdita with me, thought Liz.

She sat listening to the music coming from Duncan's studio; something she didn't recognise this time. A piano piece. She and Duncan alone in the house. Duncan painting, she doing the chores. Liz got up and went over to the sink. If we had married it would have been like this, she thought, except we wouldn't be living in a house. Two rooms somewhere, that's all we would have been able to afford. We'd have moved around – Provence one year, Italy the next, Greece, Egypt. We would have wandered the world, scraping a living among people similar to ourselves. bohemians, artists, eccentrics . . .

It was like a moment out of time, standing here at the sink sharing music with Duncan. Was he really here? Or was she dreaming again, as she had dreamed of him so often in the past? It had always been like that with Duncan. Their whole relationship had been dreamlike since there had been no space in real time for them to be together. When she was with him she used to keep looking at him to check he was still there, that he wasn't a mirage she had conjured up in her brain to defeat despair. Moving in and out of time, for their meetings had always been short and hurried, oblivious to everything going on around her, but seeing him, her lover, in the sharpest detail – his badly cut hair, his long dark lashes, his tough-looking Spanish skin. And every meeting provoking afresh that mixture of peaceful recognition and astonished joy.

What Duncan had felt, she'd never been able to work out exactly. Had he married the wrong sister? He'd never said so. But after her, he had turned back to men; she, eventually, to women. It must mean something. What had Kate said the other day, worrying herself half to death over this business with Chris? 'It might have been different with you. With you, Duncan might not have felt the need to have affairs –' And Liz had broken in swiftly, unable to bear the sight of Kate tearing herself to bits. 'He would have been the same with me, Kate, I'm sure he would.' A lie. She could have kept him. With her there would have been no space for anyone else in his life. They were two mad, emotional people, two of a kind. Rolling around on the floor, tearing at each other's clothes, crazy for each other. Duncan had been hungry when he'd come to her. Kate had left him hungry.

As for herself, someone had only had to mention his name in her presence to set her nerve ends tingling. She had been eighteen years old. Too young for the kind of passion that comes only once, or at most twice, in a lifetime. She had been marked by it. Yet the number of times they had been alone together wasn't so very many. They had met in friends' rooms; the sort of friends Duncan had didn't raise an eyebrow at lending their rooms for a couple of hours, no questions asked. Once, riskily, after making love, they had shared fish and chips on the pier, the rain dripping into their newspaper. Brother- and sister-in-law eating together – what could be more innocent? He perhaps giving her some paternal advice about her future. Since her father died, she's been running rather wild, you know. Good for her to have a steadying influence . . . That was a laugh.

Liz finished the washing up and spread out the dishcloth on the draining board to dry. There was a noise behind her. She turned round. Duncan was standing in the doorway. He looked startled to see her. Had he forgotten she was in the house?

'Has – er – has Kate gone already? I wanted to ask her to buy . . . Never mind.' He turned away.

He was scared of her.

'Duncan . . .' Her voice failed her.

'Yes?' He turned back.

Don't be scared, Duncan, she wanted to say. There's no need.

'If there was something you wanted to buy – I'm going to the shops.'

He stared at her. 'Well, all right,' he said eventually. 'It was paint. The shop on the corner has it. They get it in specially for me so that I don't have to go into town. Hang on, I'll write down the name.' He tore off a scrap of paper from Kate's memo pad hanging on the wall. 'Thanks. Well. Better get back to work.'

'Do you want lunch?' She flushed. 'I mean, I could make some for you.'

He looked at her doubtfully. 'Kate generally brings me a sandwich in the studio but –'

'I'll bring you in one when I make my own.'

He hesitated, then with a scarcely perceptible shrug of his shoulders, said, 'All right then. Thanks.' He turned and padded down the corridor to his studio.

It was better when Kate was there. In her presence they were less awkward with each other. Still, the brother-in-law, sister-in-law relationship begun, then smashed up, was slowly beginning to creak into operation again. Liz picked up Kate's basket and her list and went out to do the shopping.

At one o'clock she took his sandwich into his studio, intending to set it down on a table and tiptoe out without disturbing him, but he turned round to mix some paint as she came in and saw her.

'What do you think of it?'

He pointed his brush in the direction of the portrait on the easel. He seemed more relaxed than he had been earlier, on home territory.

Liz gazed at the lean youth with the grey, pockmarked skin. 'It's realistic.' She hesitated, wanting to say more. 'It does look like a real person.' But if Chris looks like that, she thought to herself, what on earth's the attraction?

Duncan leaned his head on one side, studying his picture.

'I haven't got there yet. Chris has a lonely, abandoned look about him that I haven't managed to capture. It's so bloody difficult!'

He sighed and wiped his brush on a rag.

She hesitated again. 'Are you going back to him?' she said, in a low voice.

'I don't know.' He sighed, more heavily this time. 'Everything's in a kind of fog at the moment. So what's new, eh?' He gave her a small, ironic smile.

Liz touched the end of a brush with her finger. 'Kate's terribly upset. She thinks you're going to leave her for good this time.'

'I know. I can't make up my mind what to do. The thing is, Chris depends on me. No one's ever been there for him. His mother married again when he was two. His stepfather didn't want to know. He's been in and out of institutions all his life. In one place, they beat him up, in another they tied him to a chair, not even letting him get up to go to the toilet. Nobody's ever bothered about him. It's good to feel needed for once.'

'Kate needs you,' Liz said softly.

Duncan looked at her. 'No, she doesn't. Not really. She's got her life sorted. Job. Colleagues. Supportive women friends who think I'm shit. Enough money to live on. This house is hers. What would she need me for?'

'She needs help with Perdita.'

'Not from me. Look what a mess I make of things. Thanks for helping out with Roger, by the way,' he added. 'Kate told me he's not going to press charges.'

'That was nothing to do with me. He did it for Perdita. Said he didn't want her to have to see her father up in court.'

Duncan snorted. 'He's so bloody responsible!'

'Yes.'

He glanced at her. 'You know why I did it? You know why I got so mad?'

She looked away. 'I didn't. Kate told me. About you feeling

207

guilty.' She wandered over to the French window and stared out for a moment, then turned and said, 'You needn't, you know.'

He ran paint-spattered fingers through his grey and chestnut hair. 'You see, I thought you'd think of me, if you thought of me at all, as the person who had ruined your life. I saw parallels with Roger. My anger against him was really anger against myself. My younger self,' he added. 'And fear that Roger will ruin Perdita's life as I ruined yours.'

'Not ruined it. Changed it, I suppose.'

'For the worse.'

'Who knows? Perhaps it was for the better. I took a different turning from the one I was expected to take, that's all.'

He rubbed his chin. 'You never did get properly educated. I always felt bad about that.'

'Even if I had gone off to university, I don't know that it would ever have amounted to much. I lack Kate's stamina.'

'Yes, Kate follows things through to the end.'

'Unlike us,' she replied.

He pulled a wry face. 'We're two of a kind.'

She hesitated, then said lightly, 'I suppose you saw that even then. I suppose you knew it wouldn't work.'

His eyes dropped to the floor. 'I saw nothing clearly then,' he muttered.

There was a moment's silence. Liz wondered whether now would be the time to leave. Then he looked up and said, 'Why did you never come back?'

'I was afraid.'

'Of Kate? Or of me?'

'Of both of you, but most of all of Mother. I was afraid of what she would say to me. Well, what is there to say about a daughter who pinches her elder sister's husband?'

'You should have come back. It was me your mother blamed. We had one short conversation, ended as soon as it had begun, in which she made it quite clear she knew everything –'

'Oh.' Here was something even Kate didn't know. Or did she?

'Yes. Then she cut me out of her life for ever. I ceased to exist for her. She would put down the phone if I answered it.'

Liz shook her head. 'It's so difficult to believe. I was convinced it was me she would blame. Mother used to think the world of you.'

'I know, it was hard to lose an admirer. No, that sounds vain and crass. It was more than that. Your mother had been good to me in all sorts of ways since I'd married Kate. I missed that warmth. It had begun to make up for the fact that my own mother died so young. Then the warmth vanished.' He paused. 'The worst of it was that it affected her relationship with Kate. Your mother never quite forgave Kate for having me back and bringing up her grandchild under the same roof as me.'

Liz played with some tubes of paint on the table beside her.

'Duncan,' she said, at last, 'why did you answer my letter so warmly and then never come? That's not a reproach,' she added quickly. 'Only it's always puzzled me.'

He picked up a brush and examined it. 'I was afraid,' he said at last. 'I'd tried to simplify my life as much as possible – painting, Perdita, Kate –'

In that order, wondered Liz. Poor Kate. Poor Perdita, if it came to that.

'– I couldn't go back to the lies, the concealments, the being split in half, I couldn't. Kate's never been jealous of my affairs with men – until now, that is.'

'In other words,' she said quietly, 'it wasn't worth the effort?'

'That's not *quite* what I meant. I was looking for simplicity. I was afraid of introducing a – a complication into my life.' He glanced at her. 'Not that I didn't want to see you again. Part of me did, very much.'

'Really?' she said, offhand because she felt so nervous.

'Yes.' He turned away. 'But you see I'd become comfortable again with Kate. After you, I went back to her, not knowing if I was saved or done for. It was Kate who got me through that. And Perdita gave us a place where we could be together, freely, whatever else was going on in the rest of our lives.'

She chewed over this in almost physical pain.

'You know what children are,' he went on, then stopped, flushing slightly.

'Go on,' she muttered, through clenched teeth.

He hesitated a moment, then continued. 'I mean they give grown-ups the chance to share things – smiles, winks, a joke – over their heads. A child creates a bond.'

'Yes,' she said, the muscles in her face suddenly gone stiff. 'Yes, I can see that it would.'

I gave you that bond, she thought. It was because of me you had Perdita.

There was a silence.

'We passed it off well, all of us, didn't we?' she said, half cynically. 'What would people have said if they'd known?'

'Thank God they didn't. Other people's sex lives always look squalid from the outside.'

That gave her a little shock.

'Do you think it was squalid?'

'No, I think we did our best. Every one of us.'

'That's what Kate said.'

'It was good, you know. It did mean something to me.'

He stepped forward and touched her lightly on the arm. Liz went absolutely rigid. She looked at him, beseeching him to let go of her. His dark eyes widened in sudden realisation. He took away his hand as if it burned him. Yes, Duncan, she thought, some things, if they happen too early in life, are never got over.

The room hung heavy with their silence. To help them both, she said, 'I've got something of yours.'

She fumbled in her pocket and brought out the silver florin dropped by him all those years ago in the café by the harbour. She laid it on the table. He looked at it without recognition.

'What is it?'

'Oh, I thought you . . . Never mind. It was something you used to value. You carried it around with you for luck. You said it had helped you through your exams.'

'I remember!' He picked it up and turned it over in his hand. 'My lucky coin. I lost it years ago. Where on earth did you find it?'

There's nothing wrong with his memory, she thought, whatever Kate says. 'I didn't find it. I stole it. I thought it might bring me luck, but I think it must only work for you.'

'Well, thanks anyway. I'm glad to have it back.' He juggled it up and down in his palm. 'Lizzie, I . . .'

He can still call me that, she thought, with a rush of relief.

Then she became aware that Duncan had stopped talking. The door opened. Kate came into the studio. Neither of them had heard the front door. How long had she been home? Had she been listening outside the studio door? Kate glanced from one to the other. They both looked stricken with guilt. Liz was rapidly going over in her head the last parts of her conversation with Duncan. What would they have sounded like to someone listening?

'You're back early, Kate,' she said nervously.

'I decided to bring my work home,' replied her sister. 'What's that?' she asked Duncan, coming further into the room and noticing that he was holding something in his hand.

'An old good luck charm of mine. I . . . found it.'

Liz's eyes dropped to the floor. They were beginning again, the lies to Kate. Yet, in the circumstances, what else could he have said?

Kate stared at Duncan, then glanced at Liz. A childhood incident, long forgotten, flashed into her mind. She had become friendly one summer with a boy who lived down their street. Matthew, his name was. The same age as herself. Twelve. They used to go exploring together for fossils down on the beach or wander around the graves up on the cliff, reading out the headstones to each other. It was a simple, uncomplicated friendship. Matthew gave her a warm feeling. She trusted him. The days she dreaded were the days when her mother said, 'I'm busy this morning, Kate. Take Elizabeth with you. And mind you take good care of her.' Liz must have been about four at the time. How tiresome she'd been, tagging along behind them, slowing them down, bothering them with her endless questions, shouting 'Wait for me!' at intervals.

One particular afternoon, Matthew had promised to show Kate a beck he'd discovered. They planned to build a dam across it. 'And me!' yelled Liz, eavesdropping on their conversation. She had given them no peace till they'd agreed to take her along with them. Naturally, she'd fallen into the beck. Matthew, who had his lifesaver's badge, rescued her. The pair of them had their photographs in the local newspaper. *'Young hero saves little girl's life.'* After that he and Liz had been inseparable for the rest of the summer. She adored him and he, it turned out, had always wanted a younger sibling. Kate was the one left to tag along behind. What had once been simple had suddenly become enormously complicated. Watching Liz and Duncan now, Kate remembered all this.

She doesn't trust us, thought Liz. She came back early to check up on us. And found us together. Muttering something about going out for a bit, Liz left the studio, walked down the hall and opened and closed the front door behind her.

Duncan and Kate were left staring at one other. Slowly Duncan's hand closed over the silver florin.

'Is it coming along all right?' said Kate eventually, with a nod towards Chris's portrait.

'Slowly.'

'I'll let you get on then.'

She picked up her bag and left the room.

Chapter Nineteen

Liz didn't return until after supper. She'd had hers in a pub down the road, she told Kate. In reality, she'd bought a sandwich from the corner shop and wandered the streets till it was late enough to return home and go plausibly straight to bed. The next morning she got up only when she heard Duncan safely moving around his studio. She went into the centre of Hull with Kate. That solved the problem of lunch. When they returned, Liz disappeared up to her bedroom, saying she needed a nap. At seven, as Kate was beginning to prepare supper, her sister emerged from her room saying she was going to a poetry reading she'd seen advertised. Kate scoured the *Hull Daily Mail*. She found no reference to any poetry reading. The next morning she said, 'This is ridiculous, Liz. You can't keep avoiding Duncan.'

The three of them had an uncomfortable lunch together, Kate gamely trying to keep the conversation going, Duncan uttering the occasional grunt, Liz doing her best to contribute but lapsing now and then into unaccountable silences. She went out again for supper (another sandwich) but she miscalculated and on her way back to the house she met Duncan having his evening stroll.

He stopped dead in the street when he saw her.

'We must talk.' He took her arm and steered her into the nearest pub. 'What will you have?' he asked.

'This is like – '

'Yes.'

She wondered whether he had deliberately lain in wait for her. 'I'll have a whisky please.'

'A double?'

'No. Single.'

He nodded. 'You've calmed down. You used to drink too much. I worried about that. It's always a mistake to bring up children in a teetotal household.'

'We know now why my mother would never have drink in the

213

house. My grandfather was an alcoholic who beat his wife.'

'Was he? I never knew that.'

'It was in Laura's diary.'

'Ah, the diary. It's meant a lot to Kate finding that.'

'And to me,' she replied.

His hand tightened round his whisky glass. Liz could see his knuckles turning white.

'Why have you come back?' he said in a low voice.

'The day before yesterday, you asked me why I'd never come back.'

'I meant at this particular time.'

'To help Kate . . .'

'We both know Kate doesn't need help. She could have made these arrangements about the house on her own.'

Liz studied her feet. 'I felt the time was right. If I had known how ill Mother –' Her voice faltered. She swallowed a couple of times. 'I'd have come back earlier.' She paused. 'Also there's nothing, at the moment, keeping me in the States.'

'Louise?'

She shook her head. He flinched slightly. Perhaps the thought of her partnerless, when he had a choice of two, Kate or Chris, made him nervous.

'To tell the truth, Duncan, I'm wondering where to spend the rest of my life.'

'You're surely not thinking of moving back here?'

'Why not? It's where my roots are. Or aren't I allowed to think of that?'

'Of course you're allowed, Lizzie. It's just that –'

'It would be awkward? But I've no intention of settling in Hull. It would be Whitby, if anywhere.'

'What would you do?'

'Waitress. Try to get the poetry going again. I wouldn't need much money to live here. It's cheap. And safe. A good place to grow old in.'

'I can never think of you as old, Lizzie.'

'So how do you think of me?'

'I don't know.' Duncan stared into his beer for a moment. 'I wish I did.'

'An added complication, perhaps?' she suggested.

'No. Never that. You're deep inside me, Lizzie. So deep, I sometimes can't find you. You're part of me, as Kate is. The trouble is, the two parts don't fit together.'

'So you thought you would make a fresh start with Chris?'

He hesitated. 'It seems to – to simplify things.'

He looked at her. She had such a strong desire to ask him to kiss her that she had to turn her head away.

'And will it?' she asked, in a voice that was not quite steady. 'Will it simplify things?'

She felt his hand cover hers as it lay on the seat between them. His touch sent shock waves through her body. Her temperature seemed to rise suddenly by about a hundred degrees. She snatched her hand away.

'Don't!' she whispered. There was silence. She turned and found that he was crying. Crying silently in the way she remembered, in the way only Duncan could. He sat back in the shadows, tears running down his cheeks. 'Don't,' she said again and touched his wet cheek. 'Don't cry over me.'

He shook his head, unable to speak. After a while, he took out his handkerchief, dabbed his eyes and blew his nose.

'Come on.' He grabbed her hand. 'We're getting out of here.'

'Where are we going?' she asked, as they stood outside on the pavement. 'There's nowhere we can go,' she added, in panic. 'Nowhere for us to be.'

'Pearson Park,' he replied. 'Come on, I know a way in.'

They walked swiftly down the road and pushed their way through some bent railings, like a couple of delinquent children.

In the park, he pulled her towards him and kissed her on the mouth and kissed her and kissed her again, like a drowning man.

'Lizzie,' he murmured. 'My girl.'

They circled around each other, half dancing in the dark. He stood behind her, his hands lightly clasped around her waist. She leaned her head back and kissed his neck above the open shirt. He turned her around to face him and pressed her against him. She felt him harden against her. Dizzy with desire, she burrowed deep into his neck, biting and kissing him. He took her breasts in his hands and squeezed them till they hurt and her knees went weak.

'Is it you?' she whispered. 'Is it really you, after all this time?'

'It's really me.'

Her eyes shone in the darkness. She rested her head on his shoulder. 'I can hardly believe it,' she said. She threw back her head and laughed. But it was laughter tinged with sadness. 'Hold me tight,' she said. 'Hold me very tight.'

'Lizzie, I could hold you like this for ever,' he muttered, nuzzling into her neck. 'Let's run away together. Let's go to Greece.'

'And live in a whitewashed cottage.'

'Two rooms. Very bare.'

'You'd paint. I'd work in a bar.'

'We'd spend our evenings down by the harbour, drinking retsina and chewing the fat with the locals. Life would be so simple.'

Then, 'Kate,' she said.

He dropped his arms. She moved away from him. That word, that single word, driving them always apart.

They walked once round the duck pond and sat down side by side on a bench, only just not touching.

'I read your poems,' he said. 'I thought they were marvellous.'

'Did you? Did Kate ever read them?'

'I don't know. I don't think so.'

'I've never dared ask.'

He looked at her. 'Lizzie, what have we wasted? Is it too late to try again?'

'It would kill Kate.'

'Kate's stronger than you think.'

'Or maybe I meant it would kill us. Could we live with ourselves?'

'I don't know!'

He began to cry again, loud, shattering sobs this time.

'Don't. Don't!' She took his head and pressed it against her, like a child's, till his sobbing and shuddering ceased. She was crying too, large silent tears that wet the top of his head. She'd forgotten till now. They had always known how to make each other cry.

He took out his handkerchief and handed it to her. 'I've been running away from you for most of my life, Lizzie. I'm tired of running.'

She sat beside him on the bench, feeling drained and exhausted, good for nothing but to crawl off into a hole somewhere.

'Tomorrow,' he began.

'Tomorrow?'

'Eleven o'clock at the Station Hotel? We've got to talk. There must be some way out of this.'

'I'll be there.'

'Don't be late,' he whispered, running his hands through her hair, lifting it up at the back in the way she remembered from all those years ago. 'Don't be late, or I'll get frantic.'

'I'll be there, Duncan, on the dot. As if my life depended on it.'

'Not your life. Mine.' He kissed her again, then sat up. 'We've got to get back.'

'I know. Kate.'

She slid off the bench.

They returned home separately. Liz went straight up to bed without seeing Kate. Moments later she heard the front door close. Duncan had arrived home. She heard Kate come out of the sitting room. There was a murmur of voices, then the sitting-room door closed behind them.

The next morning, when Liz awoke, the house was silent. She came downstairs to find a note from Kate. 'Gone into the office. I'll be back around five. Duncan is out all day seeing friends, so you'll have the house to yourself. Make yourself at home.' Liz stared blankly at the note. Nothing about it made sense. Poor, ignorant Kate. What a bombshell they were preparing for her.

She pushed open the door to Duncan's studio and stood in the doorway, looking at his paintings. I gave him up once for her, she thought. I can't do it again. Kate's had him all these years, it's my turn now. If only I can convince him he will still be able to paint with me. She closed the door softly behind her and went into the kitchen to make herself some coffee. It was nine thirty. In less than two hours, she would be seeing Duncan again. She felt light-headed with excitement. She could eat nothing. She left her coffee untouched. To kill time, she decided not to take the bus but to walk into the centre of town.

Outside, though the sky was grey, the shabby streets of Hull seemed sunlit. Liz almost laughed aloud as she walked towards the hotel. What a beautiful day. How good it felt to be alive. What was the matter with everyone? Why did they look so dejected? Didn't they know, didn't they feel, how great life was?

Duncan was sitting in the hotel foyer, a pot of coffee on the table in front of him. He was making surreptitious sketches of the people around him. He stood up when he saw Liz and crammed his notepad into the pocket of his jacket.

He smiled at her. 'You made it.'

'I made it,' she agreed gaily, laughing a little from the sheer joy of seeing him.

He sat down again. 'I can hardly believe it. I was sure something would prevent you at the last minute.'

'Such as?'

'I don't know – a broken leg or something.'

'Looking on the bright side!'

She sat down opposite him.

'Coffee?'

'I'd love one, Duncan, but just at the moment I feel as if I couldn't swallow a thing.'

He gazed across at her. 'My love. My girl.'

Meeting his eyes she was flooded with such desire that she had to turn away for a moment to catch her breath. When she looked back he was still gazing at her.

'What's the matter?'

He glanced around. The foyer was filling up with shoppers coming in for their mid-morning coffee.

'We can't talk here,' he muttered under his breath.

The old problem.

She hesitated. 'I suppose they have rooms?'

He pressed his hands together. 'Do you want to?'

'Yes,' she whispered, so softly that he almost didn't catch it.

He went up to book a room, leaning against the desk with such a casual air that she thought, he's done this hundreds of times before. She would have preferred, as in the past, to have borrowed a room from one of his friends. Yet what else could they do? Duncan's friends were now Kate's friends. Had been for years. There was nowhere for them to be. She remembered that song she'd heard once in an Irish bar in Boston. Something about hiding in shadows at the dark end of the street. Yes, that was it. They had always had to hide their love.

He turned round at that moment and smiled at her so tenderly that in her love for him Liz forgot all about the sordidness of their surroundings. She stood up, went over to him and tucked her arm through his, as if she was his wife. Together they went up the stairs, arm in arm, like an old married couple.

Once inside the room, she began to feel they had made a terrible mistake.

'Not a bad room, is it?' She walked across to the window. 'That picture of the Dales – I must make a trip over there. These curtains remind me of some I had in Paris. Oh, here's a kettle. Would you like a cup of tea? No?'

Duncan sat on the edge of the bed looking quizzically at her as she wandered around the room, keeping up a stream of chatter to hide her nervousness.

'Come here,' he said eventually.

'What?' She turned round to face him.

'Come here.'

Liz walked slowly over to him.

He reached out a hand and drew her towards him.

'It's strange –' she began.

'Ssh,' he said, as he might do to a child. He laid a finger on her lips. 'Ssh.' He drew her down on to his knee. 'You're shivering.' He took her hands in his and began rubbing them gently. 'You're afraid. Lizzie, don't be afraid. It's going to be all right.'

'Oh, Duncan, I love you so much.'

'I love you too, Lizzie, my Lizzie.'

He bent and kissed her hand. Then he lay back on the bed and drew her down beside him. For a while she lay shivering next to him. She felt him nuzzle into her neck. She turned and kissed him. They lay entwined in one another's arms.

'It's not like it used to be, is it?' she whispered. 'We're not so driven by passion.'

219

'Nothing can ever be as it was, Lizzie. We're different people now.' His hands rested lightly on her breasts. 'We've lived through so many years apart. Am I a disappointment to you?'

'Of course not. I only meant you've become gentler. I can feel your tenderness in a way I couldn't before.'

'My love. Was I rough with you?'

'Not rough, only I was never exactly sure whether it was me you were making love to.'

'It was always you, Lizzie. Always you. I was a young man then. Young men are crude in love. We have to be taught tenderness.'

She turned over and began kissing his shoulder.

'Lizzie, my Lizzie.'

She started to unbutton his shirt, then his trousers. He stood up and undressed. She did the same on the other side of the bed. He pulled back the sheets and they lay together naked beneath them. She heard the sharp intake of his breath as she touched him.

'Now you're the one who's shivering,' she said. 'What's the matter?'

'I'm frightened, Lizzie. Seeing you again . . . my life seems to be spinning out of control. Everything familiar has suddenly vanished. It's like when my mother died and nothing was ever the same any more.'

'Don't be afraid,' she whispered. 'Lie quietly.' She rubbed a hand up and down his back. 'Nothing need happen. We didn't come here to do anything except talk. Let's think about our life in Greece.'

'The sea.'

'Our cottage.'

'The light.'

'Your painting.'

'Your poetry. Will you be able to write poetry with me, do you think, Lizzie?'

'Yes. Ever since I saw you again I've realised it's not time or money that's been lacking all these years, but inspiration.'

He turned round, covering her body with his and began kissing her, holding her hands above her head, clasping them tightly.

'I love you,' he said.

'I love you too.'

'Are we going too far, I wonder?' he murmured.

She smiled up at him. 'It's our usual destination.'

He pulled away a little and lay on his side gazing at her, running his fingers through her hair. 'How do you feel?'

'All right. Surprisingly. And you?'

'I don't know.'

Abruptly he took his hand away from her hair. There was a long silence. Liz began to have a terrible feeling in the pit of her stomach. She sat up.

'What's the matter? I mean, apart from the obvious fact that on any ordinary scale of morality this is totally wrong,' she added, turning ironic to conceal her nervousness.

Duncan shook his head 'I don't know what I feel. Are we confusing fantasy and reality?'

'Is that what this is for you – a fantasy?'

'I don't know.'

He swung his legs sideways off the bed and began tugging on his trousers. He went over to the window.

'Can we survive outside this room, Lizzie?' he mumbled, his back to her.

She reached round behind her, grabbed a pillow and sat hugging it for comfort.

'Of course we can. Duncan, just because Kate got you first doesn't mean she's entitled to have you for ever. I kept away for eighteen years. She's had all that time with you. Don't I deserve some of you?'

He stared out of the window. 'It's not only Kate.'

'Chris?'

'He needs me.'

'I need you.' She felt as if she was fighting for her life.

He turned round to face her. 'Do you?' he said doubtfully.

'Yes.'

'You've survived all this time without me.'

'Not very well. Some time I'll tell you about it. And I kept away because I loved you, not because I didn't. Duncan! Don't hold that against me. It's not fair!' She pummelled the pillow in frustration.

He sat down again on the edge of the bed and put his head in his hands. She looked at the bent nape of his neck, wanting to reach out and touch him, yet not daring. The future of all of them was hanging in the balance – hers, Kate's, Chris's, even Perdita's, for if Duncan went away with her what would that do to Perdita? Too many lives were at stake. She dared not make even the slightest movement that might tilt the balance in her favour. Oh, she had plenty of arguments in her head. She knew how good their life together would be. How good for Duncan – and for his painting. She would know how to inspire him, how to release his creativity in a way Kate never could. But it had to be his decision. Taken freely and without pressure from her.

At length, he raised his head.

'I can't think in this room. I have to get some fresh air.' He stood up and put on his shirt and jacket. 'Stay here, darling. I won't be long. Wait for me.'

'I've been waiting for you all my life,' she whispered, but he had already gone.

She drew the curtains and lay back on the bed, one arm curled above her head. Shut in the womb-like stillness of that room, she heard the distant hum of cars going past, the shouts of children returning home from school. In the corridor from time to time footsteps sounded, but none of them stopped at her door. She lay for hours like that, with his smell on her body, in her hair, waiting for him to return.

Eventually she got up, ran a hot bath and lay soaking in it. She was paying now, paying for the love she had stolen. All her life she would pay for it. Slowly, sadly, she made love to herself in the bath, trying to ease the desire he had begun in her.

Chapter Twenty

When Kate arrived home, she found Duncan in his studio packing up his paints.

He turned round when he heard her come in.

'What are you doing?' she asked.

'I – I thought I'd go back tonight.'

'Back?' said Kate rather blankly, her head full of niggling questions left over from the office.

'To Middlesbrough, I mean.'

'Ah.' She sat down on a stool. 'That's a pity, because I'd booked us a table at that Mexican restaurant you're fond of.'

'Sorry.'

'Never mind. It's not important.' She gave her head a shake as if to clear it. 'Do you mean you're leaving me? Or are you running away from Liz?' she added quietly.

Duncan turned sharply, wondering how much she knew, or had guessed.

'I'm not running away from her, Kate. The past doesn't repeat itself like that.'

Oh yes, she thought, it does. She remembered the incident with Matthew and that time some old aunt had commented, 'Your little sister certainly knows how to fight for what she wants, doesn't she? She's really quite unscrupulous.' We never leave the past behind, she thought. We go on repeating the same mistakes over and over again. She put her head in her hands and felt about ninety.

'Kate, are you all right?' Duncan bent over her, a look of concern on his face.

What do you think, she wanted to snap. Liz. Perdita. Roger. Chris. My life's tumbling around my ears. She couldn't say that. Any sign of weakness in females made Duncan uneasy. He depended on her. So she lifted up her head, smiled at him and said, 'I'm all right. A bit tired, that's all. I'll be OK after I've had a drink. Want one?'

'Please.'

Kate got off the stool and dragged her weary body down the hall to the kitchen. It was like hauling along a sack of potatoes. She took a bottle of wine from the fridge and poured out two glasses. She drank one of them straight off and poured herself another. Everything was miasmic, nightmarish. She went back to the studio.

'Duncan, I've got to know,' she handed him a glass, 'are you leaving me for good? Are you moving in permanently with Chris?'

'Chris doesn't have a permanent home. When I'm not there he goes to hostels for the homeless. When I'm with him –'

Duncan stopped and looked at Kate doubtfully, as if wondering how much of this she wanted to hear.

'Go on,' she said, through gritted teeth.

'We stay in cheap B and Bs.'

'I see.'

How long would they be able to keep that up on what Duncan earned? Kate began to feel anxious. How on earth would Duncan cope on the streets? How would he get any painting done? She forced herself to calm down. If the situation was like this, Duncan would come back to her, she was sure of it. Then he said, sending an icy shiver down her spine, 'We've been looking at flats to rent. Actually "flat" is rather a misnomer, they're mostly grotty bedsitters.' He glanced away. 'We haven't made a final decision yet.'

'But you've seen one you like?'

Some kind of masochistic desire to know everything once and for all impelled Kate to go on questioning him.

'Yes.' He gazed at the floor. 'At least Chris likes it. I . . . well, it's not like this place. You've looked after me so well, Kate.' Finally his eyes met hers. He took a step forward and put his arms round her. 'I don't know what I'm going to do, Kate. And this is one decision you can't help me with.'

'No, I can't,' she said, standing with his arms around her.

Duncan looked down at her. 'I miss you already, Kate. How am I going to manage without you?'

'Don't!' Her eyes filled with tears. 'Don't!' She turned away from him and ran upstairs to her bedroom.

A while later, there was a tap on her door.

'Yes?' she mumbled, from the depths of her pillow. She turned over on to her stomach to hide her tear-stained face.

'Kate?' he said softly. 'Kate, I've packed up the car. I'm off now. I'll ring you tomorrow. Take care of yourself.'

She muttered something incomprehensible. Duncan closed the bedroom door softly behind him and tiptoed back down the stairs. In the hall he met Liz.

'Oh.' He groaned and sat down at the foot of the stairs.

She gave him a quick, nervous smile. 'You didn't come back.'

'No. I –' He mumbled something.

'What?'

'I thought it best.'

'To dump me?'

'No, Lizzie, I –'

She considered the suitcase standing in the hall. 'You're going away? Was it something I said? I didn't mean . . .' She stopped. 'Don't be scared of me, Duncan, there's no need.'

'I'm not scared of you. Why should I be scared?' he said in a sharp little voice, putting her in her place. Only the tightening of the muscles around his eyes told a different story. Yes, I am scared, they said. Go away. Please go away.

'Then why are you leaving?'

'To be with Chris.'

'Well that's not the way to avoid hurting Kate, is it?'

'Of the two options . . .'

'This would hurt her the least,' she finished for him, 'you thought.'

'Y-yes. Lizzie, listen.' He stood up and took a step towards her. 'I can tell the truth to you. I've always been able to tell you the truth when I couldn't to – to other people.'

'Yes,' she agreed, clenching her hands together. But what does it cost me, your truth?

'In the past I frightened myself with you. Up until you and I . . . got together, I'd thought experience was the great thing. Nothing mattered except that. Getting as much of it as I could. After you, I learned there have to be limits. Maybe not the limits other people set themselves – out of timidity, convention or whatever – but limits all the same.'

'Yes,' she said quietly. 'We both learned that. So why do you have to go?'

'In the hotel room back there, I could feel it starting over again. I got scared. Lizzie, years ago I gave you up. I had to. To have gone on would have done neither of us any good. But all my life I've been searching for you, for that lost waif look of yours. Women hardly ever have it – though Perdita does sometimes and it makes me afraid for her. Boys, young men, they have it. Chris has been the only one who has made me forget it was you I wanted. I have to go.'

Liz bowed her head. She'd been defeated. Life had defeated her. She had come back too late. Not by much. It was only in the last year, it seemed, that Duncan had found someone who gave him the strength to resist her. Someone he could choose over her, knowing that, though Kate would be hurt, he was saving her from a greater hurt. Liz bit her lip. Physical pain was better than mental.

'I didn't realise –' She stopped.

'What?'

'That I'd meant so much to you.' She raised her head to look at him. 'If I'd known, I would have come back earlier. When you didn't turn up in response to my letter I thought you thought it had all been a ghastly mistake.'

'Not that.' He shook his head. 'Never that, Lizzie. But I didn't know how to go on with you. I didn't know how I was going to take care of you –'

'I don't need taking care of.'

'– nor you of me,' he added.

'Ah. That,' she said slowly. 'For that you needed Kate.'

His eyes dropped to the floor. He stood before her with his head bent. Presently, picking up his suitcase, he went away.

Chapter Twenty-one

After Duncan's departure, Liz stood for a moment in the hall, then walked rapidly along the corridor to the kitchen and poured herself a whisky. She drank it straight off, poured herself another and drank it more slowly, leaning against the sink, looking out on to Kate's garden with blank eyes. I'd started to trust him again, she thought. When will I learn? After a while, summoning her courage, she went upstairs to Kate's room and tapped lightly on the door.

'Yes?' muttered Kate.

Liz came in and sat on the edge of the bed. She rubbed her cheeks with her hands in a gesture of anxiety Kate, lying back among her pillows, recognised from childhood.

'I – I met Duncan on his way out. Kate, I'm so sorry.'

Kate sat up in bed. Her hair was tousled, her eyes red-rimmed from weeping. Weep, weep, thought Liz. Weep for us all. As for herself, whether from whisky or from shock, she felt totally numb.

'The worst of it is,' Kate smiled a little shakily, 'I don't know whether Duncan's running away from you or leaving me for Chris.' She dabbed ineffectually at her eyes with a sodden tissue.

'Here, have another.'

Liz got up and brought the box over to her.

'Thanks.'

Liz sighed. 'I'd better go back to Boston. Ever since I've come here there's been one disaster after another.'

'No, stay.' Kate reached out and touched her sister's hand. 'This thing with Chris has been brewing up for months. I don't really think Duncan's running away from you,' she went on. 'It was only seeing you both together again and remembering . . .' She swallowed and stopped.

Liz looked down at Kate's patterned bedspread. 'Kate, the past's gone now. Gone for ever,' she added dully. Never, never, nevermore will I see him. She looked up. 'And if I could undo the past, I would. You know that, don't you?'

'I do. At least I think I do. Sometimes I forget.'

'Don't forget. None of us should remain trapped in the past.' What we had can never come again, I know that now. Though I also know I would have taken him from you, Kate, if it had been possible. I shall have to live with that knowledge for the rest of my life.

'But we are trapped in the past, aren't we? Our whole lives, yours and mine and Duncan's, have been shaped by the past. Even Perdita . . .' Kate's voice failed her. Perdita didn't know yet that Duncan had left.

'Shall I ring her?' asked Liz. 'Try and persuade her to come home?'

'Yes,' said Kate, giving up and lying back on her pillows. 'Perdita oughtn't to be left on her own with news like this.'

'On her own? Isn't Roger with her?'

'Didn't I tell you? He's still in hospital. The scan showed up a fragment of glass. He's had to have a minor operation. They're keeping him in for a few more days for observation. Give Perdita a call. She ought to come home.'

Liz went blankly down the stairs to phone Perdita in Whitby.

'Dad's left? For good?'

'We're not sure.'

'Poor Mum!'

Yes, poor Kate. No one else had any right to sympathy. To claim any, at this point, would be outrageous.

'Won't you come home, Perdita? Kate needs you here.'

'That's a turn-up for the books,' responded Perdita drily.

'What is?'

'Mum needing me.'

'Well, she does. *Please*, Perdita.'

'I'll come. Of course I'll come. I'll take the train.'

'I'll meet you at the station in Kate's car.'

'You're not insured to drive it.'

'I'll risk it.'

'Better not,' said Perdita, sounding, all of a sudden, maturer than her years. Sensible, cautious, Kate's daughter. 'I'll catch a bus.'

'Thanks,' said Kate, when Liz told her the news. 'I'm sure the summons was more acceptable coming from you.'

'No. She wanted to come.'

'Good.' Kate turned over in bed. 'I feel done in. I'm going to try to sleep for a while. Tell Perdita when she arrives that I'll drive her over to the hospital to see Roger tonight, if she wants.'

'Right.'

Liz tiptoed out of the room, shutting the door behind her. Downstairs, she pottered around in the kitchen. She washed a few dirty pots and watered Kate's plants. She switched on the radio, then switched it off again. Picked up a newspaper, then threw it aside as the print began to dance in front of her eyes. Overcome by grief, she fled to Duncan's studio, closed the door and wept. Soundlessly, so as not to disturb Kate sleeping upstairs.

Later, she washed her face, combed her hair and went and sat in the front room to wait for Perdita, who arrived looking calm and sensible. There were still studs in her ears and her skirt still trailed along the floor, but she had got rid of the cross, her face was scrubbed clean of make-up and her nails had returned to their natural colour. She looked more like the daughter Kate might have had.

'How's Mum?' she asked, dumping her small canvas bag in the hall.

'Asleep, but she said to go up as soon as you arrived. She'll take you to see Roger later, if you want.'

Perdita nodded briefly, then sprinted up the stairs two at a time to see Kate.

Twenty minutes later they came down, arm in arm, to eat the cold supper Liz had prepared. Kate looked pale but rested. Perdita watched over her carefully during the meal, passing Kate things before she asked for them. Liz, sipping her glass of wine, ate nothing. Neither of the other two noticed her lack of appetite.

In the end, they all went to the hospital. Liz felt that her last meeting with Roger had been filled with bitterness, and she wanted to make it up with him before he returned to Whitby. She couldn't imagine she would have many more chances of meeting him; her stay in England was nearly over. She wanted to put things right between them before she left.

Perdita went in first. Kate and Liz sat in the car park, seeming to listen to a play on Radio Four, but in reality absorbed in their separate thoughts. After half an hour Perdita reappeared through the hospital doors, looking subdued.

'He's all yours, Liz,' she said, getting into the car. 'I told him you'd like a word with him.'

'Was he all right about it?'

'Oh yes.'

'Thanks.' Liz got out of the car. 'Don't wait for me, Kate. I'll take the bus back.'

'OK,' agreed Kate, glad to have this newly mature Perdita to herself for a while.

With the sense of an uncomfortable duty about to be discharged, Liz walked into the hospital and took the lift up to the ninth floor.

Roger was sitting up in bed. His face was all colours of the rainbow and his head was still bandaged but the swelling over his eye had gone down. His first words were, 'How was Perdita?'

'Perdita?' Liz drew up a chair. 'You saw her yourself. She's taken the news of her father's departure remarkably well, she's being surprisingly mature about it, looking after Kate and –'

He interrupted her, 'No, I meant just now, when she came out after seeing me.'

'Fine. She was a bit quiet but she wasn't distressed or anything. Why?'

'Thank goodness for that!' Roger sank back on his pillow and shot Liz a sideways glance. 'We've agreed not to see one another, at least for a bit. Perdita wants to be with her mother and she wants to take her exams, to please Kate. I've encouraged her in that. Duncan was wrong about me, you know. I'm not out to ruin her life.'

'I know.'

'I gather Duncan's led Kate quite a dance over the years. Perdita feels she hasn't been as understanding of her mother as she might have been. She wants to make it up to her now.'

'Thank you, Roger,' said Liz quietly.

'What for?'

'This was your doing, wasn't it? Getting Perdita on Kate's side for once.'

'I did try to encourage her to see her mother's point of view, yes.

But I'm not trying to turn her against her father, whatever I might think of him. Perdita's very attached to him.' He shook his head. 'Of course Duncan could always charm anyone when he wanted.'

She swallowed painfully. 'Yes.'

'I never thought as much of him as everyone else seemed to,' Roger went on. 'At one time he had the whole town idolising him. Your mother was the worst,' he added.

'She liked you too,' put in Liz quickly.

'I was nowhere compared with Duncan. You know, lying here, doing nothing for the first time in years, I've been turning over the past in my mind. I could never quite work out what you felt about Duncan. Sometimes in your house, when your mother praised him for something he'd done, I noticed you looking quite jealous, as if you resented him taking her attention away from you. Were you jealous of him?'

'I suppose I was.' Not in the way you mean, though. I was jealous of anyone who came between Duncan and me, anyone who seemed closer to him than myself. And that included Mother. 'Duncan could do so many things – teach, paint, entertain, charm Mother. Now I don't know. He seems changed.'

He's shrunk a little. Yes. Something over the years has shrivelled Duncan up inside. He used to be so sure of himself. That's all gone. Will he get it back with Chris? He could have got it back with me, I know he could.

'We've all changed.' Roger looked at her. 'You're calmer.'

'Am I?'

'And sadder.'

'Ah.'

He gazed down at the patched and grubby hospital blanket. 'You know, you were right,' he said. 'I hadn't realised till I saw you again that first time, standing with Kate in my office, how angry I still was at you. Seeing you brought it all back. I felt like I was eighteen again. I actually had to go for a long walk after you'd left, I suddenly felt this enormous rage against you.'

'So you tried to hurt me through Perdita, was that it?' she said softly.

'No, I . . .' He shook his head. 'I suppose that might have been part of it,' he admitted. 'There is – was – an attraction there though, all the same.' His voice dropped a fraction. 'She reminds me of you at that age.'

Liz looked up in alarm. He hadn't guessed, had he?

Then he added, 'I don't know why,' and she judged that, on the whole, he hadn't. All the same, she thought, as she left the hospital a short while later (what more did they have to say to each other? everything had been said), Roger must have loved me deeply once to remember, all these years later, how I used to be and see the resemblance with Perdita. She waited by the bus stop. I never gave him enough credit. I must have hurt him very much, disappearing suddenly like that without telling him where I was going or why, and never writing.

But what could she have written? She got on the bus, paid her fare and sat down. 'Roger, I'm carrying Duncan's child. I'm going away so that no one will ever know.' Could she have written that? Roger, imbued by his mother (wretched woman!) with middle-class notions of respectability, would have come after her and pleaded with her to marry him, have the baby and bring it up as their own in a two-up two-down house with a patch of green out the back. Roger would have seen the baby as an ideal opportunity to trap her while she was vulnerable. He'd have complicated everything till she would have had to be cruel to him in order to make him go away.

The merit of Kate's plan had been its utter simplicity. But if she had explained it to Roger, or to anyone else outside the immediate relationship of the three of them, it would have seemed crazy, impossible, undoable. And Liz had been afraid she would begin to think it impossible too. So she had said nothing and Roger had chewed over his bitterness for eighteen years until it finally exploded in a way that might have, though thank God didn't seem to have, harmed Perdita.

If she were to write a letter to Roger now, explaining everything, explaining why he saw a resemblance between Perdita and herself, what would she say?

Would she tell him about that awful scene with Duncan? The two of them in a dingy café, the sort they normally frequented, the sort where no one they knew was likely to enter. She'd had to nerve herself up to it. When Duncan put the sugar into his coffee, then she would tell him. He shook in the sugar, stirred it and took a sip. She said nothing. They went on chatting about this and that, her studies perhaps, or his painting. And all the time, beneath the surface, she was wondering when she would tell him. His cup was half empty. When would she tell him? When? He drained his cup. Now? Now.

'Duncan, I'm pregnant.'

The words sounded stagey, melodramatic. Surely it wasn't her mouth they'd come out of? She felt as if she had seen the sentence written down somewhere – on the wall opposite perhaps – and flatly read it off. Some words, used often, hardly sound real any more. They have become common currency, tarnished and worn. They are pure cliché, the stuff of farce.

Only neither of them was laughing. Duncan stared at her for a moment in stunned silence. Then he leaned back in his chair and half closed his eyes. He stayed seated opposite her but he wasn't with her any more. He'd blanked her out. Liz wanted to walk round the table and shake him, to wake him up, but how on earth can you wake someone who isn't there? After a few minutes of this Duncan, mumbling something about how he would think of a plan, grabbed his jacket and ran out of the café. The next she heard was that he'd fled down to London to stay with friends. He'd had some kind of brainstorm at work, apparently, and the headmaster had given him two weeks off.

Would she tell Roger that? Would she tell him about the terror, the nightmare moment, staring at the positive pregnancy test in her mother's bathroom? Pink for positive. Pink, as it had turned out, for a girl. Would she tell Roger how she had crept round for weeks feeling sick and faint and terrified? Her school work fell off, she was unable to concentrate, her brain was wrapped in a kind of fog.

It had been Kate who found it out first. She who was so used to checking her body anxiously for signs of new life, who had gone through two failed pregnancies, quickly guessed why Liz was looking pale and ill, why she kept running off to the bathroom. She'd taken her younger sister aside and asked her sharply, 'What are you going to do about it?'

Put like this, Liz hadn't denied it. It was a relief that someone had finally broken through the miasma that lately had separated her from the rest of the world.

'Have an abortion, I suppose,' she had replied. 'Down in London where nobody knows me. I'll think up something to tell Mother.'

Duncan will help me, she'd thought. She hadn't yet lost her trust in him. She believed he would see her through this.

'You're going to kill your baby?' An angry flush appeared on Kate's face.

'It isn't a baby. It's a mass of cells,' responded Liz, reciting the literature she'd been reading in secret.

Kate slapped her. 'It's a human life,' she muttered, on the verge of tears. Her first pregnancy had lasted ten weeks, her second twelve. She thought of them as her two lost babies. Now Liz seemed to be denying them their identity.

'Kate, I can't look after a baby. I'm not cut out for it. I'm so unmaternal that the only doll I ever had dissolved when I bathed her. It was like she was trying to get away from me.'

'Dissolved?'

Kate's attention was momentarily distracted.

'Yes, don't you remember? Dad brought her back from one of his sailing trips. Underneath the paint, she must have been made of cardboard.' She laughed tremulously, on the verge of hysterics.

Kate gave her a little shake. 'Pull yourself together, Liz. For the baby's sake.'

'It isn't a —'

Kate shook her again. 'Who's the father?'

And then, gradually, because Liz was so adamant about not revealing the name, Kate ran through the list of likely men and came up against the one name that wouldn't go away. Liz denied it and denied it, but she flinched every time Duncan's name was mentioned. That was enough for Kate. It suddenly made sense of Duncan's mysterious attack of hysteria and his flight to London. When Kate phoned him, he broke down and sobbed.

'Darling, I'm so sorry. I never meant to hurt you like this. What can I do? Tell me what to do.'

'Stay in London,' Kate ordered, putting a clamp on her emotions and letting her practical side take over. 'I'll think of something.'

So Kate had taken charge of their lives, sitting down and working out calmly and logically what would be best for all three of them. What did Liz most want? Her freedom. What did Duncan want? Space and time to paint, with a few home comforts thrown in, such as Liz could never provide. What did she want? A child. The answer seemed obvious. It was only the practicalities that remained to be sorted out.

Liz would take a gap year – not so common then, very common now. She would do her A-levels in a few weeks' time, before the baby began to show. Then she would announce that she'd found a job somewhere – London, probably – and wanted to take a year off before starting university. The only problem was Mother: Kate would persuade her this wasn't some hare-brained scheme of Liz's but a well thought-out plan to gain some experience of life (as if she needs that! thought Kate to herself) which would return her, refreshed, to her studies. Kate, informing her department that she was pregnant, would apply for a sabbatical and join Liz in London. They'd rent a flat together. The baby would be born. Liz would stay down in London, find a job for the rest of the year and then go on to university. Kate would return to Whitby with the child, having left Duncan alone long enough to sort himself out.

A perfect plan. Dates all worked out. Duncan summoned back to Whitby to be told the news. Their final meeting in that café by the harbour . . . Mother won over. She would never dream of coming down to London to visit them. She hadn't been further south than York in her life.

Kate had found them a flat in Camberwell. She worked long hours in the British Library, wanting to get ahead with her research before the baby was born. The rest of the time she fussed over Liz, telling her to eat properly and put her feet up. After her two miscarriages, Kate couldn't believe any pregnancy could be straightforward, but this one was. After the first fourteen weeks of sickness, Liz had never felt better. It was a textbook pregnancy.

Liz found temporary work looking after a thirteen-month-old baby in the mornings while its mother went out to work. The baby slept most of the time. She spent the afternoons lying on the battered old sofa, reading magazines and books left behind by previous tenants. Occasionally she summoned up the energy to go for a walk in Ruskin Park. She had never in her life felt so deliciously unoccupied. In the evenings Kate cooked nourishing meals and made bright and cheerful phone calls to their mother in Yorkshire saying how well her pregnancy was progressing. In the course of these conversations, all Liz's symptoms became, eerily, transferred to Kate.

Both women were glad, in different ways, that Duncan was not with them. This was women's time, a time out of time, unreal time governed by the life quickening in Liz's womb.

Would she tell Roger about Perdita's birth? That cold December day. Kate was there, of course, had organised it all, phoning the hospital as soon as my waters broke, on exactly the day that had been predicted. Unplanned pregnancy, very planned birth. Kate went with me in the taxi to the hospital. She helped me undress, reminded me how to breathe, held my hand and counted the intervals between contractions, which seemed to get shorter and shorter, told me when to push and when to rest. Standing at the foot of the bed for the delivery, she saw Perdita before I did. She couldn't wait to get her hands on my baby. No, that's not fair. It wasn't like that. She took care of my baby. She took care of us both. All the same, if I'd been older or less ashamed, I might have kept Perdita with me a little longer, enjoyed a few days, or weeks, of motherhood. All I had was twenty-four hours. The hospital discharged me early. They were short of beds and there was obviously a competent person at home to care for me.

In the taxi back to the flat I handed my baby to Kate. I can still remember that moment. One minute my arms were full, the next they were empty and Kate, her face suffused with tenderness and pleasure, was cooing over my baby.

Perdita — I can't remember who first came up with the name. Probably it was Kate. She'd been rereading *The Winter's Tale*. We hadn't discussed names beforehand. Kate was superstitious about that and anyway we didn't know whether it would be a boy or a girl. I think both of us secretly hoped for a girl.

After the first few days, Kate thought it best Perdita be put on the bottle. I wasn't the world's most skilled breast-feeder and Kate was worried that Perdita was losing weight. So after that there wasn't much need for me to do anything for her. When she cried at night, it was Kate who got up to her, while I lay in bed, wide awake, my painfully full breasts leaking milk. After a few days, they dried up altogether. My body returned to its normal shape. There was nothing to show that I had become a mother. No mark, no wrinkle, nothing. My motherhood had been completely erased; it was as if it had never been. 'Oh, I'm not complaining, Roger,' I'd say. 'I've travelled, met all sorts of different people. I've been free. Kate set me free.' All the same, when I look at Perdita now, I wonder what I've missed.

One hitch in Kate's plans: I didn't do as well in my A-levels as expected. What had been intended as a gap year became instead a year out to resit my exams. I had to follow Kate and her baby back to Whitby. I stayed two days. Then I fled Kate, the baby, Mother's prying eyes and Duncan's slow descent into lethargy and depression. I took the coach down to London, leaving Kate to make up some story. I found a job with an escort agency. My clients were men seeking to escape their wives grown flabby and irritable through childbearing. What would they say, I sometimes wondered, if they knew this slender nineteen-year-old they lusted after was also a mother? But they didn't know. Nobody knew. I had reinvented myself. Except that, in the early hours of the morning, lying awake in some hotel room with a stranger beside me, it would all come flooding back and I would have to stuff a pillow into my mouth to stifle the sobs. So began the years of searching for a way to leave the past behind me, of struggling to forget because that was the only way I could survive. And it nearly worked. With Louise, it very nearly did. Until I met Duncan again.

Would she tell Roger all this? Liz got off the bus and walked up the avenue to Kate's house. No, she wouldn't. Such things didn't happen in Roger's world. Or if they did, they shouldn't be spoken about. He'd been knocked off course once by her. She had better keep quiet.

Chapter Twenty-two

The next morning when Liz woke, the house felt strangely silent. Flinging on a pair of jeans and a T-shirt, she went downstairs. She found Kate sitting in the conservatory, looking miserable.

'All alone? Where's Perdita?'

'Gone off to school. She got up early, came into my room raring to go, talked about borrowing notes and catching up on what she's missed. Let's hope she'll have enough time before the exams. This new motivation on Perdita's part is the one good thing that's come out of all this.' Kate stifled a yawn. 'I ought to get down to some work myself, but somehow I can't seem to raise the energy this morning.'

'Take the day off.'

'I don't know what to do about Duncan's studio,' Kate went on, as it Liz hadn't spoken. 'Should I tidy it or leave it as it is?' She frowned.

'Leave it as it is. For God's sake, Kate, it's too soon to begin making changes. Let things slide for a week or two.' We all need to let things slide We need to be kind to ourselves for a while. Liz patted her sister's arm. 'Let me make you a cup of coffee.'

She came back with two steaming mugs and sat down in a wicker chair beside Kate.

'I can't get used to Duncan not being here,' muttered Kate. 'I know he's often away, but this is different somehow. It feels like it's permanent. I miss . . .' She started to cry. 'I miss the sound of him in his studio. I miss the music he used to play. The way he would pop out to ask me things.'

'I know,' said Liz softly. 'We never know what we're going to miss about a person till it happens. Often it's the most surprising . . .' She stopped. For her own safety she needed to get off this subject fast. 'I like Duncan's paintings,' she added quickly.

Kate took out a handkerchief and wiped her eyes. She smiled through her tears. 'They don't sell very well.'

'I know, Roger told me. I can't think why. He uses bright, bold colours. His people look like recognisable human beings. I would have thought anyone would have been glad to have them in their sitting room.'

'Duncan doesn't know how to market himself.' Kate blew her nose in determined fashion and sat up in her chair. She took a sip of coffee. 'He'd rather paint fifty pictures than sell one. I've tried to help but I don't know enough about that side of things. And he simply won't butter up gallery owners. Duncan's attitude is that his work should speak for itself; if they like his pictures, they'll buy them. If they don't like them, well, he'd rather they didn't hang them in their galleries. But the art world doesn't operate like that. You have to be prepared to put in a bit of effort.'

'When did he give up teaching and start to paint full time?' asked Liz idly, sipping her coffee.

Kate hesitated. 'Shortly after Perdita was born. Well, about a year afterwards.'

'That soon!' Liz's hands began to tremble. She set down her coffee carefully so as not to spill it over Kate's wooden floor. 'I hadn't realised Duncan had begun to earn money from his painting so early on.'

We could have gone away together, she thought. We could have gone to Greece. If only I'd waited; if I hadn't let Kate organise everything; if I'd had courage. With Duncan's pictures bringing in money, we would have been free to travel anywhere in the world. He could have painted and I would have looked after Perdita and written poetry. What a wonderful life we would have had, the three of us.

There was a silence. Then Kate said, 'Duncan's pictures have never made money. The reason he was able to turn professional was that I offered to support him. The teaching was making him miserable. I got Perdita into a nursery and went back to work full time.'

Liz stared at her sister. So that had been the deal. Stay with me and I will give you, buy you, your freedom. It wouldn't have been spelled out so crudely. But that's what it had amounted to. Kate had bribed Duncan to stay with her. And I thought it was her charms.

He chose the easy option. And the daughter whom Liz had left in Kate's care had been pushed into second place, which was not what she had intended at all. To be fair, perhaps not what Kate had wanted either.

'I know what you're thinking,' Kate said, in measured tones. 'You're thinking I bribed him.'

'No, I . . .' began Liz, caught off balance.

'Well I did. I bribed him. Out of sheer panic. It was the only way I could think of to bind him to me.'

Liz remembered what Duncan had said, that Perdita had made a bond between himself and Kate, and how she had thought bitterly, I gave you that bond.

'What about Perdita?' she asked. 'Surely Duncan would have stayed for her?'

Kate shook her head. 'Not even Perdita would have made him stay. It was his painting, first and foremost and before everything and if he thought he was being stifled . . .'

She broke off, remembering that dreadful time. The first year of Perdita's life. Coping with her new baby, ecstatic one minute, in despair the next, thinking that life would never be normal again. Desperately tired, desperately trying to get some reading done in between feeding Perdita, changing Perdita, playing with Perdita. And Duncan, empty and drained, going out to do his teaching every morning on automatic pilot. Returning home in the evening, after a day wrestling with his pupils, a pile of essays to mark, saying life was hardly worth living any more. He had been too tired, too spaced out on Valium, to play with Perdita or even take much notice of her.

Unreal time. Waking in the night, snatching catnaps during the day, her body moving to the rhythm of another human being. She had lost touch with most of her friends. Then, gradually, things had begun to settle down. Perdita got into a routine of only waking once during the night. Slowly Kate began to emerge from the drugged days of early motherhood and look around her. She realised Duncan hadn't smiled for months. He tiptoed about the house, very polite and careful with her, his glance, when it came her way, strained and remote. She could imagine this going on for years except . . . those mysterious phone calls, late at night. Not from Liz, she was sure. Was Duncan planning to leave her? Would she wake up one morning and find him gone? There was only one way to stop him. She suggested going back to lecturing full time. For the first time in over a year, she saw hope in Duncan's eyes.

She had gone back to work, sacrificing her daughter to him. Duncan had resigned his teaching job and picked up his paintbrush again. He became relaxed, joking, practically his old self. The mysterious phone calls ceased. He started to show signs of being fascinated by Perdita, would carry her around in his arms for hours, chatting to her, pointing out shapes and colours (though Perdita was not artistic, hadn't an ounce of talent in her body when it came to making pictures). Yes, it had been Perdita, in the end, who had drawn Duncan out of his period of blankness, of withdrawal from the world, of mourning almost. Perdita and his painting.

'Didn't you mind?' Liz's voice broke in on her thoughts.

'Mind what?'

'Leaving Perdita in the nursery.'

'Of course I minded,' snapped Kate. 'Losing two babies makes a child, when you finally have one, that much more precious. I wanted to stay at home with Perdita. I didn't have a choice if she was to have a father in her life.'

Liz reflected that in Kate, too, the maternal instinct had been thwarted.

'I never wanted anything so much as I wanted Perdita,' murmured Kate. 'From the moment I first saw her.'

Which was before I saw her, thought Liz.

'You gave me Perdita,' added Kate, looking at Liz as if she had only just realised this.

'I dumped Perdita on you.' Careless, careless girl, ignorant mother.

'It came to the same thing.' Kate smiled across at her sister. 'I owe you one, Liz. I can say it now. It's taken me years to be able to. But Perdita is grown up; she belongs to none of us now. She's her own person.'

'Yes,' agreed Liz. 'She's her own person.' Not yours, not Duncan's, not mine. I came back too late.

'What will you do, Liz?' asked Kate softly. 'What are your plans?'

'I don't know,' replied her sister. 'Suddenly it seems like I have nowhere to go.'

'Louise . . .?'

Liz shook her head. 'She hasn't written, she hasn't phoned, all the time I've been here. No. Louise is gone for good.'

'I'm sorry. Eight years is a long time to be with someone.'

'It's over for me now, Kate. I'm beginning to think I'm incapable of living with anyone.' If I can't have Duncan, if I can't have Louise – second best to Duncan and perhaps she knew it and that's why she left, Louise has never been second best in her life . . . Liz sighed. 'I've got old and cranky, Kate. All I feel like doing is crawling into my shell to lick my wounds for a bit.'

'Why don't you stay here?' said her sister in a low voice.

'Here? With you?'

She must have given up hope of Duncan, thought Liz. If she thought there was a chance he'd come back, Kate would never have suggested this.

'Here. Or in the house in Whitby, if you prefer,' said Kate. 'We could keep it on as our base. You could live there. I'd sell this house – with Perdita away, it's too big for one person to live in. I'd move into a flat near the university and come over to Whitby at weekends. That would be our home, for Perdita to return to during the vacations.'

'Kate, I . . .' Liz didn't know what to say. It was so unexpected and yet, like all Kate's plans, somehow so simple. She would get a job waitressing in Whitby and in her spare time write poetry. 'Kate, how long have you been planning this?'

'Nothing's planned. It just sort of came upon me, as we were sitting here talking, that this might be a way of providing some sort of future for both of us. We've both run through love. At our age . . .'

'Remember Uncle John,' said Liz mischievously.

'Ursula is the great love of Uncle John's life. He found her again when he thought it was too late. He's luckier than we are. We've lost our loves. I've lost Duncan, you've lost Louise.'

'Yes,' replied her sister, 'we've lost our loves.' But it wasn't Louise she was thinking of.

'Mum would have liked the idea of us living together,' Kate added.

'Would she?'

Kate hesitated. 'Since we're in confessing mode, I might as well tell you that Mum did guess everything and blamed me. She blamed me for hanging on to Duncan.'

'He told me that.'

'Yes, but Duncan thinks that Mum blamed me for letting him back into the house. It wasn't quite like that.' Kate paused, then spoke in a rush, as if trying to get rid of the words. 'Mum felt it was you Duncan was in love with. She felt he ought to have been allowed to go to you.'

'To me! Mother! No, you must have got it wrong, Kate. Mother disapproved of me.'

'She didn't. She didn't know how to look after you. She didn't know what you wanted. After Dad died and you went so wild . . . She thought Duncan might have been what you were looking for.'

'Mother uncertain of herself? l can't believe it, Kate. Why did she cut us all off, then, if she felt like that? It looked so much like she was judging us.'

Kate shook her head. 'I don't think it was judgement, I think it was fear. The situation was beyond her, outside her experience – she never knew how to react to Perdita, for instance – so she turned her back on us, more or less. It was her way of dealing with it.'

Mother afraid? Kate had seen a different mother from the self-righteous policeman who had haunted Liz's conscience for years. A frailer, more vulnerable woman, a woman who had sometimes not known how to act. Kate had succeeded in seeing their mother as a grown-up woman. Liz envied her. I went away too soon, she thought. I never got to know Mother in an equal relationship, adult to adult. And now it's too late.

'Later,' Kate went on, 'Mum thought I neglected Duncan and that was why he had affairs with men. I hadn't been able to keep that from her. But it wasn't like that. What Duncan wanted from me was to make a home for himself and Perdita, a refuge for him to come back to.' She smiled wryly. 'To tell you the truth, I don't think Duncan much likes women, except in the mothering role. As you know, his own mother died when he was seven. In some buried part of his mind he's never quite forgiven her for that; holds it against all women, that they're unreliable. His father, the old colonel, packed him off to boarding school. All male in those days. Duncan got used to loving men,' she added sadly.

You don't know him, thought Liz. He would have stayed with me, I'm sure of it.

Aloud, she said, 'If this is true, why did Mother never get in touch with me?'

'She wanted to. She was waiting for some kind of, I suppose, forgiveness, on my part. I . . . couldn't.'

'You called for me to come though. Why did you, Kate? You needn't have. You could have sorted everything out yourself, disposed of the house and sent me a cheque. You'd have had a perfect right.'

'The strange thing was, as soon as I knew Mum was dying, all I wanted then was to carry out her wish. Hence those frantic phone calls.'

'Which didn't reach me till too late.'

'She never saw us together again. I'll always regret that.'

'Perhaps she sees us now. Who knows?' said Liz, her heart breaking open for her mother after all these years. For a moment she felt like a little girl again, playing quietly on the kitchen floor in the shelter of her mother's presence.

'Perhaps,' said Kate, surprised. She had never associated Liz with any kind of belief in the afterlife.

They were silent for a moment.

'Kate,' began Liz, presently, 'I think I would like to stay here. I mean in the house in Whitby. I've seen the world now, or as much of it as I want to. I like the idea of putting down roots at last.'

A curious expression flashed across Kate's face. 'Are you sure?' she said.

'Yes, it's been growing on me ever since I arrived in England, the feeling that here is where I belong.'

'If you really feel like that,' said Kate slowly, 'then I think we should tell Perdita.'

'Oh.'

'A feeling's been growing on me too, since you got here, that Perdita has a right to be told the truth about her birth. She's old enough now to understand. I hope. But I would only tell her if you really are planning on staying. It wouldn't be fair otherwise. It wouldn't be right for us to tell her and then for her to watch you drift out of her life again.'

'I know.' Liz sat quite still for a moment as a kind of joy long buried, often despaired of, began working its way to the surface of her mind. 'I'll stay,' she said finally.

'Then we'll tell her at the weekend. Tomorrow's Friday. When Perdita has finished school, we'll drive over to Whitby where it all happened and tell her there.'

Chapter Twenty-three

'Are you sure this is the right thing to do?' Liz kept asking at intervals during the day. 'If we tell Perdita the truth about her birth what on earth will she think of us?'

'She has a right to know, Liz. In the past few years, I've sometimes caught her with an expression on her face – a sort of lost expression – as if she had mislaid a piece of jigsaw. Subconsciously I'm sure Perdita feels there's something odd about her situation, but she can't quite put her finger on what it is. I think, when we tell her, she'll have a feeling of something having been cleared up at last.'

'I can't help thinking we've left it too late. That if we were going to tell her, we ought to have done it years ago, so that she could have grown up with the knowledge.'

'You weren't around then. She would have wanted to fit into your life in some way and how would that have worked? She would have felt torn, wanting to be here and yet also wanting to be off wherever you were. No, it's better like this. Perdita's ready for it now. She's grown up a lot in the past few weeks.'

'Let's hope so. It's a great deal for her to take in.'

'You're not getting cold feet, are you?'

'Yes,' admitted Liz. 'It's all right for you. You come out of this rather well. But what on earth is she going to think about me? A mother who abandoned her baby.'

'You didn't abandon her. You found her a home. Perdita's old enough now, almost the same age as you were then. She'll understand why you couldn't look after her yourself. Teenagers nowadays are much more aware of these issues than we ever were. They come across them all the time in the newspapers or on the television.'

'I'm terrified of her reaction.'

'Don't worry.' Kate touched her arm. 'It will be all right, you'll see.'

They picked up Perdita from school and drove over the moors to

Whitby. It was wet and windy. The house smelled faintly damp. Kate lit a fire in the sitting room and made soup for them all. When the rain had eased off, Liz set out across town to do what she ought to have done weeks ago – visit her mother's grave.

She found the granite headstone with William Miller's name on it and the space beneath where her mother's name would go. Liz knelt down and brushed a stray paper off the grassy mound. She removed the dead flowers that still lay scattered around from the funeral and began planting the bulbs she hoped would flower in the autumn.

Strange how differently she felt now about her mother, that she understood her at last, that everything had fallen into place. Little Jessie Chapman, ripped from her safe, comfortable home, her father dead, her own mother accused of murdering him. Impoverished, sent out to work at sixteen. No wonder she had been so anxious for her two daughters to get on in the world, to climb back to the place she had once occupied in the town as Arthur Chapman's daughter.

As she knelt by the grave, digging the soil, Liz remembered the mother of her earliest childhood, before there had come a distance between them, before she had turned into a rebellious teenager. As a child it had always been her mother she'd turned to for comfort, her mother who had defended her. Yes, there'd been no one like Jessie Miller for standing up for her daughters. How we must have disappointed you, Liz thought. You had planned such brilliant futures for us. Kate was to marry and have children. I was to go to Cambridge. Instead Kate had miscarriages and I became a waitress. I never did anything to make you proud of me. When Dad died, I ran away at night to escape the sound of your sobbing. Yes, that's when the night prowls around the town began. I couldn't bear lying in bed hearing you cry for Dad. So I ran away. And met Duncan. You took my side over that, though you never said and I never knew till Kate told me yesterday. How I wish I had known you were on my side. Things might have turned out very differently.

Liz patted down the earth with her trowel and stood up. We're going to make it all right, Kate and I. We're going to be friends again and make a home for your granddaughter. I wish you could see us. Liz imagined herself in the kitchen of the house in Whitby, saying this to her mother as she stood at the sink doing the washing up. Slowly, as Liz was speaking, her mother turned round from the sink to look at her. For the first time in years, Liz was able to picture her mother's face, with its pointed elfin chin and the dark eyes that were so much like Perdita's. She walked back to the house filled with hope.

She found Kate and Perdita sitting in their dressing gowns by the fire drinking cocoa and, in the absence of the television which had been given away to a neighbour, listening to a concert on Radio Three. Liz made herself a coffee and joined them. From time to time as they sat there, Liz found herself stealing a glance at Kate. Her eyes often rested on Perdita, watching her. Once, Liz caught an expression of yearning on her sister's face as if Kate was imagining a time when Perdita would no longer be there, as if in some strange way she was saying goodbye to her.

Was this truth-telling going to be fair on Kate? What if Perdita were to come to want her, Liz, more than Kate? If Kate were to lose both Duncan and Perdita? What would she have left? What do *you* have left, she thought, her hands tightening around her mug of coffee. Not Louise. Not Duncan. But Kate deserves Perdita more. She's put in all the work of bringing her up. I only gave birth to her. It's a little thing really, compared with raising her and disciplining her and educating her. A little thing, and yet everything. I gave her life.

She glanced across at Perdita, who had abandoned the pretence of listening to the concert and was sitting gazing down into her mug of cocoa. Who was she seeing there? Roger? Duncan? 'Perdita has always preferred Duncan to me,' Kate had said earlier that day, in the kind of resigned tone people use to cover up an old hurt. Normal for a child to prefer one parent over another, but Kate must never have been sure that Perdita's preference was not dictated by some deep-seated yearning for her proper biological parents.

We'll see, thought Liz, looking over at the young woman sitting there so calmly, unaware that in just a few hours the world she'd thought she had begun to know was to be changed for ever.

The concert ended and they prepared to go to bed. Liz thought that Kate kissed Perdita especially tenderly this evening, almost like a farewell kiss. Liz and Perdita never kissed. Perdita merely nodded in her direction, saying casually, 'Night, Liz' as she made her way up to bed.

The two sisters stood for a moment in the sitting room, looking at one another.

'Tomorrow,' said Kate softly.

'Tomorrow,' Liz responded.

Chapter Twenty-four

The next morning, coming down first to breakfast, Liz saw a letter with an American postmark lying on the doormat. Her heart began to thump. With shaking hands she forced herself to pick it up.

'Is that from Louise?' asked Kate, entering the kitchen some time later in her dressing gown and noticing the letter lying unopened on the table.

'Yes. Do you want coffee? The kettle's just boiled.'

Leaning back against the cooker, as if she was trying to put as much space as possible between herself and the contents of the letter, Liz took a sip from her mug.

'Are you going to stand there all day and look at it, or are you going to open it?' Kate moved briskly towards the kettle.

'I . . . I can't.'

Kate glanced at her sister's white face. 'Do you want me to open it for you?'

'No.'

Liz set down her mug on the cooker, plucked the letter off the table and with a muttered 'Oh God!' ran up the stairs two at a time to her bedroom.

Upstairs she tore open the envelope with trembling hands and let her eyes skim over the – quite short – letter inside. Then she lay down on her bed for a long time, staring at the ceiling and thinking.

When she came downstairs again, she heard the sound of voices in the kitchen. Perdita had obviously woken early. Liz let herself out of the front door. She walked up the street and stood for a moment leaning against the railing, looking down at the harbour. The good weather had gone. A grey mist hung over the boats. How many times had she seen it like this? The town was not, after all, much changed since that evening when she had stolen out of her mother's house and stumbled across Duncan down by the harbour. Out of that simplest of chance meetings had come all this. Out of it had come Perdita, unplanned, unwanted really, by any of them except Kate.

She took Louise's letter from her pocket and read it through once more, as if to make absolutely certain of its meaning. Then she tore it into shreds and tossed it up into the grey morning air for the seagulls to chase.

Drawing her jacket more tightly around her, Liz climbed the steps to the abbey, to the spot where the wonderful St Hilda had once ruled over a community of women and men. If your spirit is still here, St Hilda, she prayed, give me wisdom, wisdom to know what is the right thing and strength to do it. She walked a little way along the cliff path, hearing through the mist the peculiar wail and whine of seagulls as they circled the steep red cliffs to her left. It came on to rain more heavily. She turned back towards the house.

She ran into Perdita on her way out, a shopping list in her hand.

'Some things Mum's asked me to get,' she said cheerfully. 'Do you want anything, while I'm down at the shops?'

Liz stared at her for a moment, then shook her head. 'No. Thanks, Perdita. There's nothing I want.'

'See you then. Bye.'

'Goodbye, Perdita.'

Liz went inside the house and found Kate sitting in the kitchen in her dressing gown, a mug of coffee in front of her and an untouched slice of toast. Liz looked at her. There was a sadness about Kate this morning. She'd withdrawn a little, as if she was preparing her strength for some battle to come. What had Kate said? 'I never wanted anything in my life so much as I wanted Perdita.' She didn't wish to do battle with Kate over Perdita. Her daughter should not, must not, be fought over.

Liz sat down at the table.

'Kate, this letter from Louise. She wants . . . she wants me to go back.'

Kate looked at her for a few moments without saying anything. 'And will you?' she said softly.

It was there, you needed bat's ears to catch it, but it was there and Liz heard it, the faintest, infinitesimal note of hope in Kate's voice. Liz glanced down at her hands resting on the table. For a second they seemed like a stranger's hands. Then she raised her eyes to meet her sister's.

'I think I will.'

There was a silence in the room. From somewhere outside came the sound of a child's laughter dying away into a sob. Then Kate asked, 'What will we do about Perdita?'

Liz swallowed. 'We'd better not tell her, had we? At least for the time being.'

'Perhaps that would be best, if you're not going to be around.'

'Kate, I know this sounds odd but I . . . I'd like to leave at once, if that doesn't seem awfully rude and ungrateful, after the way you've put up with me these past weeks.'

'What? Now? Right away?' said Kate, startled.

'I think I would like to.'

'Are you afraid Louise will change her mind?'

'Yes.' Or I'll change mine. 'You do understand, Kate, don't you? I have to go at once.' I have to get out of the house before Perdita comes back and tears my heart in two.

'I understand,' said Kate. 'You need to make sure of her. I'll miss you, Liz. I've got used to having you around. A lot's happened these past few weeks, hasn't it?' She suddenly sounded quite cheerful and even began absent-mindedly to eat the slice of toast on the plate in front of her.

'Yes, a lot has happened.'

'Well.' Kate stood up, all brisk practicality now that a decision had been made. 'I'll drive you back to Hull.'

'No, don't worry. I'll take the train from here, then catch a connection to London. I'd rather,' she added, seeing a look of doubt on Kate's face. 'I'm going up to pack straight away. Would you be a dear and ring the airport to reserve a seat? I'll find you the ticket.'

She flew upstairs to get it.

'Are you sure you want to do this?' Kate looked at the ticket in her hand. 'It seems so sudden.'

'I know, but that's me, remember? I don't make plans. I go with the wind.' Liz forced herself to smile at Kate, though her face felt as stiff as a board. 'I'm leaving Perdita with you, I'm afraid, like last time.'

'Only this time she's grown up and able to take care of herself.'

'Yes. I can't help it, Kate,' she added apologetically. 'That's how I am.'

Duncan's argument. That's how I am. I can't help it. Kate felt the past echo around her. We don't change, she thought, any of us. We go on repeating the same old actions. She went to phone the airport.

Ten minutes later, Liz was back downstairs, her holdall packed and ready.

'I'll drive you to the station.'

'No, it's OK, I'll walk.'

'Sure?'

'Yes.'

The two sisters hugged.

'You will go on with Laura's stories, won't you?'

'Of course. They must be published,' replied Kate.

'And you'll go over to Paris?'

'As soon as I've seen Perdita through her exams.'

'Good.'

Liz opened the front door. Outside it was an exhausted grey day. The wind was whipping up the waves on the sea and the litter in the streets. Just the kind of weather she usually loathed. This morning she felt grateful for it. It made it easier for her to leave.

'Keep in touch, Liz.' Kate's hand rested on her sister's shoulder for a moment. 'Now that we've finally met up again. I haven't so much family that I can afford to lose members of it. And don't let Louise walk all over you,' she added.

Standing on the pavement outside the house, Liz screwed up her eyes. Against the wind? Or was she in pain? Kate took a step forward.

'You will be all right, won't you?'

'Oh yes, I'll be all right. Don't worry about me. I'm used to looking after myself. Take care of Perdita . . .' she turned away and started down the street '. . . for me,' she added under her breath.

She walked down the cobbled street, past the tourist shops and over the bridge, retracing the steps she had taken what seemed like half a century ago but was really only a few weeks. As Kate had said, a lot had happened. She had seen Duncan again and understood why, at eighteen, she had fallen for him and would go on falling for him for the rest of her life, if only she were allowed to. She had met her daughter and been touched, finally and too late, by motherhood. Yes, she was a changed person from the carefree woman who had arrived in Whitby such a short time ago. No wonder she was seeing everything this morning through a veil of tears.

Head bent, she hurried through the town, not wanting to bump into Perdita. At the station she turned to catch a last blurry glimpse of the red-roofed houses nestling into the cliffside and to take her last breath of that peculiar English seaside air.

There was no one to meet her at Logan airport. She took a cab to Beacon Hill and let herself into the empty apartment. There was no one there. She wasn't expected. She dumped her holdall on the floor, walked into the bedroom and flung herself down on the bed she had once shared with Louise. Later, opening cupboards and drawers, she found that Louise had moved out all her things. She was gone for good then. As she had said in her letter.

Chapter Twenty-five

Some weeks later, Liz received a letter from Kate.

Dear Liz,

No news from you so far. Is all well with you? Guess what? Duncan has come back. He says he needs me and the support I give him. It didn't work out with Chris. He couldn't get any painting done. Of course I forgave him immediately, as he expected me to. If I wasn't so bloody reliable he'd probably be less promiscuous. Irony.

So we're staying put in Hull for the time being. Perdita's glad to have her father back home. They've been going for long walks together and having chats about Cambridge. She has caught up on the work she missed and feels quite confident about her exams. Fingers crossed. There's been no more talk of taking a year off. Roger's had his nose put out of joint – his role as father figure has been quite usurped. A good thing too!

I thought I would put Mum's house on the market after all, if that's OK with you? I suppose you're planning on staying in Boston? Let me know. I'll be using a different estate agent this time!

By the way, I think I may have found a publisher interested in Laura's stories. At least what he's really interested in is her life – the murder, the trial, the lesbianism in Paris – but I'm hoping I'll be able to slip in the stories as well.

I hope things have worked out for you with Louise. I suddenly felt quite worried as you were leaving. Please write and tell me everything is all right. You know you are always welcome here. For as long as you like.

Love, Kate

Liz sat down on the edge of the bed. It was stripped of sheets. On the floor beside her stood a suitcase of clothes and two cardboard boxes, one filled with books and tapes, the other with odd bits and pieces she had collected over the years of travelling around. Fewer possessions than one might have expected for someone her age.

She held Kate's letter between her fingers and stared into space. Presently, with a rustle, it dropped to the floor unheeded. Liz went on staring blankly at the bare wall opposite.

Kate had ended up with everything. Liz had gone away from Whitby because she had been afraid she was about to rob her sister; another theft, this time not perpetrated. She had thought she was leaving Perdita with Kate to make up for Duncan going – and now Duncan had come back. Kate had her family around her again, her happiness shone through the letter. No lucky florins needed for Kate. She had it all.

And me, Liz thought. I have nothing. She lay back on the stripped bed and contemplated the rest of her life. The apartment was to be put on the market. Louise's letter had made that clear, even specifying the date by which Liz must move out, which was today.

Well, she was packed and ready. But where on earth was she going? New York, perhaps. She'd never lived there and it was large enough; she would be bound to find some sort of work. Yes, perhaps New York would be the next place for her to perch in for a while; not to settle, never to settle, not now, not any more. Forever searching for what she knew had been lost years ago. It was better to face facts. Kate's way wasn't her way. Her sister pandered to weaknesses in people – Duncan's desire for a comfortable life, the publisher's wish for scandal about Laura's life. Oh, let it go, let it go, she thought. What does it matter? What does it matter that Duncan loves Kate in his weakness when he could have loved me in his strength? But then, to be that strong, he would have had to be a different person, I see that now. He was never the person I thought he was.

A phrase of Philippa Hamley's echoed in her mind. 'It is possible to survive on very little.' That was it, that was how it was going to have to be, learning to survive on very little. Liz picked up her notebook, now at last half filled with fragments of poems. She felt the past slide past her, nudging her lightly as it went, an almost weightless weight. It was time to move on.

And if things didn't work out, well, there would always be Kate. I hope she doesn't die before I do. I hope she will always be there.